MW01672015

Dillon was as white as a ghost. Clearly he was losing his mind. "Hearing voices is never a good sign," he muttered to himself as he slid down his bedroom wall. His heart was racing and he wished he could believe the radio or TV was on, but unfortunately he knew they weren't.

"First off, you are not hearing voices. It's just one voice. I wanted to talk to you, but it took me a while to figure out how. So I've spent the last two months figuring it out and then waiting for the right time to talk to you, and you know what? There is no right time for a spirit to start talking to a kid, so I just decided today was your lucky day."

"You're a spirit, as in dead?" Dillon whispered.

"Thank you, Captain Obvious."

ALSO BY MARILYNN HALAS

Mom's Choice Award Winning Fuzzwippers Series

Hello, We're The Fuzzwippers
Fuzzwippers Find Good Listeners
Fuzzwippers Play Fair
Fuzzwippers Make Good Helpers
Fuzzwippers Make Great Travelers
Fuzzwippers Have Feelings Too
Fuzzwippers Learn About Family

Coming Soon

Hot Spots
Tennis Anyone
More from our Fuzzwipper Friends

PLAY ON

Marilynn Halas

4 sunflowers media

This is a work of fiction. Names, characters, places, and incidents either are the product of the author's imagination or are used fictitiously, and any resemblance to actual persons, living or dead, business establishments, events, or locales is entirely coincidental.

4 Sunflowers Media
Publishing books that celebrate and support families since 2010.
Connecticut.

Library of Congress Cataloging-in-Publication Data
Halas, Marilynn.
Play On/ Marilynn Halas.
ISBN 978-0-9915092-0-1
ISBN: 0988356244 (Limited Edition)
ISBN 13: 9780988356245
LCCN: 2012955565 Limited Edition)
LCCN: 2014933076

Marilynn Halas

For my husband, Stephen: in your eyes I can see our future
and I know that we will always play on together.
- mph

JULY 4, 2004

The sound of the mortar's blast left Danny with a ringing in his ears. Only in Afghanistan one month and the experience was like nothing he had ever known before. If he'd had time, he would have thought about his horse and his family's farm in Tennessee, but happy memories couldn't distract him from the terror all around him. His trembling hand reached for his M-4 rifle, and he released the safety. His squad was advancing through an abandoned warehouse; at least, they thought it was abandoned. Clearly, the intel was not much good. As soon as Captain Grainger threw the flash-bang grenade he was answered by twenty rounds from an insurgent. Then an older man stepped out from the shadows and brandished something. At first, Danny thought the guy was literally throwing rocks, but then it began to glow. It glowed with a white-hot light as the man threw it at them. When it exploded Danny was almost blinded. This was no ordinary grenade.

His Captain gave him the sign and he began to move. As he stepped over the rubble and crouched down, he saw them. The Taliban insurgents were hiding behind a low wall and Danny was coming up from behind. In their arms Danny saw a struggling little girl. He guessed she was no more than maybe five or six years old. There was no way to capture the enemy without risking the child's life, and that was exactly what those cowards were counting on. Danny was trying to figure out what to do next and he looked around for his Captain's orders. That was his fatal mistake.

The first bullet caught him in the neck, just above his body armor. The spray that followed landed everywhere and brought down the last of the crumbling ceiling hanging above him. The whole thing was surreal. Danny was covered in dust and blood and debris, but he had no pain; well, almost no pain. He couldn't feel much below his neck and his head was way too foggy to for him realize how much it hurt. There was a small part of him that could hear the shouting and exchange of gunfire happening around him, but mostly his brain was already back home.

He was sitting on the porch strumming his old guitar and breathing in the best smells he knew. Fresh cut grass and fried chicken. He thought about his mom, he thought about his girl, and just before he closed his eyes for the last time, he thought about heaven.

Within twenty-four hours his parents saw the military detail in dress uniforms pull up to their door. His mother was numb as they told her that her son, Private First Class Daniel Charles, had made the ultimate sacrifice for his country. On behalf of a grateful nation, they thanked her and they were gone.

The next few weeks passed in a blur for everyone. Danny's girlfriend started wearing black. There was a funeral with full military honors once the body was stateside again. The choir sang "Danny Boy" and there wasn't a dry eye in the church. There were at least a dozen requests for Danny's picture from local media and even from friends. They put his picture up at the town hall and in the church vestibule, and his old football coach dedicated the Wildcats' next season to Danny's memory. His dad tried to remember how proud Danny had been to serve his country, and his mom prayed that no one else's son would ever have to die to protect this nation. They were even surprised by a flurry of angry letters from so-called pacifists who wanted to blame their son for the war, saying that with no volunteers, there would be no fighting. Danny's dad thought those letters made especially good kindling.

That's when time seemed to stop for the Charles family. Clint and Sara Charles closed the door to Danny's room and never touched it, except to keep it clean. It was almost as though they thought that if they left his room the way it was, life could return to the way it was before their only son was killed. Danny's bed was made, his curtains drawn, his guitar stood in the corner, and nothing changed for seven years.

JULY 4, 2011

"Hurry up!" Dillon's father yelled up the stairs. Dillon used to think the yelling would stop after the divorce, but it seemed to only grow more intense.

"Move it! The meter's running!"

Dillon ran down the hall and saw his mom, Maggie, pretending to be asleep on the living room couch. She winked at him and held her fingers up to her lips. He knew she didn't want to deal with his dad when they were running late. She worked the night shift as an ER nurse and now she was finally getting a break. Dillon grabbed his bag and a warm cookie from the kitchen and headed downstairs to meet his dad.

His father had an important client in the Hamptons and they were invited out for a Fourth of July barbeque. Normally his father wouldn't bring him on a business call, but this was different. This client had a son who played soccer in the same park as Dillon. The boys had never even met each other, but their fathers thought it was a great way to keep them busy so the men could talk. All Dillon knew was that the family summered in the Hamptons and the rest of the time this client and Dillon's dad were neighbors on the Upper East Side. From soccer at the park to lemon pancakes at Mary Beth's Restaurant, Dillon loved where his dad lived. Unfortunately, they weren't going there today. Instead they were taking the train to Long Island to spend a day with his father, Ryan, pretending he had time for Dillon, and Dillon hanging out with a boy he didn't know. Dillon put on his earphones and zoned out.

Sometimes it was hard not to think about the way things used to be. There was a time when they all lived on the Upper East Side. Now, Dillon spent most of his time commuting there on the subway. Dillon went to the same school he had since Kindergarten, Madison Country Day. He and his friend Tom thought it was ridiculous to call anything on the Upper East Side "country." But it was still a great school, and it would feel weird to graduate after being there from Kindergarten through high school. After the divorce he and his mom moved to Morningside Heights to be closer to her job. It was okay, but it still didn't feel much like home to him. At his mom's place Dillon had a room the size of the walk-in closet at his dad's. Still, that wasn't the real problem. Dillon liked the apartment fine and he didn't care too much about the close quarters. He just didn't like the feeling that it was temporary. At fifteen, Dillon knew he would be off to college in three short years. He didn't know what would happen after that, and he hated the thought of his mom alone in that place. There was nothing really wrong with the apartment; it just felt sad, no matter how bright Dillon and his mom painted the walls.

An hour later the cab from the train station wound its way up a huge hill, and they could see the ocean in the distance. The house in the Hamptons didn't have an address; it had a name. Villa Victoria was a magnificent stone-and-clapboard mansion with a four-story turret that looked out over the sea. The driveway went on for miles and Dillon had never seen so many people except, of course, at the Thanksgiving Day Parade. He was reminded about his manners and that the boy's name was James, and then his father disappeared into the crowd of guests and was gone.

Dillon didn't have to wait long to find James. James was waiting for him at the top of the stairs and Dillon could hardly believe his eyes; James was not alone—he had his nanny with him and his thumb in his mouth! James was about three years old, and the closer Dillon came, the further behind his nanny the little boy hid.

"Sorry about him," she said. "He's real shy and his dad wants him to start hanging out with other boys." She looked as surprised to see Dillon as he was to see James. "I thought you boys would be a lot closer in age, but I guess you'll just have to help me keep an eye on him. Can't imagine you like playing with dragon trains nearly as much as he does."

Dillon wished he was shocked by the turn of events, but he wasn't. This must be a big client if his dad was so desperate to keep him happy that he dragged Dillon along. Dillon sighed and smiled at the little guy.

"You know what? I love a good game of dragon trains," he said. About an hour later James was napping and Dillon went down to the party.

There were about a hundred guests and at least two hundred staff members. There was every variety of passed hors d'oeuvres, from sushi to shish kabobs, but none of it felt much like Fourth of July food to Dillon. He wished he had a hot dog, but a minute later he was completely distracted. Out of nowhere a magnificent bald eagle flew over the garden. A moment later it was joined by the biggest bird Dillon had ever seen. He heard someone say something about the eagle and the condor that Michael McIntyre liked to show off at all his parties, and Dillon shook his head. He didn't think anyone was supposed to keep a bald eagle as a pet. But then the birds were gone. That's when he noticed the banner over the bandstand.

It had an abstract drawing of the eagle on one side and the condor on the other. In the middle were the words *Eagle and Condor Uniting Power With Potential.* Dillon didn't understand it, but he knew it had something to do with Mr. McIntyre's company. Either way, Dillon had something better on his mind.

There was a makeshift bandstand at the edge of the garden. The red, white, and blue bunting blew in the breeze and the ocean crashed over the rocks below. Dillon could see the musicians taking their places and he moved closer. The drummer wore a cowboy hat, but Dillon tried not to hold it against him. There was no doubt it was an unusual thing to see in the Hamptons, but maybe it was part of the act. A young man in blue jeans stepped up to the mike with a guitar, and the most beautiful girl Dillon had ever seen walked up beside him. The piano began a simple melody, and one by one, each musician added a layer of sound until the young woman began to sing.

Dillon was mesmerized. The bass had his heart thumping and the drums had his toes tapping. The girl was what caught his attention, but the music carried him away. For two hours he never left the band. The twang of the steel guitar and the sweet sounds of the fiddle filled his head, and the lyrics made more sense to him than anything he ever heard on the radio. Most of his friends listened to songs about going to clubs and talking tough, and while Dillon loved the music, he couldn't really relate to the lyrics.

This music was different. There was a song about the thrill of learning to drive and a song about not having the nerve to talk to a girl and that was like a page right out of his life. Dillon felt more understood in that moment than ever before.

The even a song about a guy who didn't know he liked country music. Dillon made it his business to find out more.

From across the lawn Michael McIntyre watched Dillon. He knew there were years between his son and Ryan's, but he needed to get Dillon here. He had to find out whether it had started yet. If Dillon had already made the contact that would change everything. A moment later and the bird handler walked by with the eagle.

"Where's my condor?" Michael wanted to know.

"I'm sorry Mr. McIntyre, the condor broke its wing when the wind shifted and it hit your sea wall. I'm on my way now to free it."

Michael's stare was as cold as ice. "Don't free it, shoot it. A condor with a broken wing is of no use to me."

"Sir,. . . I think I can fix the wing. It will heal. The bird is young and . . ."

Michael didn't wait to listen to the trainer's pleas. "A trainer who can't follow orders is also of no use to me. Clear?" The trainer nodded and walked away.

JULY 5, 2011

The next day Dillon went over to his dad's place. His buddy Tom was planning to meet him there, and Dillon wanted to check something out before Tom arrived. The doorman tipped his hat, and Dillon just smiled. He missed his old building and it was always nice to be back. The mahogany elevator doors closed behind him and soon he was on his way to the twenty-first floor. The lobby was like an old English library on some estate in Surrey. Persian rugs and fresh roses filled the space, and only Marco, the doorman, ever smiled. The twenty-first floor was different. There were only two apartments on this floor, as opposed to six on all the others. When the doors opened, it was a total transformation from the traditional elegance in the lobby to the sleek, modern energy of a life lived above it all. Black marble and chrome covered the floor and walls, and Venetian glass mirrors stood ready for a final check before the residents ventured out into the city. The door was stainless steel, and when Dillon swiped his fob over the sensor, a cool automated voice offered the regular greeting, "Welcome home, Dillon."

Dillon called out to his dad as he walked down the hall, but he would have been shocked if Ryan had answered. Dillon knew his dad would be out running for at least another hour, and that was one more reason to miss this place: privacy. Privacy was in short supply over at his mom's.

Dillon grabbed his laptop and plopped onto his black platform bed. He searched for country radio stations and was shocked to discover that New York City barely even had one.

He searched online for country music only to discover he didn't have a clue what he was looking for.

"What are you doing?"

Dillon jumped at the sound of Tom's voice.

"I ran into your dad in the lobby. He's in the shower, by the way." Tom made himself at home as he always did. Dillon closed the laptop. He was embarrassed, but he didn't know why.

"Nothing, I'm just looking for a song I heard."

Tom grabbed the laptop and laughed out loud.

"Country music stations? Seriously? Why?"

Now Dillon laughed. "Shut up. You ready to go?" A minute later and they were on the street heading for the skate park.

That night Dillon asked his dad about the client who had a country band flown in to play for the party.

"Michael McIntyre is a real player," said Ryan. "He's a corporate raider who grew up in Nashville." Ryan could see that Dillon was already lost. "He buys companies and sells off the parts. He has a real gift. It's almost like he knows the future. He can pick up a company just before it discovers the next big thing. Then he sells off all the parts he doesn't need and develops the best. The guy's a genius."

Dillon's dad might have gone on, but Dillon's eyes were starting to glaze over. Just then, Dillon heard something that brought him right back to the conversation.

"Anyway, I'm going to Nashville next week to close a real estate deal for Mr. McIntyre."

Dillon heard himself asking the question before his brain had a chance to tell his mouth to shut up.

"Dad, can I come?"

From the minute he said it, all he could think about was how bored he would be in a strange city, wandering around while his dad was too busy to hang out with him, but it was too late now. He didn't know why, but he knew he needed to get to Nashville. It was like the music was calling him, or some fantasy about spending time with his dad, or something. Dillon couldn't explain it, but he felt like there was a part of him that he needed to bring home.

JULY 14, 2011

The flood of May 2010 took a toll on Middle Tennessee. The Grand Ole Opry was under four feet of water, the Bridgestone Arena and L. P. Field were all but washed out, and the Cumberland River swelled up and over its banks and flooded countless homes and farms. More than a year later, most things were either restored or under construction, but the Charles family farm was still struggling. The river had always been a source of cool breezes and catfish, but now Clint Charles looked at it with nothing but contempt. It flooded his fields, which he understood was just a force of nature. It flooded his home, which he accepted as a risk his great-granddaddy had assumed when he built the house. What he could not accept, what was nothing short of a personal insult, was the fact that when the waters uprooted the old live oak, it fell onto the back porch and took out Danny's room.

The roof was torn off and there were leaves and branches all over Danny's broken bed. The glass littered the floor, and Danny's prized guitar was all scratched up with two popped strings. The last time Clint had been in Danny's room, it was immaculate: nothing out of place and furniture so polished that it all but glared at him. Now it was destroyed, a fitting monument to the life he and Sara were living. Ruins. Clint picked up the guitar and sighed. He knew where to take it, but he just couldn't bring himself to part with it.

Clint and Sara had been living in the old farmhand bunkhouse for the last few years. There were just too many memories in the farmhouse, and they maintained it like a museum. If Sara wasn't cleaning Danny's room, she was working hard somewhere else on the farm. In their thirty-one years together, Clint had never seen Sara work so much. She mucked out the stalls, turned out the horses, and worked the Internet to market their barns and boarding facilities. She never sat still and never cried; she just worked and ran. Sara had been a runner all her life but now she ran with desperation to get away from her own broken heart. The thing was, her broken heart ran right along with her.

"Okay, that's it," Clint muttered to himself, and he carried the old guitar outside. "I ain't never been a coward before and I can't keep going like this."

He walked back into the farmhouse and took out two things: family pictures and Danny's folded flag from the burial. Sara saw him but just shook her head. She had no idea what he was up to, and she decided she was too busy grooming her foal to get involved.

Clint was on the massive old tractor and heading straight for the house. She screamed to him, but there was no way he could hear her even if he wanted to. The sound of the first wall breaking was like a firecracker, and soon there was a dust cloud so thick Sara could hardly see through it. She climbed onto the tractor and saw a single tear running down his face.

"I can't do this anymore. Our whole life is like a monument to pain and I can't do it anymore. We need a clean start and I'm making it."

At first Sara didn't understand, and then Clint put the tractor back in gear and she remembered how much she missed his crazy side. Sara nudged him over and put her hand over his on the throttle. Together, they pushed the old bone-shaker right through their living room and got back out just in time to see the roof cave in. Sara and Clint laughed, cried, and cheered as they brought that old, wrecked house to its knees. It was a huge mess, but it was a new beginning. Clint took the guitar to Nashville to be fixed up, and he and Sara began to breathe a little deeper each day.

Down the street from Rosalie's Lounge on Broadway was the Lead Guitar Shop. It was a busy place full of tourists and country music. Jake Fabler, the owner, was at least a hundred years old and knew just about everyone. He held Danny's guitar in his gnarled hands and smiled. He promised Clint that he could get it fixed up with no problem at all.

"Aw yeah, this is what I'm lookin' for," Jake mumbled under his breath as he put the guitar in the back room.

The plane touched down on runway 20R at Nashville International Airport at 4:30 in the afternoon. Dillon loved to fly as much as his dad hated it. "What a waste of time," his dad complained. Dillon's dad was used to private jets, and after the stock market crash of '08, he was still adjusting to his new reality. Dillon, however, loved to travel any way he could. They grabbed their bags and were the first off the plane. No need for baggage claim because Dillon's dad didn't trust airlines enough to check anything. An hour later and they were settled in at the Heritage Hotel and heading down to the Nashville Grille for dinner.

The food was ridiculously good, but Dillon couldn't wait until the meal was over. They were headed over to Rosalie's Lounge after dinner, and the music there was supposed to be better than the barbeque—no small feat in Tennessee. A quick ride in a taxi and they were there. Under normal conditions, Dillon was too young to be allowed into a place like Rosalie's, but tonight was different.

His dad's big client, the same Michael McIntyre from the Hamptons, was throwing another one of his famous parties, and everybody who was anybody was there: record producers from New York, L.A., and, of course, Nashville; publishing execs; and plenty of musicians. Michael McIntyre was the sole owner of Big Game Music, the first music label to produce exclusively for digital downloads. Since McIntyre had bought Big Game, profits were way up because everyone knew he sold more music for less money than anyone else. He was famous for saying that hard copies were history and soon CDs would go the way of vinyl, 8-track, and cassette. When the digital market became the only choice, Big Game Music was poised to pounce. It was no surprise that Michael McIntyre was at the cutting edge of any industry he entered.

After the party Michael McIntyre took Dillon and his dad to a small honky-tonk around the corner. The adults just sat at a table in back to talk. Apparently the guy at the mike was Mr. McIntyre's latest find and McIntyre could hardly wait to show him off. Dillon made his way up to the stage. Different from the party in the Hamptons on the Fourth of July, there was no bandstand here. The stage was just a small platform near the front window with an old neon sign flashing on the wall. No five-piece band either. There wouldn't have been enough room anyway. There was just one guy and his guitar. He sang about love and trucks, and even a song about how much he loved his truck, but it was a funny song and Dillon laughed. Dillon's dad was busy with Mr. McIntyre, so when the set was over, Dillon spent some time talking to the singer.

"Hey, kid, where're you from?" the guy with the guitar wanted to know. Dillon looked down at his feet and realized how the singer knew Dillon was from out of town. There were a lot more boots than high tops around here.

"I'm from New York. My dad is Mr. McIntyre's lawyer, so I got a free trip to Nashville." Dillon shrugged.

"My name's Jason and I'm from Georgia, but I live here now. I see you like the music. You play?" Jason held out his guitar, and Dillon held up his hands to wave it away.

"No, I played the violin when I was younger, but I'm no musician." Dillon wished he had something more interesting to say.

"Tell you what, I've got a break for a minute and I'm feeling generous tonight, so I'm gonna show you something that changed my life when I was just about your age." Jason stood up and pointed to his chair. Dillon sat down and before he knew it the guitar was in his hands.

"The difference between being a musician and being a technician is that anybody can learn what notes to play; that's just technical. Being a musician requires something that can't be taught: you gotta love it in your bones. It's gotta be the only way you can imagine getting through the day, the only way you can tell your story. That can't be taught and that's good, 'cause that's what you got. Any fool can see you love it, so here you go." He showed Dillon a C chord. It sounded pretty weird when Dillon played it, but he didn't care. It was as if a huge piece of him just slid into place.

"Remember kid, they say that country music is just three chords and the truth. Now you got one of the chords, go get yourself some more, and good luck." After that, the singer was back to work. As soon as he heard the first word, Dillon recognized it. The guy with the guitar was a big deal here in Nashville, and Big Game Music wanted to make him global.

JULY 15, 2011

The next day Dillon was on Broadway again. Broadway in Nashville was more than just a little bit different from the one in New York, but one thing was the same: throngs of tourists. Slowly he made his way down the street. He knew where to meet his dad, but he still had plenty of time and he wanted to find something to bring back for his mom. She worked really hard, and he wanted to find something to make her life a little easier. So far, all he saw were cowboy hats and T-shirts, and since he couldn't really see how they would be useful to his mom in New York, he kept looking.

He decided that between grocery shopping and changing her clothes for work, his mom could always use another tote bag. Besides, he didn't think she had one with a rhinestone buckle on the front. The store was a definite tourist trap, but that was fine with Dillon. Proud of his purchase, he had just decided to head back to the hotel when something stopped him dead in his tracks. The Lead Guitar Shop had an electric blue acoustic guitar in the window and it was the most beautiful thing Dillon had ever seen. Dillon had never given much thought to guitars until recently, but now they were all he could think about.

The neck of the guitar was inlaid with mother-of-pearl and the body was the color of a blue flame. He just had to hear it. There was no doubt in his mind that his one C chord would sound better played on such a beautiful guitar. The shop was bustling with tourists and professionals alike. There was a sea of blue jeans and cowboy boots, and he could hear at least three different guitar riffs as he walked around the store. The wide floorboards creaked with every step, and the smell of stale smoke hung in the air. It was like a honky-tonk on a Sunday morning, or at least it was what Dillon imagined a honky-tonk would be like on Sunday morning. He tried to get a salesperson's attention, but no such luck. Still, he waited and kept trying until a nice girl, not much older than he was, came over to help.

"Sorry about the wait. We're kinda busy today. I'm Annie and I'm just here to help out my grandpa today, but I'll help you if I can."

Five minutes later Dillon held that magnificent, blue beauty in his hands. He sat down and threw the strap over his shoulder. He was a little embarrassed to try to play his one and only chord in front of Annie, but he did it anyway. The guitar was just too sweet not to play, no matter who was around.

"How much is it?" Dillon heard himself ask, as if he had any money anyway.

"I'm not sure." Annie smiled encouragingly, "but I know we have special sale today."

Dillon couldn't believe his luck. Maybe there was a chance he could bring his dad over here later on and he could go home with the ultimate Music City souvenir. Then reality struck. Who was he kidding? Even if it were free, his dad would never get him a guitar. His dad got him that stupid violin years ago and now he hated the violin, Beethoven, and especially his teacher, Maestro Posano. Dillon could not imagine his dad giving him a chance with a guitar.

Dillon explained that he really couldn't afford it at any price, and Annie sighed and nodded. He was nearly out the door when she called after him.

"Grandpa will seriously kill me if he finds out about this, but wait a minute." She disappeared and came back a few minutes later. In her hand was a beat-up old guitar case and a brand new strap.

"Sometimes we get old guitars to fix up and the customer just forgets about it, or can't afford it, or trades it in toward something else. This one was in the back closet where we keep the Christmas lights. I figure if we've had it that long, no one's really gonna miss it. Besides, it's a good first guitar. Nothing fancy, like the blue one in the window, but if you get new strings on it, I bet she'll sing. Tell you what, for seventy-five dollars it's yours. I'll even throw in the strings."

Dillon had $80.00 in his pocket and he quickly handed it over before she changed her mind. He thanked her at least twenty times and she smiled and hurried him out the door. He half expected to hear sirens behind him at any minute as he headed back to the hotel. The whole way up in the elevator he clutched his prize and tried to figure out how he would explain this to his dad.

Safely tucked away inside room 302, he opened the case. There it was, a miracle of spruce, mahogany, and strings. Gently, he lifted it out of its case and placed it on his lap. He wrapped his hand around the fingerboard and drew the pick across the strings. No doubt about it, it was the best C chord he'd ever played.

He barely even noticed when his dad came into the room an hour later. He was lost in his own world, trying to figure out the G chord he'd found online.

"Where'd you get that?" his dad said as he crossed the room. "I haven't seen one like that since high school."

Dillon gave his dad the guitar and was stunned to hear

the first few bars of a classic rock anthem fill the air.

"You know how to play the guitar? You never told me."

"Well, your old man has to keep a few surprises up his sleeve, right?" His dad reached for the strap and fastened it to the base and back of the guitar. "Here you go. That will make it easier for you to hold."

"Aren't you mad? Aren't you gonna tell me it's too big to take back to New York or something?" Dillon was really confused.

"I'm gonna assume you didn't steal it, so I guess if that's what you want to spend your savings on, you could do a whole lot worse. Music City, right? Well, rock on."

It was as though Dillon had just met his dad for the very first time. Who was this guy who played guitar riffs (he had just learned that word) and didn't freak out when surprised? *Who knows and who cares, as long as he is here to stay*, Dillon thought. He smiled as he put the guitar away. When he tried to fasten the case, Dillon noticed it was stuck on something. He lifted the guitar and found a piece of paper he hadn't noticed before. When he turned it over, he saw only one word: *Remember*. Dillon felt chills run down his back.

AUGUST 2, 2011

By the time they got back to New York, his dad was back to business again, but at least he didn't hassle Dillon about the guitar and even paid for it to be carried on board. When they got back to his dad's place, Dillon opened the case to show his dad the note.

"Hey Dad, check this out." Dillon waited for his dad's response and then discovered why he was being ignored: his dad had fifty emails in his inbox and from the look on his face, every one of them was more interesting than Dillon.

Back at his mom's, Maggie smiled when she saw the tote bag and put it discreetly in the back of her closet. Life got back to normal with one small change—Dillon was obsessed with country music. He knew three chords now, but judging from his musical abilities, he was not convinced they were the same three chords that singer told him about.

His friends thought the guitar was cool, but they were so over his "hillbilly phase."

"What the freak, man? What is that?" Tom looked disgusted when he scrolled through the music on Dillon's phone. Dillon was getting his jacket and boots on, and they were going for a slice of pizza and to walk over to the park. "Oh, no! No way, my friend. Step away from the boots!" Tom looked and sounded like a cop trying to talk down a jumper.

"Relax. I like these. You should get a pair," Dillon said.

"No man, you should get a pair—a pair of sneakers or loafers or even flip-flops, but cowboy boots in New York City? You see any cows around here?"

Dillon laughed, but Tom didn't. Instead, he just handed Dillon a pair of sneakers and walked out the door.

"And one more thing," Tom called over his shoulder. "Put back that denim jacket and put on a hoodie like a normal person. Jeans and a denim jacket look like a freakin' hillbilly tuxedo." Tom shook his head and muttered something about saving Dillon from himself as the boys headed out onto the street.

Dillon thought about staying home to play the guitar a little longer, but he didn't think Tom would understand. No matter where he was, whether at his mom's or his dad's, playing the guitar was where Dillon felt most at home and least alone.

Back at The Lead Guitar Shop, in Nashville, chaos was king and old Jake was as mad as a cat forced to snorkel.

"What do you mean it's not there?" Jake yelled at his clerk. "I specifically put it there so it would be out of the way and safe from all you meddlers!"

Everyone scurried around the store and looked again where they had already looked at least five times. No one knew where the old guitar from the Charles farm was hiding. In truth, no one except Jake really wanted to find it anyway. Jake had no right to do what he was doing: he was just supposed to fix that guitar, not sell it, but the old greedy rat couldn't resist. He knew the Charles family didn't realize that Danny's old six string was worth a fortune on the collector's market, and anyway Danny wasn't coming back to play it, so why shouldn't Jake make a little money and let the Charles family get on with their lives? If the New York collector saw it, he would buy it for sure, and Mr. and Mrs. Charles would be okay, eventually. Jake planned to give them a different guitar and let them think the refurbishment changed the color a little.

Jake sold a lot of guitars on consignment and he was good at it. If the guitar itself wasn't enough to entice the buyer, Jake was a masterful storyteller who would "embellish" the details just enough to make the collector want it as a conversation piece if not as a musical instrument. The only problem was that this particular guitar was not there on consignment. It belonged to the Charles family and everyone knew it was all they had left of their son. The only things that came back from Afghanistan when he was killed were his dog tags and his broken body, so they held onto his old guitar.

The clerk still recalled the day Clint had dropped it off to be fixed up. He almost didn't let it go, but Jake was a very convincing man. Now it was lost or stolen, and the New York collector and the Tennessee farmer were both out of luck. This was a disaster all the way around. The search was called off a few minutes later when Mr. Jay Warrington walked in. He looked around the store like a general inspecting his troops—a decidedly unimpressed general.

"I'm here to see Jake Fabler and I've come a long way."

Annie walked toward the back door and pretended to keep looking for the guitar. Her grandfather smiled and shook the man's hand. No one knew what would happen next, and even though everybody tried to look busy, they couldn't quite look away.

"Mr. Warrington, what a pleasure to meet you." Jake flashed a giant grin.

Good grief, thought Annie, *my grandpa has turned into a used car salesman!*

"Come right this way. Here is the special little beauty you have come so far to meet." He'd found it? No way. Annie was the one person in the whole store who knew that simply was not possible. Relieved as she was that the guitar wouldn't go to a collector, she was sick over the fact that the guitar they were looking for must be the same one she had practically given away a few weeks ago.

An hour later Mr. Warrington was insisting they call him Jay, and thankfully Grandpa was acting like his old self again. *The whole used car salesman thing must have been some kind of nervous reaction*, Annie thought. *You know, like a rash.* The guitar Grandpa sold him was a limited-edition acoustic that had once belonged to Johnny Cash, maybe or sort of. Well, technically Johnny Cash might have only played it once while he was in the store, but Grandpa liked to say that any instrument played once by a true legend belonged to that legend forever. Jay was thrilled and Jake and his professional reputation were still intact, so all in all, it was a pretty good day.

When the door closed, Jake locked it and turned the sign on the door to *Closed.*

"Somebody better explain to me what the heck just happened. Where in the world is the miserable guitar that guy really flew all this way to see?"

AUGUST 26, 2011

It took a week to clear the land and a month to get the permits to build a new house on the other side of the Charles family farm. They decided to build a small cottage with a wrap-around porch that would be perfect for sipping sweet tea and watching the sunset.

Ever since they started working on it, things were slowly getting better. Clint put Danny's flag and wrecked dog tags in a shadow box in the new front hall, and he and Sara spent their days working with the horses and their nights working on the house.

"Mr. Charles? Hi, this is Fred Monroe. I work over here at The Lead Guitar Shop."

Clint was delighted to hear from someone at the guitar shop.

"Hello. I bet you have some good news for me. Is the guitar ready to be picked up?"

"Not exactly. The thing is, it appears to have been lost in shipping. Mr. Jake sent it to Memphis for a special sealant and now we don't have it." Fred felt sick. He hated covering for Jake, but he needed his job. "Sir, I'm really sorry."

When Clint put down the phone, he was heartbroken.

"I can't believe that fool lost Danny's guitar! I never should have left it with him. How could I be so stupid?"

Sara just gave him a hug, and what she whispered into his ear put the whole lousy thing into perspective: "We already lost the most precious part of our lives when Danny was killed.

I don't need a guitar to remind me of our son and neither do you." With that she sat down and announced that they were going to New York for Christmas.

"New York City?" Clint was confused.

"Here's the thing: Danny always wanted to go there and he never got the chance, so I thought maybe we could go for him." It made perfect sense; Sara wanted Danny's dreams to live on.

SEPTEMBER 9, 2011

Dillon came home and threw his new backpack onto his bed. What a day! School had just started and he was already counting down to Thanksgiving vacation. He had more homework than he knew what to do with, but there was no way he could start yet. He needed to unwind at least a little bit, so he picked up his guitar. He was about halfway through a new song when he screwed up the bridge, again!

"Man! You think you're ever gonna make it all the way through?"

Dillon flew off his bed with the guitar clutched in his white-knuckled hand. "Who said that? Who's there?"

"Aren't you supposed to wait until I say Knock, knock before you ask who's there? No wonder you can't get that G7th chord. You're always moving too fast and getting way ahead of yourself."

Dillon was as white as a ghost. Clearly he was losing his mind. "Hearing voices is never a good sign," he muttered to himself as he slid down his bedroom wall. His heart was racing and he wished he could believe the radio or TV was on, but unfortunately he knew they weren't.

"First off, you are not hearing voices. It's just one voice. I wanted to talk to you, but it took me a while to figure out how. So I've spent the last two months figuring it out and then waiting for the right time to talk to you, and you know what? There is no right time for a spirit to start talking to a kid, so I just decided today was your lucky day."

"You're a spirit, as in dead?" Dillon whispered.

"Thank you, Captain Obvious."

Dillon started to sweat. In his mind he kept telling himself that he was fine, maybe just a little too stressed or tired, or maybe he just had a crazy imagination, but his brain could not persuade his ears not to listen. That's when his eyes joined the mutiny. He could feel his fingers loosen their grip on the guitar. It was like he was handing it to someone, but there was no one there. His guitar began to move, and then it began to play. In fact, it wasn't just playing: it was playing perfectly.

Dillon watched his floating guitar, and what he saw next had his gut churning and his lungs gasping: the longer the music played, the more clearly Dillon could see a young man materializing. He wasn't ghostly at all, at least not in the Hollywood way. He wore blue jeans and a red T-shirt. His hair was brown and he had big blue eyes. The only part of him that was hard to see were his fingers, but not because they were translucent or made of some kind of cosmic vapor. They were hard to see because they moved so fast over the strings.

"If you look real close, you'll see sparks flying from my finger tips," he joked as he played. When he was finished, he put down the guitar and began to fade out of sight. "My name is Danny and this used to be my guitar. I guess I just missed it more than I realized, because when I heard you trying to play it, I had to come."

Not really up to date on astral etiquette, Dillon stammered, "I'm Dillon, nice to almost meet you."

A moment later Danny was gone. Dillon sat down on the bed with a thump. He took a deep breath, willing his heart to return to its usual steady rhythm. Did he really just see what he thought he saw? Hear what he thought he heard? Slowly, he turned his head and gazed at the guitar. The same guitar that had just risen into the air and then was being played by a . . . no, not possible.

He reached over and grabbed the guitar. “Okay,” he told the instrument, “I’m either schizophrenic, seeing things and hearing voices . . .” Dillon frowned. “Or maybe I’m psychic and really seeing ghosts.” Dillon didn’t know what to think, but he kept coming back to the same two indisputable facts: someone or something put that note in his guitar case, and someone or something had just appeared out of thin air and played his guitar.

“You’re not crazy or sick or even particularly gifted, as your massacre of that G7th chord has painfully pointed out. No, man, you’re just a normal kid hearing from a normal guy who happens to be dead. Really, this is no big deal from my side.” Danny said in his smooth southern drawl.

“What are you talking about? Dead is a pretty big deal on any side! And speaking of sides, why the heck didn’t you stay on yours? Isn’t this against the rules or something?”

Danny began to float back into view and then fade out again. Only his voice remained clear and steady. “By the way, much as I hate to admit it and much as I love teasing you, I think you may have a gift for music, in spite of your abominable chord progression.”

Dillon decided right then and there, even if this was the first symptom of schizophrenia, he was going to just go with it. Whoever or whatever this guy was, he was funny and friendly and a great guitarist, so as long as no one found out about it, why not? Hanging out with a ghost could be fun. And who knew, maybe he’d learn something too.

SEPTEMBER 11, 2011

Dillon hated the divorce, he hated 9/11, and he hated the vacant look in his mom's eyes whenever she talked about her brother, Joe. Dillon couldn't remember life before the War on Terror, but those who could remember said that 9/11 changed everything. Dillon didn't know. All he knew was that there was no way to measure the toll taken on that day because some families would live in the aftershock forever.

Dillon walked to church between his mother and father, a rare occurrence on any day, but nearly unheard of in the five years since the divorce. The tenth anniversary of 9/11 was a tough day in New York City. There were all kinds of memorials and Dillon couldn't figure out how Mayor Bloomberg could possibly be in so many places at the same time. Dillon didn't remember much about Uncle Joe, but he knew he had been a firefighter who gave his life on that day, and he knew his mom was never the same again.

After the service Dillon grabbed his guitar and headed over to the park. He needed to be alone. It was weird to see his parents together and he needed to shake off the strangeness and overall sadness of the day. He sat down on the end of his favorite bench beside the gate. The sun warmed his face and the smell of a hotdog vendor made his stomach growl. As he began to play, he breathed a little easier and soon he was lost in his music.

"Man, I hate sad songs." Dillon was startled to hear Danny talking to him here at the park, but he tried not to show it. "Seriously, don't you know something else?" Danny asked.

"In case you haven't noticed, I'm ignoring you," Dillon muttered. "This cannot start happening out in public."

"And in case you haven't noticed, you are talking to me, out here in public, looking like a fool sitting on a park bench playing sad songs on my guitar."

Dillon and Danny were both startled when a passerby threw a dollar into Dillon's guitar case.

"Whoa! Looks like you've officially gone pro." Danny laughed.

Dillon smiled and started playing again. This time, he decided to sing a little louder. By the end of the afternoon, he had made $82.35. Not bad at all for a kid from New York playing country music in the park. At one point, a man asked him if he wrote the song he was singing. It was an old country song about an unsolved murder. Dillon couldn't resist the joke.

"Yeah, I wrote it. Do you like it?"

"No, I do not!" the stranger replied. "It freaks me out."

Dillon could not believe that no one else heard Danny laughing. "It freaks him out? That's awesome! That means you sang it just about perfect."

Dillon started spending all his free time at home playing the guitar. He still saw Tom at school, but he just couldn't bring himself to talk about the World Series when all he could think about was the ghost in his guitar. And there was absolutely no way he was going to talk to anyone about that. Tom was his usual self, reading *Popular Science* and trying to look cool with a skinny tie hanging from his skinny neck. "Hey Cowboy," Tom offered, "let's hit *Coffee Crème* after school. I could seriously use a latte."

Dillon just shook his head and shrugged, pointing to

his earbuds as if he couldn't hear a word Tom said. Tom would have been furious if anyone else had done that, but Dillon looked so lost that Tom wondered whether Dillon even realized just how weird he was becoming. He spent less and less time with his old friend and more and more time with his old guitar. Dillon's parents were glad he liked to practice, but they were starting to notice that he was always alone. The thing was, Dillon was never actually alone.

That night when Danny arrived, Dillon had a question. "Why are you here? I mean, not that I don't enjoy your company or anything, but why? Heaven must be lame if you'd rather hang out in this place."

"Let me tell you something: heaven is ridiculously awesome, I think. Anyway, I'm here because, well, technically I'm not exactly sure why I'm here with you, but I know it's for a good reason."

"That sounds lame all right."

"Look, I'm a spirit, that's true, but I never said I was a psychic. I don't know why I get to be here, or why you can see and hear me. What I do know is that there must be *some* reason." Dillon thought that was a wholly unsatisfying answer, but he let it go.

Dillon and Danny were sitting on Ryan's couch after school the next day. "Unbelievable!" Danny exclaimed. "I cannot believe you missed that one." Dillon played the video game as player one, but lately he always had advice from his ghostly wingman.

"You couldn't hit that either," Dillon retorted.

"Hit it? I would have crushed it!" Now it was Dillon's turn to laugh.

Later that night at his mom's place, he found another

note in the guitar case. It made him more than just a little bit nervous, but Dillon reached into the case and pulled out a crumpled piece of paper. He flattened the note out by pressing it against his jeans and then held it up to the light. When his eyes wandered from the note back to the guitar, he thought about Danny. Dillon didn't know why Danny didn't just talk to him, but he figured that the whole thing was so strange anyway, one more weirdness didn't really matter. He unfolded the note and saw one word scrawled across the page: *Death.*

Dillon's hand trembled as he held the paper. What kind of note was this? Danny seemed like a nice guy. Why would he send such scary notes? For that matter, why send notes at all? Dillon could see Danny and hear him, so why not just get to the point? Why the drama?

Dillon hated drama. He hated it during his parents' divorce, he hated it at school, and he sure as heck hated it in his paranormal encounters. At that moment, he wished he could curl into his mom's lap and feel safe again. It had been a long time since he felt safe. His parents' divorce made him feel like a drifter in his own family. In fact, he was literally drifting in between his parents' homes, rules, and friends, and each place kept a strict border so that the two would never overlap. He had separate wardrobes, games, books, and rules at each house. The only thing that crossed the border with him was this guitar and Danny; and if now Danny was going to go all psycho about it, Dillon was pretty sure he couldn't bring him along much longer.

No doubt about it, Dillon would have to confront Danny and find out just what the heck was going on. *Remember*? *Death*? Was someone about to die? What did the notes mean?

Dillon put away the guitar and climbed into bed. His mom was working late as usual and he was too tired to warm up dinner anyway. Dillon fell into a deep and heavy sleep right away.

"Dillon! Dillon! Wake Up! Can you hear me? Dillon, please!"

Dillon fell like a brick onto the floor and tried to shake himself awake. He felt groggy and sore. When he could focus his eyes, he felt sick. There was something sticky all over his hands.

Dillon's mother knelt beside him on the floor. She examined his hands and looked into his eyes. "You're a mess. Eyes bloodshot, pupils dilated, but given the darkness of the room, I guess that's to be expected." Dillon's mom helped him up, but he couldn't tell if she was more mad or upset. Dillon's stomach turned and he felt the room spin. His mother's tight grip on his arm began to throb as he staggered toward the bathroom. When the lights went on, Dillon gasped. Why were his hands covered in blood?

"Where does it hurt?" his mother wanted to know as she turned his hands over and examined the other side.

"I . . . I don't know, Mom. I know it's weird, but actually my hands don't hurt at all."

"You mean they're numb? Do you have any feeling in your arms?"

"Mom, you don't understand. My hands aren't numb. In fact, they feel fine. My hands don't hurt at all, but where did all this blood come from?"

Dillon's mother couldn't quite decide if she was relieved that his hands were uninjured or horrified about what must be a serious head injury if he really thought he was okay. She slowly walked Dillon over to the bathroom sink. There was no doubt about it; Dillon seemed fine in every way. She turned on the water and put her son's hands under the tap. As the bloodstains disappeared, Dillon's flawless hands were revealed. The only injuries he had were the tiny blisters on his fingertips from playing the guitar.

"Mom?" Dillon's voice crackled with rising panic. "What's happening to me?"

The nurse in Dillon's mom took over and in her best "It's not so bad" reassuring tone, she told him to try to relax because everything would be all right soon. She put a salve on his blisters and made him promise to lay off the guitar for a few days. Even though neither one of them believed it, she blamed the blood on the blisters and declared that they must be a lot worse than they looked. Dillon was about to object, but stopped. Maybe the guitar was getting to be a little too much for him. A break from the whole thing might be a good idea after all.

Dillon tried to remember something about his dream. What little he could remember was more of a feeling than an actual narrative. He had a feeling of overall sadness about time wasted, and he thought maybe Uncle Joe was in the dream, but that was probably just because of all the 9/11 talk all around him. He wished he could remember the details, but it was like trying to catch a bubble: every time he almost had it, the memory just popped and disappeared.

Dillon flipped on the TV and heard the news blare. "This just in: Thirty Americans military personnel presumed dead after a helicopter attack outside Kabul, Afghanistan, this morning." Pictures of fresh-faced soldiers in new uniforms flashed across the screen. One guy reminded Dillon of Danny, and he began to wonder about how Danny died.

The more he thought about it, the more he realized he didn't know too much about Danny at all. He knew he was young, a ghost, and a great guitar player. Judging from his southern drawl, he was definitely not a New Yorker, and he seemed like a good guy or ghost or whatever, but Dillon really didn't know much else about him.

Now that he was getting notes that would freak out a monster, Dillon wasn't so sure he could just keep going along for the ride. He needed answers from Danny and he needed them now. He knew what he had to do. Dillon didn't believe Danny would hurt him, but he had to find out what was happening before things got worse.

The next morning Dillon was up early. He played the guitar for a full hour before school. Nothing. He called for Danny and he even prayed that Danny would come, but nothing. Tired and frustrated, he went to school. At lunch Dillon's friend Tom could tell something was wrong, but he didn't mention it. Things just weren't the same between them anymore. Dillon tried to catch Tom's eye, but Tom looked away. "Maybe it's better that way," Dillon said mostly to himself. A few months ago he would have walked right up to Tom and within fifteen minutes he would know everything. He would know what Tom had had for breakfast, his weekend plans, and which girl he was hopelessly crushing on, but not now. The sound of the people shouting in the cafeteria reminded Dillon of the fight he and Tom had last week.

Dillon didn't want to think about it, but he couldn't help but remember. Tom wanted to go to the park and kick the ball around after school, maybe get a hot dog, but Dillon blew him off. All Dillon cared about was the guitar and a new riff he was learning. Tom reached the end of his patience and thundered, "That stupid guitar is all you can think about! You can't even play it right!" Dillon was sure that Tom didn't mean for the words to come out as roughly as they did, but still Dillon stumbled under the weight of them. If Tom had thrown a box of razor blades at Dillon, he couldn't have hurt him more. After that they had just avoided each other.

Now everything was just odd and awkward between them. Tom might have missed Dillon, but Dillon let Tom think that he was too busy to care. If Tom only knew what was really going on in Dillon's head.

Dillon was distracted by an annoying drumming sound. *Tap, tap, tap, tap*. It was getting right on Dillon's last nerve when he looked down and realized it was him. He put his hands on his lap, took a deep breath, and tried not to look quite so nervous: not an easy feat, because the more Dillon thought about the notes and the blood on his hands, the more scared he was. No matter how he tried, he couldn't figure out what the notes meant, and now he couldn't even get Danny to talk to him.

"Shoot, boy. You look like a long-tailed cat in a room full of rocking chairs."

Dillon jumped and spilled his soda all over his shirt.

"Seriously? Now? I tried to call you for over an hour this morning and you were nowhere, but you show up here in the freaking cafeteria at school?" Dillon was scared about the notes and everything, but right now he was even more worried that anyone else in the cafeteria could either see Danny or, worse, see Dillon sitting there looking like a crazy person talking to himself. Tom thought Dillon was acting weird again, but he just shrugged it off. Dillon guessed that Tom would think he was just mumbling along with the music on his phone.

"Relax," Danny drawled. "This is a private party. So what the heck is going on? You never called on me before and now I have like twenty messages from you."

"Messages? You mean there's voicemail in heaven?"

"You know what? I think maybe you're right. You are nuts." Danny chuckled.

"Whatever. If you knew I was calling, why didn't you come?"

"I did come, you fool. I'm right here, aren't I?"

Dillon decided it was a waste of time to keep this up. Besides, other people were starting to stare, so he stood up and prayed that Danny would follow him outside. Once he got out into the sunlight, he just kept walking. Dillon had never cut school in his life, but he needed to talk to Danny and there was no way he could say what he needed to say there. Danny tried to make Dillon smile by pointing out the absurdity of a sign for jumbo shrimp, but Dillon practically glared at him. After that, they walked in silence the whole way home to Dillon's mom's place.

Dillon pushed open the door to his room and opened the guitar case. Danny just sat down, watching him. Dillon planned to confront Danny with the notes, but when he reached into the guitar case, he was the one confronted, not with notes, but with a nail. When Dillon reached into the velvet lining, the back of his hand caught on a rusty nail that had pushed through the velvet lining from the hinge on the lid. Dillon jerked his hand out and shrieked. Danny was up in an instant and immediately put himself between Dillon and the guitar case.

"That's it. Straight answers. What in the hell is going on here?" Danny wanted to know. "What happened?" Danny fumed when he saw Dillon's hand.

Dillon didn't answer, he just pointed into the case. This time it was Danny's turn to be surprised. He read *Remember, Death,* and on a third blood stained page, *Honor.* Danny turned to Dillon and even for a ghost he looked pale.

"What is this? Have you seen these before?" Danny held the notes in his fist.

"That's why I was calling you," Dillon began. "I got the first one in Nashville, just after I got the guitar. The next one arrived after I got back home to New York. The third one, I've never seen before."

Danny's military training kicked in. "In what order did they arrive?"

"*Remember*, then *Death,* and now *Honor*. What does it all mean? I thought maybe they were from you and I couldn't figure out why you would send me scary notes when we talk to each other all the time. Judging from your face though, now I see how stupid that theory really was."

"Dillon, I did not, would not, and will not send you anything that scares or threatens you. I tell you what though, someone or something is trying to freak you or us out, and you know what? It's working!"

"There's more. Last night I fell asleep and when I woke up, my hands were covered in blood. I wasn't hurt. They were just covered in blood."

"Oh, is that all?! Why didn't you tell me?"

Dillon felt the throbbing in his left hand and grabbed a towel from his pile of laundry in the corner. "Last night, there was no cut, but today . . . well, you can see for yourself." Dillon held his hand out, and Danny winced. The cut from the nail was oozing blood over the back of Dillon's hand. The good news was that there was no doubt in Dillon's mind that Danny wasn't the one sending the notes. The bad news was that the notes were still coming. Dillon felt three things all at once: scared, overwhelmed, and grateful that because of Danny, he wasn't in this alone.

SEPTEMBER 30, 2011

All Dillon could think was *Thank God it's Friday.* It had been a week from hell, and this weekend was shaping up to be just swell. His dad wanted to take him up to Connecticut to some tourist-trap farm to go pumpkin picking and get fresh cider. Dillon could hardly believe that the same guy who played classic rock wanted to go pumpkin picking. For Pete's sake, didn't he realize that Dillon was fifteen years old? *Gee Dad, could we go to the playground too?* Ugh!

Still, Dillon knew that he would go and pretend to like it because the pathetic truth was that he would do just about any lame thing if it meant he could hang out with his dad. The guitar and Danny were the constants in Dillon's life. Even though the old guitar brought unexplainable things, even scary things, into Dillon's life, he still loved it. Playing it wasn't really a choice; it was more of a need. He packed up the guitar and his bag and headed downstairs to wait. His mom was busy cleaning up the kitchen, and he felt the same pang of guilt he always felt when he left. He knew she would work pretty much all weekend, just to get out of their empty house. He knew she would eat Chinese food and sleep on the couch, and he knew she would say she had had a "fabulous" weekend when he returned.

A horn beeping startled Dillon, and he looked out the window and laughed out loud. There was his father in a truly ridiculous minivan, all smiles and waving as he parked in front of the building.

"Well, that confirms it. He's a lunatic," Dillon

muttered before he realized his mom had heard every word.

"He may be crazy, but that's still your dad, buddy." His mom smiled as she opened the door. For a moment, it was like old times. Ryan might have been any dad coming home from work and being greeted by his family, but only for a moment. The tension entered the room before he did.

"Make sure he gets some rest this time," Dillon's mom, Maggie, said. "I'm still worried about the way he is sleeping or not sleeping, I guess." His mom had left and *Nurse Hardknuckles* had taken her place.

"Don't worry, I won't break him. I promise I'll return him to you in full working order." Dillon's dad tried to smile but just looked tired. Dillon almost felt sorry for him. Dillon's mom had a way of making a person feel incompetent sometimes. "Come on, Dillon, let's get you out of here before we get any more instructions."

"Dad? Why did you rent this thing?" The closer he got to the minivan, the worse it looked. It had a dent on the side and alarming green stains across the back seat. The bonus was the somewhat less-than-delightful, musty smell that blew all over them when Dillon's dad turned on the heat.

"I rented this thing because we are going to the farm in Connecticut tomorrow and I am most certainly not driving the Lexus on the farm."

"You know I'm fifteen, right? Pumpkin picking? Why can't we just get the pumpkin at the grocery store like normal New Yorkers?"

"Because it's not just us going. I invited a friend to join us. There is someone I want you to meet. Her name is Jane, and I want you to promise you'll be nice."

Dillon felt like someone had just punched him in the

gut. He noticed his hands were trembling, so he sat on them and stared straight ahead.

"Jane? Is she your girlfriend or something?" Dillon felt like his throat was closing.

"She's a nice person, Dillon, and clearly she is both a girl and a friend, so yeah, I guess you could call her a girlfriend. Why not?"

"Are you getting serious with this woman? How long have you been seeing her?" Dillon's parents had been divorced for a few years, but this was the first time his father ever talked about dating.

"Take it easy, kiddo. I'm not in the habit of answering to my son."

"And I'm not in the habit of putting on some happy father-and-son dog-and-pony show!" Dillon railed.

"Oh boy, here we go." Dillon knew that southern drawl in an instant, and then he felt Danny's hand on his shoulder. "Take a breath, Dillon. This might be okay."

"No. This is most certainly not okay." Dillon was surprised to find he was trembling with rage. His dad looked confused. "Does Mom even know?"

"Yes, she knows. She's not exactly happy about it, but yes, she knows. I asked her to let me tell you about it, so she is giving me the time to do that."

Not another word was said as they drove across town. Dillon waited in silence when his dad ordered dinner from the bistro around the corner and glared at him when he suggested a game of cards. About halfway through dinner, Dillon's dad gave up trying to resurrect the evening and turned on the TV. Dillon disappeared into his room and began to play. The first few chords fell off his fingers like water rushing in a stream, smooth, easy and effortless. He was barely paying attention to what he was playing when his dad opened the door, sheet-white and breathless.

"Why are you playing that? Who told you to learn it?"

Dillon had to think for a minute about what he was doing. He was just strumming his mom's favorite song. He liked to play it for her, and tonight he just started playing it without even realizing what he was doing. He didn't know why, but the whole idea of meeting his father's girlfriend made him want to declare some kind of loyalty to his mom.

"It's just an old song. Mom and I like it and I felt like playing it. What's the problem?" It was the first time Dillon had spoken to his dad in hours.

"That is more than just some old song to me. It's from a time in my life when I believed in fairy tales and miracles. Do me a favor, play something else, play anything else." His dad closed the door and for the first time in a long time, Dillon was actually worried about him. He looked worn out and really sad. Until that moment Dillon always thought his dad had a sort of selfish invincibility.

He remembered the night his dad left and how he barely looked at Dillon in the front hall. "Dillon, it's time you learned," he had said, "that everything in this world has a beginning and an end and this charade is over." Dillon's mom cried in the other room and he just stood there watching his father walk out of their lives.

Before the divorce, Dillon and his dad used to ride their bikes from one end of Central Park to the other and then stop at Franny's Market on West 57th Street for strawberry banana smoothies. They loved Saturday mornings on the town: his mom could relax and they could have their "guy time." Dillon didn't even know if his dad still owned a bike, but it didn't matter. It's not like there was any chance of them going for a ride now anyhow.

Dillon put down the guitar and closed his eyes. Ten minutes later he was out cold, and anyone looking at him would have sworn he was sound asleep. They would have been dead wrong.

Dillon looked around but couldn't see anything. The cold, damp walls were pitch black and less inviting. Was this a dream? Slowly, he stepped forward. He heard glass crunching beneath his feet and a sickening sound of wailing in the distance. As he inched forward he reached out his hands and tried to feel his way out of this horrible place. His hands met some kind of slime oozing down the wall, and when he pulled his hand back, he was sure it was bleeding. Dillon took a deep breath to steady his nerves, but gasped instead. There was some kind of rancid odor coming from the slime all over his hands and no matter how hard he tried, he just couldn't shake it off.

He began to whisper to himself to stave off the abject terror building inside him. "Okay, everything is still okay." Slowly he inched forward again. In the darkness he felt a cold breeze pass over him. Hoping it was coming from outside, he pressed on. The glass under his feet was starting to cut into his feet and it hurt. Desperate to know where he was and, more importantly, how to get out, he kept walking. Step after step, he walked on through the inky blackness with only the breeze for company. Then he finally got a break.

The breeze really *was* coming from outside, and as he lifted his head, Dillon nearly cheered when he saw the night sky. Never before had the stars and the moon looked so wonderful to him. Faster now, he followed the breeze, and the night sky came closer and closer. A few more steps and he was sure he would be out of this cave or tunnel or whatever it was, and then he could try to find his way back home.

The moonlight was warm and welcoming as he took the next step and left the awful cave behind. He expected to stand on soft ground, maybe even grass or a path. At the very least he expected to leave the crunching of broken glass behind. Dillon didn't know he had already seen the best this place had to offer.

The last step from the cave was much more than Dillon bargained for. As soon as his two feet touched the ground, it began to shake. What started as a tremor grew into a full-blown earthquake and the breeze became a whirlwind. In the moonlight Dillon saw trees uprooted and felt splashes of icy rain on his face. The field was like a moonscape, barren and dark. Dillon tried to keep moving but stumbled. His feet were sore and his hands were bleeding, but he didn't give up. The adrenaline from his terror pushed him on. Anxious and alert, he crouched down to grasp onto the roiling earth.

There was no way to walk on the ground, so he crawled. The ground heaved and churned around and the noise was so loud it felt like the world was vibrating. Thunder cracked in the distance, but the lightning struck inches from Dillon's head and burned the ground around him. When he couldn't even crawl forward because of the seething and quaking of the field, he crouched down low and looked around for some kind of shelter. There was none.

Another thunder crack and Dillon looked up just in time to see a tree limb falling. It crashed to the ground and began to roll right for him. Dillon got up to run but it was too late. Dillon, the tree, and at least a million raindrops fell into some sort of great abyss. Down and down they fell, and on at least three occasions Dillon was sure the tree would hit him. In a truly exhausted moment, he almost wished it would.

He landed with a thud only inches away from where the tree had crashed down moments before. Convinced that every bone in his twisted body was shattered, Dillon lay very still. Even opening his eyes took a monumental effort. Afraid of what he might see, he gingerly opened one eye. What he saw confused him almost as much as it was a relief.

"Well, I guess you wanted to know, so here it is. Can't say I ever wanted to come back, but there is no way I'd let you go without me." Danny reached out his hand to help Dillon stand.

"Where are we? Is this hell?" Dillon was afraid to hear the answer.

"War, hell, really I don't reckon there's much difference. You wanted to know about how I died, right? Well, you're about to find out."

"Can you read my mind? How did you know? Why can't you just tell me? Why did you have to bring me here? How . . ."

"Slow down and back up! No, I can't read your mind, but wanting to know how I died would be a logical question to ask, right? And I didn't bring you here. Man, I wouldn't bring anyone here." Danny shivered and looked over his shoulder. Dillon was amazed to discover that he was all right. Nothing was broken and nothing was bleeding, either. Great.

"What should we do?" he asked Danny.

"I'll tell you one thing, the next time you want to know something, just do us both a favor and ask about it upfront. Don't go putting us through this kind of thing any more."

Danny was getting annoyed. “Shoot, I don’t know what I’m so freaked out about, I’m already dead. It’s not like I’m in any danger. I need to shake this off.”

“Danny? Why did you come with me? You’re right, I did wonder how you died, but it’s not an easy question to ask. Still, I had no idea that I could cause a vision or nightmare or whatever this is. Anyway, I know why I’m here, but if it makes you so nervous, why did you agree to come with me? Are you my guardian angel or something?”

Danny burst out laughing. “If you could meet my father, he would surely tell you that I’m no angel! I’m not quite sure why I’m here yet, but I’m guessing it must be important to both of us. Either way, I ain’t letting you into my nightmare without me.”

The sky lit up with an explosive blast that shook the ground. Danny threw himself over Dillon and swore. For a ghost, he felt remarkably solid, and Dillon hoped Danny couldn’t tell that he was shaking.

“Now! Move! We need to take cover!” Danny shouted in his ear. The next moment they were up and running across the fields. They ran into an old building that was equal parts decrepit and dilapidated. They needed the shelter, but Danny wished they had anywhere else to go. As soon as they got inside, they both knew it was a mistake, but only Danny knew why. The place was dark and falling down around them. The floor was dirty and piled high with broken crates and sandbags. A second explosion rocked the place, and bits of the ceiling began to fall. At that moment Dillon saw something he would never forget. A little girl ran past him, and before he could reach her, she was scooped up by gnarled hands covered in grease and sweat. The rest of the monster was hiding behind a low wall. They heard more crying and shouting, but Dillon couldn't tell where it was coming from.

He looked to Danny, who just put his fingers to his lips, warning Dillon to be quiet. Then Danny pointed to a pile of crates and trash in the corner of the room. Dillon watched and saw three armed men, and then three more joined them. They had the little girl, and it was clear they were preparing for something big. Dillon's eyes were wide as saucers, but he didn't want to look. Someone had to do something. Someone had to help the little girl, but there was no one there except Dillon and Danny, and Danny was a ghost!

"What should we do?" Dillon whispered.

Danny answered by shaking his head, reminding Dillon to keep quiet. Dillon could tell that Danny knew exactly where they were and exactly what would happen, but he didn't know the rules of this nightmare. Could they be seen? Heard? Were they just observers? Participants? Dillon didn't have a clue how this kind of thing worked, but he was sure he didn't want anybody getting hurt. Danny put his hand on Dillon's shoulder and moved him closer. Why Danny felt so protective of Dillon, he couldn't figure. But Danny was sure he would die all over again to protect him.

Then there was a breeze again and Dillon breathed a sigh of relief. A door opened, and the cavalry arrived. The girl would be saved after all. Eight men in uniform were coming into the building and crouching low. They were armed to the teeth and wore the American flag on their jackets. Dillon nearly ran over to hug them.

Before anyone realized it, the kidnappers were on their feet, shouting and dragging the little girl out in front of them. The American Captain was shouting too and his troops began to move. Then someone threw a strange kind of glowing grenade. That was the moment one of the kidnappers leveled his weapon and fired at the one soldier with his back turned. The soldier had taken his eyes off the insurgents looking for orders; that was a mistake he could not afford. Then the man sprayed the room with bullets and the troops returned fire.

The soldier that was shot hit the ground hard and his buddies surrounded him as they fought. In all the commotion the little girl ran to the American troops and hid behind them. Within ten of the longest minutes of Dillon's life, the American troops annihilated the insurgents and secured the area. Dillon was about to call out to them when Danny grabbed his sleeve. Danny shook his head and motioned for Dillon to wait. Dillon was pretty shaken, but he took pride in the fact that he kept his cool better than Danny did. Danny looked terrible; he even had tears in his eyes.

One of the soldiers carried the little girl out to a waiting truck and the others gathered around their fallen friend. Dillon leaned over to get a better look, and when they rolled the young man over, it was Dillon who lost all control. Before he could stop it, a bloodcurdling scream ripped from his chest. His eyes filled up with tears, and he could barely see. It was Danny, covered in blood and lying under a pile of rubble from the ceiling that had crashed around him. The Captain shouted an order as the ceiling began to cave in. The six remaining soldiers gently lifted Danny's broken body and made it outside just as the building collapsed.

Dillon didn't know what to do or where to look as debris began falling. Danny grabbed his hand and together they tried to run away, but Dillon missed his footing and fell. He kept falling and landed with a thud back in his dad's apartment in his own room. The mattress was actually bouncing with the force of his landing.

OCTOBER 1, 2011

Dillon sat up and looked around. He threw back the blankets to look at his hands and feet. He knew there was no way he could ever hope to explain blood on his hands and feet, and he hoped he wouldn't see any. His father would flip out and have him committed for sure, especially after his behavior last night. The sun was coming up over the horizon and there was just enough light in his room to see.

"Oh, thank God," Dillon muttered. His hands and feet were fine. Dillon was all set to try to convince himself that the whole thing was nothing but a terrible dream. He started to relax and unclench his fists. As he opened his left hand, he shrieked. There on his palm was a single word seared into his flesh: *Living.*

What the heck was that? Was he branded? Was he marked for something? He winced as he moved his hand, and he was glad his dad was still asleep. Now there was no way he could pretend that had been a dream and there was no way he could relax.

"Danny? Where are you? Oh please, Danny, I really need to talk to you." There was no reply. Dillon got up and took a shower. His hand stung when the water hit it, but all in all it wasn't too bad. He dressed and then sat in his room, staring out the window. He couldn't bring himself to eat and he couldn't face his dad. He sat there hoping Danny would come, trying to rationalize what was completely irrational. Before he knew what he was doing, he lifted his phone.

Tom was up early and smiled when he saw a text from

Dillon. He hadn't heard a word from him in a long time, and now here he was texting at six on a Saturday morning? Crazy, but still cool in a way. Maybe things could get back to normal between them. Tom texted back and even offered to come over with bagels.

Dillon didn't know what to say. He knew he hadn't been much of a best friend to Tom lately, and he wasn't sure he should drag him into this, whatever this was, but he had to talk to someone: ideally, someone grounded in reality who could help Dillon hold on to whatever sanity and safety he had left.

Dillon offered to meet Tom at the bagel place on the corner and headed for the door just as his dad was getting up.

"Where are you going? We need to get ready for Connecticut," Dillon's dad declared.

"I'm meeting Tom for breakfast," Dillon said. "Don't worry. I'll be back in time for your dog-and-pony show." It sounded so much meaner than he meant it, but Dillon didn't look back as he left.

New York was an amazing city; even this early there were people all around. Runners ran, dog walkers walked, and the street was filled with the smell of bagels and coffee. Dillon stepped around the pile of newspapers being dropped off at the newsstand and found Tom waiting for him at the Brew and Bagel.

Dillon put his left hand in his pocket and winced. There was an awkward silence at first, and then Tom smiled.

"So, you still like garlic bagels? Personally, I don't know how you eat that first thing in the morning, but what do I care? It's not like I'm gonna kiss you."

Dillon laughed and headed for the counter. Tom really was a good friend. Five minutes later he had his garlic bagel, Tom's cinnamon and raisin, and two coffees light and sweet. When he set the tray down on the table, he hoped Tom wouldn't see his hand.

"Thanks for meeting me here," Dillon began and then he realized he really didn't know what else to say. Dillon smiled to himself as he imagined saying something like *So, here's the thing. I'm seeing ghosts, having out of body experiences, and coming back maimed.* Yeah. No way. So instead he just looked at Tom and wished for the old days.

Apparently, Tom did know what to say. "What is it, Dillon? I know you're weird and all, why not? We're all weird, but something is happening to you. Holy smokes! You've even got a gray hair!"

This was news to Dillon. He knew about his hand, but turning gray? For Pete's sake, he was only fifteen! Dillon reached for his hair before he knew what he was doing; by then, it was too late.

"What did you do to your hand?" There was real concern in Tom's eyes as he put down his bagel and grabbed Dillon's hand to get a closer look. The word was seared into Dillon's palm and stretched from his knuckles to his wrist. "*Living*? I don't get it. Why would you have yourself branded like this? What are you involved in?"

There was no way around it now. Dillon would have to come clean.

"I don't know where to start."

"I do. Start at the beginning and tell me everything." Tom stared intently across the table.

Dillon told Tom about the guitar and then about Danny. He told him about the notes and the blood on his hands. Then he told him about the nightmare, or whatever it was, and how he discovered his brand that morning. When he was finished, Tom pushed back from the table and said, "Let's go."

Before Dillon could ask him where, or tell him that he had to get back to his dad's place, Tom was up and out on the street. Dillon caught up with him as Tom entered the subway station.

"Wait up. Where are we going? I need to get back to my dad's. He wants to go get a pumpkin or something."

Tom glared at Dillon. "Pumpkin picking? Really? You're having all kinds of paranormal experiences and now you're getting branded and pumpkin picking is what's on your mind? That proves it. You need me. You are nuts!"

Tom and Dillon boarded the Number 4 train heading uptown. Dillon was glad he didn't have cell service underground. It gave him time to figure out what the heck he was going to tell his dad about not going to Connecticut today.

They boys emerged onto 125th Street with the sun in their eyes and the wind at their backs. Dillon texted his dad that he was sorry but that he really needed to be with Tom today, and he felt better thinking that at least on some level that was the truth. Besides, it was a whole lot simpler than telling his dad he just wasn't ready to meet his girlfriend, and unbelievably simpler than trying to explain the rest of what was going on.

Tom walked with purpose and seemed to know exactly where they were going. They hailed a cab, and before long they stood before the gates of Manhattan University.

"What are we doing here?" Dillon wanted to know.

"We are doing some research."

Spending the day in the library was almost as

unappealing as spending the day pumpkin picking, but Dillon didn't say a word. He did, however, breathe a big sigh of relief when they passed the library and kept right on walking. Tom rolled his eyes. He never understood Dillon's distaste for libraries; the library was a great place to meet girls. If Dillon had known where they were going, he would have developed a whole new appreciation for the wonders of the library and the relative security of a place bound to be deserted on a Saturday.

The Northern Building, as it was currently known, was humming with activity. Desks were being moved in and so were countless boxes and machines.

"It's just about finished now, so everybody's excited to move in," Tom said with excitement in his voice.

"I don't get it. Where are we?"

Sounding more like a tour guide than a teenager, Tom began. "The Northern building is the new interdisciplinary science center at Manhattan University. This is the place to start to figure out what is happening to you."

Dillon looked as confused as ever, but his friend didn't seem to notice. "This is the place where they finally acknowledge that science is science; not biology, chemistry, or physics, but all science. One discipline will never figure out all the answers. Every discipline explores a piece of the universe." Tom was getting more and more excited as his inner nerd was revealed. "But the only way to unravel all the mysteries is to put aside the differences long enough to study the common ground that overlaps between the different areas. That's what this place is all about. Studying the universe from all perspectives, not just one angle at a time. Get it?"

"No, not really, but I'll take your word for it. This is relevant to us how?" Dillon didn't want to seem ungrateful, but he really didn't have time to congratulate Manhattan U. on its new cross-curricular approach to the universe.

"They are studying single-molecule physics here—you know, where quantum physics meets biology? Come on, tell me you don't see it now." Tom was getting exasperated. He took Dillon's hand and spelled it out for him. "You, a living being, i.e., *biology*, are crossing into other dimensions, i.e., *quantum physics*, and undergoing some sort of fundamental change as a result, i.e., *chemistry*, you idiot!"

"Oh," was all Dillon could manage before Tom was off again and heading into the building. Inside there was the smell of drying paint, new carpet, and old coffee. Dillon was surprised at how well Tom seemed to know his way around until they came upon an office door. The name read *Thomas J. Thurgood, Sr., PhD.* Tom's dad worked at Manhattan University. If he had thought about it, Dillon was pretty sure he used to know that, but most of the time "Tom's dad" was just the guy who liked pizza and drove them to the movies, not some hotshot research scientist at a big time university.

Tom didn't even knock; he just walked right into his dad's office and sat down. His dad nodded and smiled at them as he finished up on the phone. "No, no, no. We need the delivery by tomorrow at the latest. Yes. I realize tomorrow is Sunday. That's why I want it delivered today. The Board of Trustees is touring this facility on Monday morning and I promise you they will not be happy when I tell them the reason they can't see the Molecular Motion lab is because your company screwed up." He winked at the boys and waited. He was clearly enjoying his job. "Okay, great, I'll see you this afternoon." He hung up the phone and gave the boys his full attention. "Hi guys, what's up?"

Tom shut the door. "Go on, show him," he urged Dillon.

Dillon swallowed. Maybe this was a mistake.

"Don't wimp out now," Tom scolded. "Dad, something really weird is happening to Dillon. Check out his hand."

"Dillon?" Dr. Thurgood said.

Reluctantly Dillon held out his hand for Tom's dad to see. "Mr., uh, Dr. Thurgood, you have to understand. I didn't do that to myself. I know it sounds crazy, but I woke up this morning with that on my hand."

Dr. Thurgood's eyes snapped up to meet Dillon's. It was clear he was caught somewhere between disbelief, concern, and excitement. He turned up his lights and put Dillon's hand under a magnifying glass.

"Extraordinary. I've never seen anything like it. Dillon, there are three things I want you to remember from now on. One, I believe you. Two, it may take us a little while, but we will figure this out. And three, you can call me Thomas."

"Cool. Can I?" Tom wanted to know.

"Definitely not. You can call me Dad, or I guess 'Your Highness' is also acceptable," joked Thomas Thurgood.

It was the first time in a long time that Dillon actually felt relaxed. For the second time that day, Dillon did what he had thought he never would: he told the whole, mind-blowing story to Thomas. Somehow the act of saying it out loud seemed to make the whole thing more real and more manageable. It helped a lot that Thomas just listened. He only interrupted Dillon to clarify a point for his notes, and then he went back to his writing and nodding. When Dillon finished, the room was quiet and the sun was high in the sky. By now he should have been on some farm in Connecticut searching for a pumpkin, but instead he was in Morningside Heights, at Manhattan University, searching for answers.

"Did you kids ever notice that the word *university* has an awful lot in common with the word *universe*?" Thomas said. "Seems to me that you have come to exactly the right place to figure this out. We are bound to get at least halfway there, and as for the other half, well, we'll just see." The boys didn't know what he meant by that, but right now, even half an answer sounded good to them.

"The first thing we need to do is to get you a complete physical, Dillon. I know what you say is really happening to you, but we will need to prove it, and the first thing we need to show is that you are a normal, healthy kid. We need to contact your parents. Your mom is a nurse, right?"

Dillon felt sick. If his parents got involved, they would flip out for sure. There would be no medical tests; they would just have him committed. "Please, Thomas, there must be some other way. I can't tell my parents yet."

Thomas Thurgood put his hands on Dillon's shoulders. "Let me talk to them. We can't do this without their consent, and from the sound of things, your mom might be glad to make sure you are really okay after that whole bloody hands incident."

Dillon hated to admit it, but that actually made a lot of sense. Still, he didn't want to tell his parents. Thomas opened his office door and motioned to the boys.

"After you, gentlemen. I think we should stop for pizza on the way to your parents. This isn't the kind of conversation I want to have on an empty stomach." Thomas called both of Dillon's parents on the way to the pizzeria. They were pretty worried, but they agreed to meet an hour later at his father's apartment.

Tom's dad loved pizza as much as Tom and Dillon did and they polished off a whole pie in about twenty minutes. Dillon tried to stall when they were finished eating, but Tom and his dad were all about getting it done. They grabbed a cab downtown and soon arrived at Dillon's dad's apartment.

They rode the elevator in silence and all Dillon could think was that things would never be the same again. From today on, Dillon was sure his mom and dad would never look at him the same way.

When the door opened, Dillon's mom rushed to him and gave him a big hug. He could see in her eyes just how worried she was. His father stayed on the couch, but it was clear he was definitely upset. Dillon guessed he was probably annoyed about not spending time with his girlfriend.

"Maggie, Ryan," Thomas began, "I really appreciate the chance to talk to you today. The boys came to me with something this morning and I believe they really need our help."

Dillon's mom and dad looked at each other. "Go on," his dad said.

"Look, anyone who has lived in this world longer than a few minutes knows it is an unpredictable and crazy place. There is a lot we can understand and control, and a lot that we can't. Dillon seems to be going through something that we are only just beginning to discover and simply don't yet know much about." Slowly and gently, Thomas relayed to Dillon's parents all the things the boys had told him. When Ryan discovered that Maggie knew about the bloody hands, he looked hurt, but he wasn't angry like Dillon expected him to be.

"I can't pretend that I have even a small piece of

the answer we need to figure out what's going on," Thomas continued, "but I know this much for sure: *something* out of this world is happening to Dillon. What it means and how it will all turn out, no one knows. In fact there is no shortage of doctors who would recommend a psych evaluation for all of us. What we know for sure is that Dillon is experiencing disturbing sleep patterns and physical manifestations of stress as a result. I believe we can figure this out. I guess the question is, do you?"

Dillon's mom and dad looked at each other and then at Dillon. His mom spoke first.

"If we take him to the ER, I can tell you right now he'll be placed in the psych ward as a schizophrenic. Seeing things? Hearing voices? They will do all they can to medicate it out of him and there are major side effects involved. Not to mention the fact that since Dillon is not schizophrenic, no medicine will put a stop to these experiences. The only other option I can see is a priest. If we do that, it will be years before they will believe us and then they'll want to exorcise it out of him. Once again, not my first choice for my son."

Ryan looked at the guitar in the corner. "Why don't we just get rid of that thing? If it is haunted, or whatever, why not just get away from it?"

Before Dillon could object, Thomas answered. "As I understand it, these episodes are no longer tied to the guitar. Dillon can sense Danny at any time and in any place. Given that, I'm not convinced the guitar is the problem."

Dillon's father closed his eyes. "What do you propose?"

"I'm not sure yet but I know where to start," Thomas said. "I'd like your permission to give Dillon a full workup in the lab: blood tests, a physical, and most importantly an MRI. I want to have baseline readings and confirmation that he is the healthy kid we all believe him to be. Then, I'd like to do a sleep study. It seems that most serious episodes happen when he is at rest, so I'd like to study that."

"I don't want my son turned into a lab rat. How will he benefit from all this *study?*" Ryan wanted to know.

"He will get two things," Thomas replied. "Some kind of record of what is happening to him and answers he can understand. This experience may be the new normal for Dillon; he needs to know how to deal with it and he can't do that until he knows what it means."

The thought of this becoming the new normal was upsetting to everyone. Up until that moment, they thought they were looking for a cure. Thomas started up again.

"My new lab is not just the perfect place to figure this out; it is quite possibly the only place. I think what is going on with Dillon is that he is experiencing the anthropic principle of string theory."

"I think the good doctor is a pretty smart cookie." Danny's voice startled Dillon right off the couch. Everyone stared at Dillon as he landed on the floor, and if they had any lingering doubt that Dillon needed some help, they abandoned it in that moment.

"He's here, now, standing behind my mom," Dillon explained. Everyone looked at Maggie but saw nothing behind her other than a plant. Thomas smiled.

"Okay then, ask him what he wants."

Danny laughed. "If I knew what the heck was going on, I'd tell y'all, but I got nothing. Maybe this hotshot can help figure me out too."

Dillon felt like he was at a surreal family reunion. It was a relief to finally talk about what was going on, and now he felt like maybe everything would be okay. He relayed Danny's comments, and Thomas nodded. Danny took a seat on the ottoman near the window.

"Okay, let's start with some really basic string theory," Thomas began. Tom and Dillon shifted in their seats. "String theory is all about reconciling gravity with quantum physics." Everyone in the room started to feel uncomfortable. Only Danny sat up and looked fascinated. "If we accept that everything in the universe is made up of vibrating filaments, or strings, and membranes of energy, or branes, then we are just beginning to understand the space-time continuum and the fact that several extra, usually unseen, dimensions to the universe must exist."

Ryan, Tom, and Danny nodded. Dillon and his mom exchanged puzzled glances.

"Using string theory to analyze black hole thermodynamics confirms that parallel universes are not only possible," Thomas continued, "but probable. Take ghosts for example. What if it was possible to fold over the space-time continuum?" Ryan blinked and swallowed hard. "Imagine that I had a timeline and I folded it over. Now, I would have the current date lined up with some date in the past. If you believe that each universe is composed of vibrating strings, then maybe when they line up, it's possible to move from one vibration to the other. I think that's what ghosts do." Danny and Dillon looked at each other and smiled. Thomas went on. "I think when we die we leave this dimension and go to another. What if the continuum folds and the two dimensions line up? What if some people can adjust their vibrating strings long enough to move back and forth between the dimensions? What if that is what is happening to Dillon and to Danny too? That's my theory, anyway, and with your permission, I'd like to try and prove it."

Maggie rubbed her head. "Why? How? Why fold the timeline and how is it folded and why is he coming back hurt?"

Dillon looked at his mom. He knew that at the end of the day she didn't care two hoots about string theory, ghosts, or thermodynamics. She just wanted him to be safe. If he could have figured out a normal way to do it, he would have gone over to her and given her a hug; but that would be weird, so he just sat there instead. Thomas talked on and on about how string theory explained all the craziness, even how travelling between dimensions was bound to mess up a person's molecules and how blood could be displaced to outside the skin, at least theoretically, as a body readjusted from the vibrations of another dimension. It all sounded possible, but Dillon didn't know what to believe. It sure did feel like he was in another dimension, whatever that was.

It was decided then and there that Dr. Thurgood would arrange for Dillon to undergo the basic diagnostics as soon as possible. Much of it could even be done at the new lab. Everyone looked relieved except Danny; he looked nervous. "I don't think I like the idea of you being poked and prodded. This is happening *to* you, not *because* of you." Dillon shrugged. As far as he was concerned, any plan was better than no plan, so he was willing to give it a shot.

OCTOBER 8, 2011

Dr. Thurgood ordered the tests and soon Dillon's diagnostics were almost complete. As everyone suspected, he was as normal as any teenager could be. Today was the MRI, and he would be glad to get it over with. He went down to his mom's hospital and met Thomas and his dad. His mom arranged for her friends in the MRI suite to do the test after hours so Dillon didn't have to wait around. He put on the hospital gown and sat there, embarrassed and cold.

"Good Lord! You look ridiculous!" Danny laughed. "Are you sure you have to wear that?"

"Yes, I'm sure," Dillon mumbled. He wished more than anything that he had two hospital gowns. At least that way he could have used one as a robe. This business of holding the back closed was getting real old, real fast. Dillon watched his parents and Thomas talking. They were on the other side of the window in the MRI suite, trying to explain what they needed to the technician. Dillon tried to listen, but it was impossible to hear. He had a pounding headache and so he decided to just try to keep his gown closed and wait. Danny sat beside him, but no one else could tell. Dillon leaned back and rested his head against the tile wall.

Danny thought, *Dillon looks terrible*. But he figured Dillon was under a lot of stress since he was going through a lot more than the average fifteen year old and was doing it on precious little sleep. Things had been pretty quiet since Thomas got involved, so maybe this whole string theory thing might not be needed after all. Maybe Danny could just try to keep an eye on Dillon and see how long he could stick around.

Dillon sighed. He couldn't remember the last time he felt so tired. He was completely shattered and couldn't wait to go home and relax. Dillon wondered how long this test would be. At that moment Thomas and the tech came in and asked him to get on the table. Dillon nodded. "Oh, by the way, Danny's here too," he said. Thomas smiled.

"Hello, Danny," said Thomas.

Dillon felt a little queasy as he stood, and he was glad to lie down. His mom put a thin blanket over him and told him to try and relax. *No problem*, he thought as he closed his eyes.

The banging and clanging inside the machine was epic. Dillon's head was in a vise euphemistically called "the halo" and the machine was so narrow he felt like he was stuck in a coffin. Unable to move and finding it a little hard to breath, Dillon learned two things. First, he was a little claustrophobic, and second, there was no way to relax during an MRI. He closed his eyes and waited. The doctor told him this could take about a half an hour, and Dillon wasn't really sure he could take it that long.

From somewhere behind him he heard singing. Not exactly the voice of the angels, but not too bad either. It took him a minute or two before he realized the voice belonged to Danny. He hated to admit it, but listening to that guy butcher an old Tim McGraw song was a great distraction and helped Dillon to relax a little. If only he could get rid of his headache.

Dillon could hear the doctor and everything seemed fine. Thomas sounded pleased as well, and then he suddenly sounded surprised.

"What is that?" Thomas asked pointing to heightened

blood flow around Dillon's frontal lobe. "I've never seen anything like it." The screen lit up as new areas of Dillon's brain began to experience more and more activity.

"Dillon, how are you doing?" his mom called to him from inside the booth.

"Okay, I guess. Are we almost done?"

Those were the last words Dillon spoke that night. It wasn't clear exactly what happened next, but it changed everything.

Danny was singing away when he noticed that something was very wrong. Dillon's eyes were open wide and he had an expression of abject terror on his face. Dillon began to sweat and he clenched his fists.

"What is it, Dillon? Talk to me! What's going on?" Danny said.

But Dillon couldn't talk, he couldn't move, and then he couldn't breathe. Outside, everything looked okay. The doctor could see elevated respirations, but that wasn't uncommon after twenty minutes in an MRI. They had spoken to Dillon just a moment ago and all his vitals had been steady. Danny was starting to panic. There was nothing normal about Dillon. Danny had to get help and he had to leave Dillon there alone in order to do it.

The lights in the room began to flash. Dillon's mom worried that they would lose power before the MRI was complete. She hated the thought of having to come back again. Then the screen flickered.

"Come on," said the MRI technician as he hit the side of his monitor. "I just need two more minutes."

Danny was frantic. He tore into the technician's suite like a cyclone. He yelled directly into their faces, but they heard nothing, saw no one, and had no clue that Dillon was in terrible danger. He flicked the lights, messed with the screen, but nothing. Then it occurred to him, *Enough with the light show, time for battle stations.* Danny banged every door he could find. He slammed cabinets and doors and even managed to throw some keys off a counter. For a moment they just looked startled, and then Thomas figured out what was happening. He didn't know why, but he knew that Danny wanted their attention.

"Out! Get him the hell out of there!" Thomas yelled. "I think Danny is trying to tell us something." The technician looked confused, but he did as he was told and stopped the test.

Danny raced back to Dillon's side and found him struggling for breath. He put his hand on Dillon's chest and his heart raced like it was trying to break free. How was it possible that the monitors didn't see this? At first, Dillon looked scared and then he was eerily peaceful as they pulled him from the machine. His mother gasped when she saw him and grabbed his wrist partly to hold his hand and partly to take his pulse.

"Hey now, Cowboy, cut it out. You're gonna be just fine here in a minute," Danny rambled.

The doctor put an oxygen mask over Dillon's nose and mouth and Dillon became very still. Just before he passed out, he saw his mother crying and his father holding her in his arms.

"I don't understand it. He's crashing." The doctor grabbed the crash cart next to the wall and ripped open Dillon's gown. A moment later Danny saw Dillon's body jump and lurch as the machine unleashed hundreds of volts of electricity. Nothing. The doctor turned up the machine and tried again. Once again Dillon's body bounced like a rag doll on the table, but this time they got a sinus rhythm. Before anyone really understood what was happening, Dillon was rushed out the door and into the ER. They made his parents sit in the waiting room, and Thomas never left their side. The only ones who could go near Dillon now were the doctors, nurses, and Danny.

Dillon was hooked up to all kinds of machines, and Danny stood watching over him. From what he could hear, they thought Dillon had had some kind of heart attack, but there didn't seem to be any cardiac enzymes or heart muscle damage to confirm the infarction. Good news about the muscle, but a heart attack?

"Come on, Dillon. What gives?" Danny whispered.

Dillon stirred and opened his eyes. He heard Danny's whisper and expected to see him, but he didn't. Dillon was in a nice, warm bed, but he wasn't at home or in the hospital. He was in his grandma's old house in the Catskills. There was humming in the distance, and when Dillon realized who was humming, he jumped out of bed and headed downstairs. There she was, setting the table and telling Dillon to wash up. Dillon grinned from ear to ear. He was so happy to see his grandma and so happy that she was taking one of her awesome chicken potpies out of the oven. She didn't even look surprised to see Dillon, but he was shocked to see her.

When they sat down, Grandma ruffled Dillon's hair like she always did, and then Uncle Joe walked in. Uncle Joe smelled like smoke so Grandma made him shower before she would let him come anywhere near the table. Dillon thought he must have died and gone to heaven.

When Uncle Joe finally came down, they said grace and started eating. "Dillon, I want you to be sure and eat a good dinner. Have seconds or thirds if you like. I want to make sure you keep your strength up," said Grandma. Dillon looked at her with surprise. It never occurred to him that he might be going back.

After dinner Uncle Joe got all serious. "Dillon, I need to talk to you. I'm worried about your mom. Tell her not to be so hard on herself, will ya?" Then Uncle Joe looked at Dillon's palm. He traced the word *Living* and looked Dillon in the eye. "Don't forget this." Dillon nodded and then he noticed his guitar leaning against the wall. He was about to reach for it when Grandma said, "Okay boys, that's enough. Dillon, it's time you went to bed." Grandma was right; suddenly Dillon was exhausted.

When they moved Dillon to the cardiac ICU, his parents, Danny, and Thomas all waited. Thomas was feverishly scribbling notes and trying to understand what had happened and how to make sure it never happened again.

"Okay, I think I've got something. Dillon hasn't been sleeping well for some time now, right?" Dillon's mom nodded. "Travel to another dimension or contact with visitors from another dimension, like Danny, requires a relaxed mind. That's why it happens when he is either lost in his music or asleep. I haven't had a chance to review this with you yet, but the results of the sleep study we did showed that Dillon has developed an inability to sustain REM sleep for more than a few minutes. His mind won't let him fall into a deep sleep because he is afraid of what will happen and where he will end up. That's why he doesn't feel too relaxed, even when he does finally sleep. But what if there is something calling to him from the other dimension? What if the timeline wants him to go there, ready or not?"

"You mean that it's trying to pull Dillon away?" Ryan

asked.

"Exactly and it's yanking him so hard that it is scrambling the vibration of Dillon's strings in this dimension, screwing with his electrical impulses, and messing with the rhythm of his heart. Once it lets him go, there is no damage because the pull from the other dimension has released him. That other dimension cannot have a sustainable effect here in our world."

"How can we stop it? Lasting or not, he can't keep experiencing this," Ryan said.

Danny hadn't left Dillon's side. He wracked his brain to try to figure out if maybe he was the one doing this to Dillon. From time to time he looked in on his parents in Tennessee, but he never even seemed to be noticed, let alone cause heart attacks. Danny would never forgive himself if he did this to Dillon. He made up his mind to get Dillon out of this mess. He just didn't know how.

Thomas went on. "I don't think this is a random thing. I think Dillon was chosen for some reason. The other dimension needs him to know or do something and it will keep pulling him back until whatever that purpose is gets satisfied. I think we need to see what they are trying to show us and I think we better figure it out fast."

OCTOBER 15, 2011

A week after his heart stopped, Dillon was back at home and feeling great. His mother watched him like a hawk and Danny did too. He was recovering well, and there had been no other episodes. No one wanted to rush Dillon, but everyone wanted to know what he remembered. They needed any clue they could get about what the message from the other dimension might be. Finally Danny spoke up because he was starting to think there might be a method to this particular brand of madness.

"Listen, kiddo," Danny said as Dillon sat up in bed, strumming his guitar. "I need you to call Thomas. I think I may know why everything went crazy in the MRI."

"What do you mean? What do you think happened to cause my heart to seize up like that?"

"Well, MRI stands for 'magnetic resonance imaging,' *magnetic* being the key word. String theory is about figuring out the way quantum physics and gravity work together, right? So gravitational pull works like magnetic pull. The nearest I can figure it, we just about put you in a cosmic slingshot by putting you inside that huge magnet with me there pulling you. I didn't get it at the time, but what if me, from my dimension, next to you in yours, is fine, say like any of the millions of ghost stories we all grew up on. But what if the thing that bends the timeline is actually a kind of magnetic gravity. The magnetic pull of one dimension attracted to another, like a magnet and steel. The MRI is like a lightning bolt for magnetic energy and you got zapped when the two dimensions collided. What do you think?"

"I think I'm impressed. I didn't know you were so into physics."

"Yeah, I know how it is. You Yankees think you done cornered the market on intelligence." Danny smiled with a twinkle in his eyes.

Thomas came over right away, and Dillon presented Danny's theory as best he could. If Danny was right, then the key to controlling and understanding this kind of episode was figuring out what it was that attracted Dillon's dimension to the one pulling him toward Danny's. They now understood *how* the timeline folded, but they still needed to know *why.* Danny sat quietly trying to figure it out. Thomas scratched his head.

The guitar leaned against the wall and Dillon couldn't resist. He walked over to it and absentmindedly plucked the strings. The vibration of each string made a different sound, depending on its thickness and tension. Thomas watched him closely and when his mouth caught up with his brain, he rose excitedly.

"That's it! You're like a guitar string!"

"I beg your pardon?" Dillon guffawed.

"Tension is the key. The strings won't play unless they are adjusted, or tuned, right?"

Dillon nodded.

"Right, so you tune the guitar by pulling the strings either tighter or more loosely around the pegs by turning the keys, or turners, at the top of the neck. The tension is the determining factor. The same is true for you. The more relaxed, or less tense, the easier it is for you to go to the other dimension. Inter-dimensional travel seems to require a relaxed mind, a strong attraction between the universes, and something to magnify the gravitational pull, like the mega magnet in the MRI machine."

"I think you just figured out the blueprint for a time machine," said Dillon. He couldn't help feeling excited, even if it was his molecules that were getting scrambled in the experiment. He figured, *You have to break some eggs to make an omelet.*

There was still one piece missing. What caused two dimensions to be so strongly attracted to each other that the force exerted was strong enough to bend and fold the space-time continuum? Dillon tried to think back over all his visits that were, literally, out of this world. Each one scared him, but each time he was really safer than he actually felt. What was the message he was supposed to get? Whatever it was, it seemed not only important enough to send those notes, but also to let Dillon travel through time.

Danny pointed out that it wasn't really just time travel. It was travel to a completely other dimension. "I hate to be insensitive, but to put it bluntly, I'm dead. You are moving way beyond your own set of strings. Ever wonder where else you could go?"

Dillon began strumming his guitar again with a new reverence for the strings that vibrated under his fingers. They were there the whole time, but he had never considered them before. Dillon was sure the answer to figuring out the message was right in front of him too: he just couldn't see it yet.

OCTOBER 16, 2011

Danny hated to admit it, but he was getting irritated. He and Dillon had a lot they needed to talk about, but it seemed like forever since they could just sit around and hash things out. There was no denying that there was a good reason for that. They had a whole team in place now to help figure out what was going on, and Dillon needed to do what he needed to do to get that worked out. Then there was the small item of the heart attack. Danny most definitely did not want Dillon joining him as a ghost, so Dillon had to do whatever the doctors thought he should, so he could recover and be all right. Danny's fondest wish for Dillon was what he used to wish for himself before he would head out on patrols: to die an old man in his warm bed, not in the line of fire.

Still they needed to talk, and Danny had already decided today was the day. There was a lot going on and Danny knew if he waited until Tom came over later, he would lose his chance.

"Hey, sleepyhead. Wake up." Danny nudged Dillon, but he just rolled over. "Teenagers," Danny mumbled. "Come on now! Wake up!"

"No," Dillon moaned.

"Oh my goodness, I can't believe you sleep naked!" Danny sounded shocked and offended.

Dillon sat bolt upright in bed and lifted the covers. After confirming that he was still wearing the T-shirt and sweatpants he had fallen asleep in the night before, Dillon glared at Danny.

"Let's just say it's a good thing that you're already a ghost," Dillon growled, "because if looks could kill, you would die twice; and just so you know, you stink." Dillon rubbed his eyes. When he realized it was only six o'clock, Dillon practically ignited. "Man, whatever this is, I certainly hope it couldn't have waited."

"*Whatever this is*?" Danny repeated. "You and I have done some pretty extensive time travelling in the last few weeks and we need to debrief."

Dillon knew it and the truth was, he was dreading it. He didn't know what to say to Danny. How could he possibly tell him what he thought about all the things they had seen? Seriously, what could you say to someone about witnessing the way they died, especially when they died so violently, far from home and fighting to keep us safe?

So Dillon just said, "Thank you." Danny looked confused by that so Dillon went on. "That place we went, that was to see how you died, right? It really scared me. I didn't know you were a soldier killed in the war. I didn't even know what *war* really was. I used to think it was a series of isolated incidents that gave reporters something to talk about. After what you showed me, I can't shake the feeling that war is a nightmare we all get to endure together."

Danny had never thought about it that way. He remembered the day he came home to tell his parents he enlisted. His dad shook his hand and then went out to the barn. When Danny found him there an hour later, it was clear he had been crying. "I'm so proud of you, son," Clint began, "but I can't pretend I'm happy about your decision."

Danny's mom had a different reaction. "No way! I forbid it! I did not go through everything I went through to have you and raise you up to be a man, a man accepted to MIT, thank you very much, just for you to throw it all away on some stupid hero complex!" Sara had thundered around the house shouting, crying and shouting some more. It took him a while to calm her down long enough to explain that MIT gave him a deferral until after his service and it was a done deal. There was nothing she could say that was going to change the fact that he made his choice. When he shipped out the following month, it was the last time he ever saw either of them.

Still, Danny had no regrets, even now. As far as he was concerned, his nation had been under fire and there was no way he was going to sit home and let it happen again. Inspired by the passengers on the plane that went down in the Pennsylvania field, he wanted to protect his country.

That guy, Todd Beamer, who called his wife to say good-bye and then said *Let's roll!* to his buddies on Flight 93 had really impressed Danny. Beamer was a regular guy with a wife and two kids when he got on that plane, but when he realized what was happening, he stood up for his country and his family. The way Danny saw it, it was always just regular guys that stood up to make things right. Danny figured Beamer was like a modern day Minuteman from the American Revolution. Danny was proud to take his place next to guys like that in history.

The only problem was Danny wasn't next to Beamer, or anyone else as far as he could tell. He felt like he was stuck. He knew he wasn't in hell, but he didn't think it was heaven either. In fact, the whole situation was kind of embarrassing. Danny had not planned to die at nineteen in a war he didn't understand. He had planned to come home, be a war hero, go to MIT, and make millions.

Dying, while certainly not his plan, was not embarrassing, but not being anywhere since then? It made him feel like a moron who couldn't find his way to the afterlife. Danny told Dillon he was lonely, and when he heard Dillon playing his old guitar, Danny couldn't resist reaching out. Danny could hardly bear to see what happened to his parents after he died, so mostly he stayed away. Now, Dillon was his only contact and Danny was glad to have someone to talk to.

"Look Dillon, I think I need to be straight with you about something. I'm not the one driving this," Danny began. "I didn't want to take you to see how I died. Hell, no kid should see that place. I'm not leaving you notes because I can't leave that kind of mark in this world anymore. It took nearly everything I had just to slam doors at the MRI to tell the others you were in trouble. I'm not leaving here to have tea with the angels. I'm just kind of waiting and trying to figure out what is going on right along with you. I died seven years ago in your dimension, but there is no time here in mine. For me, it may have been just a day or two. I can come back here and see what's going on, but that's it. I don't have whatever it takes to just move around all the dimensions. Pretty much I can pick here or there but otherwise, I'm just along for the ride."

Dillon didn't know what to think. Dillon had already accepted the fact that the notes weren't coming from Danny; he just wasn't the kind of guy to carve words into someone else's palm. Still, Dillon realized that he *did* think that Danny knew more about this than he was telling. The idea that Danny was lonely or embarrassed had never even occurred to Dillon.

"I think I owe you an apology. I had no clue what this was like from where you are, let's talk." Dillon said. They began again at the beginning and started wading through

Dillon's experience in the cave before he met up with Danny in the Afghanistan part of the dream, nightmare, or whatever that had been. Remembering the cave and the broken glass put a shiver up Dillon's spine, but he held none of it back. At Danny's suggestion, he even wrote down some notes to share with the others. Danny guessed the cave was some kind of portal that Dillon had to travel through to get to the other dimension, and considering the fact that Danny seemed to exist between the worlds, he was glad he didn't have to deal with a place like that every time he came to see Dillon.

Most of the time, Danny was in a pretty nice place; not quite heavenly, but a long way from hell. "I guess I owe you a little explanation," Danny said. "I mean, I can look around and see your life, but you really have no idea about my life and how it is when I'm not here. I can visit you, but you can't exactly visit me." Dillon nodded for Danny to go on.

"Well, you saw how I died, so I guess I'll start with what happened next, on the other side. For me, dying was like a shock followed by peace like I've never known. I mean, you think that you're gonna have a hard time letting go of this life; but it's not like that." Danny paused to collect his thoughts. "When the moment came for me, I was shocked, but a moment later I felt such peace that I really didn't even want to come back. It felt like I didn't have to let go of my family and friends; I just didn't have to worry about anything anymore. There isn't really a separation for me. I can still be with them. What I learned is that there is a huge separation for them. I can visit, but they can't and they can't even find peace when they do feel like I'm there."

Dillon looked away. He had never thought about it like that before.

Danny went on. "I was totally amazed the first time I went back to my family's farm. I mean, I guess I should have figured that they'd be upset, but I never figured that they would look more dead than I was."

"What do you mean?" Dillon asked.

""What I mean is that they raised me to be a fighter, so I never figured them for quitters. That was the first time there was no peace on this side. Up until then, that awesome feeling of everything being fantastic was just building and building, but once I saw how destroyed my parents were, it was like someone let the air out of my balloon. No more riding high."

Danny ran his hand through his thick, brown hair.

"Anyway, since then, I'm kinda stuck," Danny sighed. "I can't go back, but I can't go forward either. I can't leave them like that and now I have waited so long, I don't know how to let go again. So, pretty much, when I'm not here, I'm hanging out in a place that's like a park. The sunshine is warm and the grass is green and the flowers are beautiful. There is a live oak tree next to a brook and I like the shade it casts over the water. Sometimes I can even smell barbeque and hear the laughter of family reunions that must be happening nearby. I can hear them calling to each other, but I can't see them. Truth is, it's a little lonely. Nice and all, but I guess it will be a while before I'm having a reunion with my family and anyway, that's cool. I seriously don't want to rush them."

Dillon was amazed. Danny shrugged and said, "Just so you know, I'd have preferred just telling you I was a soldier killed on patrol in Afghanistan. I still don't like that you saw all that. I was stupid. I knew never to take my eye off the bad guys, but I did and we all paid for it. I never saw it from that angle before. I didn't know my buddies surrounded me like that. I was such a mess. I can't believe they carried me out. I bet the whole thing made them sick."

For the first time in this whole conversation, Dillon knew exactly what to say. "Maybe that's why we were there. Maybe whoever or whatever is driving this has a message for both of us. I mean, all along we both figured this was just happening to me, but what if we're missing the point. This is happening to *both* of us. Seeing what happened in Afghanistan must have been as important for you as it was for me, so what did we learn?"

"I learned that my buddies really cared about my sorry ass even though I was only over there for a few weeks and they barely even knew me. I thought I was on my own, but I really never was," Danny said.

"What if that's still true? What if, right now, you feel like you're on your own, but there is help when you need it? If everything happens for a reason, then maybe that's part of what you needed from that tour of your last day on earth. As for me, it's not that complicated. I needed to know you better, and seeing how you lived and died makes me feel like we can handle anything together. The truth is, Danny, you aren't alone and neither am I; we're going to stick together."

OCTOBER 17, 2011

The next morning everyone gathered at Dillon's father's place. Even Tom got the day off school because his dad figured this was at least as educational as anything happening at school that day. Everyone sat around the kitchen table, eating donuts and drinking coffee.

"That better be decaf," Maggie chided Dillon, and then she took the cup out of Ryan's hand. "I know yours isn't." She gave Ryan a smile as she poured it down the drain and refilled Ryan's cup with "unleaded."

"Okay, so we are here today to figure out what happened when Dillon was in the hospital." Thomas had wanted to videotape the session, but Ryan refused. The last thing he wanted was his son labeled a nut online someday. The adults wanted to give Dillon some time to recover, but Dillon was anxious to get back to solving the puzzle. He began by telling everyone the full story about Danny and the day he died, and Maggie was visibly shaken.

"He was just nineteen? Somehow I never thought of him that way. Just a kid, really. His poor mother. Now he feels stuck? Not here, not yet in heaven? Just stuck?" Danny looked at Dillon's mom and smiled.

"Tell her I'm okay. I don't need two mamas worried over me."

Dillon told her and tried to steer the conversation back to the night he had the heart attack.

"The last thing I remember from the hospital was feeling really tired and wishing the MRI was over. The noise and close quarters were really starting to get to me."

"I'm warning you, if you tell them I sang to you, I will haunt you for the rest of your long and happy life," Danny threatened, and Dillon smiled.

"Anyway, the next thing I knew, I was getting real up-close and personal with claustrophobia. I started sweating and feeling sick and it was getting harder and harder to breathe." Ryan put his hand over Maggie's. It was hard for his parents to hear this.

"Then you guys pulled me out of the machine and I felt like I had a herd of elephants dancing on my chest. In a way, in that moment, passing out was a welcomed relief. I don't really know what happened at the hospital after that, and I'm good with never knowing, but the next thing that happened for me was something I never expected and at first, I thought it meant that I must be dead."

Dillon took a bite of his donut to stall. He was trying to get his emotions a little better under control and it wasn't easy. "I opened my eyes in a nice warm bed, but it wasn't at home or in the hospital. It was Grandma's old house in the Catskills. I could even hear her humming downstairs and setting the table." Dillon went on to tell them about the visit, the chicken potpie, and the message from Uncle Joe.

Maggie had tears in her eyes just thinking about her mom and brother. Danny closed his eyes. Oh man, what he wouldn't give for some of that. There were a lot of people he would like to see, and sitting at his Gram's house, having dinner, sounded great. Maybe he would even eat too many biscuits, 'cause really, why should he worry about cholesterol now? Heaven.

"Mom? Uncle Joe is real worried about you." Maggie

turned red and looked away. "He wants you to know that everything is okay and that you don't need to be so hard on yourself, or something like that. What was he talking about?" Dillon looked confused.

"He's just being a big brother, I guess," Maggie whispered.

"Then Uncle Joe looked at my hand." Dillon opened his palm to reveal his brand, *Living*. "He told me not to forget everything he told me. I nodded, and just before Grandma sent me up to bed, I noticed the guitar there just leaning against the wall. When I woke up, I was in the ICU with a major headache and starving, which is weird because I ate a huge amount of that chicken potpie."

Thomas was fascinated. "It makes me wonder if that's what happens to a lot of critically ill people in the hospital."

"You know, it could be," Maggie agreed. "We are trained to believe these patients are hallucinating or delirious, but most of us think they are visiting loved ones who have died."

"What if it's a regular application of string theory happening right before our eyes every day?" Thomas said. "What if the timeline folds and the seriously ill patients move between dimensions all the time?" Thomas began writing in his notes again.

"All things considered, it was the best experience I've had so far," Dillon said. "You know, except for the heart attack, which I really don't recommend, Dad." Dillon took Ryan's third donut out of his hand.

That night, Tom read over his dad's notes again and again. He knew it had to be there, right in front of him, but he couldn't see it. What was the pull that made time fold itself in half? Her brother wanting Maggie to take it easy on herself was nice, but it couldn't possibly be the only message. What was so important that it kept Danny in limbo and made Dillon time travel?

OCTOBER 18, 2011

It was two in the morning when Tom finally went to bed. He was still confused, but hopeful that Dillon's lab results would give his dad an insight soon. Maybe he should suggest that his dad get blood samples from Dillon's parents; maybe there was a genetic predisposition for this? Could time travel run in families? Tom didn't know, but it felt good to have a new theory. He got up and went to see his dad. Thomas didn't appreciate being woken up, but he couldn't help feel proud that questions of genetic predisposition kept his son awake at night.

Later that day, Thomas collected Ryan's and Maggie's blood samples and ran the tests. When the results came back, Thomas retested again and again. This was definitely not what he expected. He had known Maggie and Ryan for a long time, but he had no idea how he was going to talk to them about this. Deciding it just wasn't possible, Thomas ran the tests for a fifth time. No change. Dillon's blood type matched his parents', but his DNA did not.

OCTOBER 20, 2011

Sara was in the ring again, working with a colt she had named Shamrock. She called him "Rocky" most of the time because he was a real fighter. He kicked and bolted and was all around unpleasant once he had even a bridle on, let alone a saddle. He was a nuisance for sure, but Sara liked his spirit. "Giddy-up, come on now," Sara whispered as she led him around on the lunge line. Faster and faster he went, finally channeling his energy into running instead of resisting. It was as though he had discovered his purpose in life right there in that moment. He looked at Sara as if to say, "Thank you. Now I understand."

Thomas took off his glasses and rubbed his eyes. What the heck was he supposed to do now? He was fine dealing with string theory and inter-dimensional time travel, but getting in the middle of family business gave him the creeps. Hoping for a miracle, he checked again, but the results had no pity on him. They were unmoved by his situation and glared at him from the page. Thomas lifted the phone.

"Maggie? Yeah, hi, it's Thomas."

"Hi, Thomas. Are you finished with your tests? He's fine, right? All your tests show no lasting damage? He's healthy?"

"Yes, Maggie, Dillon is fine. In fact, he's just great, but is there something you maybe forgot to tell me about?"

"No, why? What are you getting at, Thomas?"

Suddenly, Thomas wished he had just asked her to meet

him for coffee. He thought he could hide behind the phone, but this was worse. How could he ask about Dillon's lineage on the phone? The receiver in Thomas's hand began to slip, and he realized that his palms were sweating.

"Maggie? The blood work came back."

"So? Dillon is type O negative. What's the problem?"

"I took your blood and Ryan's too, remember?"

"Yes, so? I'm O negative and so is Ryan. Again, I don't see the problem."

Thomas groaned. "Please don't make me tell you what you have got to know already."

Maggie was silent and then she let out a small breath. "Oh Thomas," she stammered. "You didn't just type the blood, or check for environmental markers did you? You ran the DNA?"

"Yes. Does Dillon know?"

"No, he doesn't have a clue and I'm begging you, please don't tell him."

"Maggie, don't you think he has a right to know the truth?"

OCTOBER 22, 2011

Dillon liked the new twist on their theory almost as much as he liked the sound of the guitar solo on Brad Pearlman's new single. He played and played it until he had it just right, and then he waited. Any minute now Danny would show up and Dillon planned to knock his socks off. Dillon was so busy playing that he didn't notice Tom was there until he heard his mom offer them some cookies.

"That sounds pretty good," Tom said as he sat down to listen. "It almost doesn't stink."

Dillon threw his guitar pick at Tom. "You're just jealous because you know guitar players get all the girls."

Tom turned red, but he answered back. "We both know there is only one girl you want: Marie Watson." Now Dillon turned red.

Dillon and Tom were both saved by the bell on Tom's phone.

"Hey, kiddo" Tom's dad began. "I've been thinking about something Dillon and Danny said. What if time was folding to correct something here, in our dimension *and* in order to correct something for Danny, in his dimension? What if there is something here that is needed over there? Maybe even something about that guitar?"

Tom knew that would change everything. Looking at it from that side of things gave him a whole new series of questions. They needed to grab that guitar and get over to the lab right away. Maybe they could interview Danny. The fact that it hadn't occurred to him before hit Tom like a ton of bricks. How could he have ignored half of the equation? Tom looked at Dillon. "Let's take those cookies to go. Call your parents; we need to get over to the lab." A minute later Tom realized his dad was still on the line. "Dad? Sorry. I think you are right. We're on our way."

An hour later everyone was sitting in the lab. Dillon promised to tell them when Danny arrived, but he warned them that Danny kind of kept his own hours and showed up when he was good and ready. He wasn't the kind of guy who just waited around and jumped the moment he was called.

They were just about to call it a day when Dillon sat up.

"You guys! My man, Danny, has arrived."

Danny waved, even though he knew they couldn't see him. "Hey, y'all. What's up?"

Dillon explained that they were pretty much at a standstill until either a new episode happened, which nobody really wanted, or until they figured out a new angle.

"Thomas has run all kinds of tests on me and even blood tests on my parents, but we don't know too much about your family, so that's why we were hoping you would join us today. Maybe we could even talk to your family?"

Danny looked down. "Nope. Y'all can just leave my family out of this. I'm happy to help you figure out what's happening to you, Dillon, but my folks have been through enough. Truth is, they almost didn't make it after I died."

Dillon told everyone what Danny said, and Thomas tried to convince Danny to change his mind. "Danny, no one here wants to hurt or even bother your parents, but it would help us a lot to know what the connection is between you and Dillon."

"The connection is the guitar. That's all." Dillon was

surprised at Danny's anger. When he warned Thomas to cool it, Thomas nodded, but then he went on.

"Danny, if it was just that guitar, then we would be crossing the space-time continuum all over Long Island every time someone brought a new antique to the Hamptons. It has to be more than the guitar. It just has to be."

Danny stared at Thomas. "What are you looking for? If not the guitar, what do you think it is?" Dillon voiced Danny's question and held his breath.

Thomas knew this question would come and he was prepared. "I believe there is some connection between you and Dillon. Something that couldn't wait. Something neither of you know, but something you both need to understand so you can move on."

Dillon was as surprised as Danny by the answer. Together they said, "What do you mean?"

Thomas had to admit at that point that he didn't know what that connection might be, but he knew that he needed to know more about Danny if he was ever going to have a hope of figuring it out.

"Tell you what," Danny began. "I'll give you name, rank, and serial number about me, but I want your word that you will leave my family out of this."

When Thomas heard Danny's terms, he was disappointed to say the least, but he would have to take what he could get. "Okay, let's start with your full name."

"My name is Daniel Patrick Charles."

"Three first names?

Danny looked annoyed. "Charles is my surname."

"Sorry. Rank?" Thomas felt beyond weird interviewing a ghost in the physics lab through a fifteen-year-old translator, but anything for science.

"Okay, here's what you get of my story. I was born and raised in Middle Tennessee on a horse farm in Franklin. I grew up riding horses and building things. My mom and dad are good people who still live there and who still can't really understand how their boy chose the army over MIT."

"You went to MIT?" Thomas asked. "No wonder you grasped string theory so well." Thomas had a whole new respect for Danny now.

"No, I never went. I deferred my acceptance and went to serve ole Uncle Sam. I could not believe what went down on 9/11 and I wanted to be a part of stopping it. I never would have believed the war would last this long. I was smart enough to get in to MIT, but I was pretty dumb when it came to politics."

Thomas nodded. Ryan asked, "Danny, do you remember giving away the guitar?"

"Heck no! I never did give away that guitar. I don't really know how y'all got it, but I left it in my room on the farm. I wanted to bring it with me when I was deployed, but my Sergeant wouldn't let me. He said boot camp wasn't for making music, it was just for singing the blues. I didn't get it then, but I sure did understand it later. Man, boot camp was the hardest thing I ever did, next to dying of course."

Dillon spoke up. "I bought it at the Lead Guitar Shop when I was in Nashville." Danny just shook his head. He could not believe his parents would have sold it to old Mr. Jake, but then again, nothing seemed to make much sense anymore.

"I remember the day I got that guitar. I was about twelve years old and my dad brought it back from a trip to Memphis. He told me it was so old that even E. Princely, The

Ambassador might have played it," Danny said.

Thomas was taking his notes again. "You know, I never gave much thought to how you got the guitar. I'm ashamed to admit it, but I guess I thought it had always been in your family or something."

"I've had worse assumptions made about me. My dad went over to Memphis to see a stallion. He passed on the horse, but brought me that guitar. I played it every day until the day I shipped out."

"Maybe we should do a little more research on the guitar. Maybe there is more to it than we thought," said Ryan. He was glad to find something he could do to help. "I'll take it to a friend of mine, Bill Butler. We were in a band together in college and . . ."

"What did you say?" Dillon could not believe his ears. "You were in a band?"

"Yeah. The Blind Ambitions. We were such a bunch of idiots. Man, this is getting embarrassing. I hope time doesn't fold over to those days."

Dillon smiled. "Cool, Dad. Was Mom your back-up singer?" Maggie rolled her eyes and Ryan laughed. "Son, you have no idea."

Danny told them about his days at school and on the farm, and apart from the fact that he got the guitar from Memphis, they didn't feel any closer to solving the puzzle. Then they turned their attention to the notes. *Remember, Death, Honor,* and *Living.* There had to be something missing. Some message or some reason time was folding itself to bring these two worlds together.

Everyone decided to meet again in a few days when Ryan would have some news on the history of the guitar.

Dillon rose and put it back in its case. He lay the neck down and a piece of paper billowed out and onto the floor. It bore a single word: *Tell.*

OCTOBER 23, 2011

There may have been a few things in Ryan's past that he wasn't proud of, but the time he shared with Maggie and Dillon was the best part of his life. Still, he knew he might not have been so lucky.

Ryan took the guitar to work and put it next to the Palladian window in his corner office. He would go and see Bill Butler after work to ask about the guitar, and in the meantime, he had plenty to keep his mind off the craziness. Michael McIntyre was rapidly becoming Ryan's biggest client. Michael and Ryan were both Southern State University alumni, and Michael joked that this was the only reason he kept Ryan around.

When the phone started ringing, Ryan knew who it was before he even checked the caller ID. "Ryan! How the hell are you?" Michael's voice boomed through the speaker. "I just wanted to let you know that I have located a great piece of land and I want you to get a sales contract out today."

Ryan was nearly afraid to ask, but he did.

"More land around our old alma mater?"

"Of course!" Michael laughed. "I may live in New York, but I intend to keep my compound in Tennessee growing."

Michael McIntyre kept everything growing. He built his reputation and his business on his ability not only to think outside the box, but also to create a world where boxes didn't exist.

He was a genius when it came to trends and always

stayed at least one step ahead of the market. Digital music had been unheard of just a few years ago and now Big Game Music was the single most powerful force in the music industry. At the moment, Michael was intent on buying up nearly all the land around his farm back in their college town. Ryan didn't know why the thousand acres around the farm wasn't enough already, and he wondered whether Michael was getting paranoid about security, but it really was none of Ryan's concern. His job was just to help Michael establish a bigger and bigger security zone around his land. Ryan spent a lot of time getting Michael the paperwork and zoning changes he needed to acquire more land and fortify it with stockade fencing, high-tech surveillance, and at least one underground bunker for emergencies. Ryan had no idea what kind of threat Michael expected, but clearly, he intended to be ready.

Dillon and Tom walked down East 57th Street and for the first time in a long time, they didn't talk about ghosts or other dimensions or even school. They were going skateboarding in the park and nothing else mattered. It felt good to have a day of normal. Since he got out of the hospital, Maggie had practically kept Dillon under lock and key. He guessed he didn't blame her. Having a fifteen year old who had some kind of heart attack and travelled between dimensions must be a serious stress for a mom.

The wind was picking up and the news was even predicting a nor'easter in a few days. Crazy! Snow in October in New York? Either way, it was cold for this time of year, and Dillon couldn't wait to get to the skate park. He had a new Zip Caster skateboard and it was so sweet. On it, he felt like there was nothing he couldn't do. It was as though the board became an extension of his body, and riding it was more instinctual and intuitive than planned or practiced.

The park was as busy as usual, and the air smelled crisp and sweet like an apple ready to harvest. When they got near the ramps, they saw a bunch of kids from school, but Dillon only noticed Marie Watson. She was beautiful, and Dillon stole a quick glance before she caught him and looked right into his eyes.

Tom and he got to the skate ramps and fastened on their helmets. There wasn't too much they couldn't do on their boards, and Dillon was psyched. Tom walked to the top of the ramp and gave Dillon the thumbs-up. Down he flew at lightning speed. The wind whipped around him, and Tom looked like he had wings. He was soaring above and around everything. Tom always said that skateboarding was the freest he had ever felt and he loved it. Dillon couldn't wait to get started. It would start getting dark earlier and earlier now, and he didn't want to burn daylight fooling around with kneepads. He wanted to fly.

Dillon climbed to the top of the ramp and put his foot on the front of his board. The wheels were made of a space-age alloy, and unlike the boards all around him, they didn't make a sound. He took a deep breath, smiled from ear to ear, and took off. Dillon knew the girls were watching, so he leaned back to make sparks fly from the board. It was just flat-out cool.

"Quit showing off, you freak!" shouted Tom with a laugh. He knew Dillon was having a good time, and he was too. The girls from school were walking nearby, and Tom knew they were talking about them. Marie was writing a note and Amanda was giggling. Tom thought her giggles sounded like music. Dillon was big news, but they didn't know the half of it. The story around school was that he had to take some time off school because he had a heart condition that was so rare, the scientists at Manhattan University were studying him to see if maybe he was the missing link between humans and apes.

It was *possible* that Tom had encouraged their confusion, just a little. It was kind of fun for them to be the center of attention for a while. Usually they were such übernerds that girls just looked at them with pity. However, since this reworking of their image, Tom and Dillon were slowly approaching cool. Well, maybe not cool, but at least not pitiful.

Dillon caught up to Tom and they walked over to the girls. It was hard to tell whether they were more excited or nervous, but either way, they were committed now. The girls saw them coming, so there was no backing down.

"Hey, guys," Amanda Armstrong said, and she flashed them a perfect smile. Tom noted that years of braces and teeth-whitening were definitely paying off. "It's nice to see you, Dillon. I heard you were sick, but I can see you're feeling better now."

"Yeah, I'm fine."

The girls moved closer. It was cool, but totally unnerving too. Dillon looked at Amanda's friend, Marie Watson. She didn't say a word, but she smiled at him and something inside Dillon lit up. Marie was in his English class and when they read *Romeo and Juliet,* Dillon thought about Marie. She wore blue jeans and her hair was always in a ponytail.

"Hey Marie, you ever go skateboarding?" Dillon was sure she never did and he wanted the chance to show her how.

"Yeah, I can ride." She reached for his new board and

he gave it to her, dumbfounded. Ten minutes later they were standing together at the top of the ramp, Marie on Dillon's board and Dillon borrowing Tom's.

"One, two, three!" she yelled as she pushed off the edge and soared down the hill.

"Whoa! That was awesome!" Dillon cheered.

It took Dillon a minute to reach her, and when he did, they were both laughing and catching their breath at the bottom of the ramp. Marie leaned down to give Dillon back his board and she lost her balance. She would have wiped out for sure, but Dillon saved her just in time. Of all the thrills Dillon had with his skateboard that day, holding on to Marie was by far the most exciting.

He held onto her a little longer than he had to, but she didn't seem to mind. Walking back to Tom and Amanda, Marie slipped her hand into Dillon's. When she let go, he found a note in its place. Unlike the scary messages he was starting to get used to, this note was welcome. Two glorious words: *Call me.* Dillon didn't know quite what to say, but it didn't matter anyway.

"Well, we should probably get going." Amanda was grinning like a Cheshire Cat, and a moment later Tom and Dillon were watching the girls head out of the park and down the street. When Dillon showed Tom the note, he smiled.

"Aw, that's nothing! Amanda kissed me!" Tom looked like he was flying again, but this time there was no skateboard involved. "It was awesome. When you guys went skateboarding, she just leaned in and kissed me!"

It was getting dark and they decided to get hot dogs and then head home. Both of them had dinner waiting, but as far as they were concerned, there was nothing better than a dirty water dog to celebrate the best day ever. Inter-dimensional time travel was nice and all, but girls were a much more interesting course of study.

Danny watched Ryan work all day. At first he felt a little guilty since he could tell that Ryan had no idea he was there, but he figured it was always a good thing to have more security around the guitar. Danny didn't know what it was about that guitar, but ever since he first got it, he had felt like it was his job to keep it safe. It was like Danny knew he was keeping it for someone; he just didn't know it would be Dillon.

Ryan headed over to Bill's store on 2nd Avenue and Danny was right beside him. It had been a while since Ryan had seen Bill, but he was his usual warm and jovial self when Ryan called.

"You do realize this is going to cost you a nice steak dinner, right?"

Ryan smiled. "Yeah, sure. We'll get together and go to the Oak Room."

"No. I don't think you get it. I mean tonight. I don't hear from you for years and then it's all hurry up and help me out. Well, that's fine, but I want to hear what you have been up to and the way I see it, now might be my only chance."

Ryan smiled again. There was nothing like an old friend. He and Bill had played together every weekend during college and even during Ryan's first year of law school, but then other dreams eclipsed the band. Now, it was pretty much down to news through the grapevine and Christmas cards. Pathetic.

"Tell you what, take a look at this guitar and tell me what you can. Then we'll head over to the Oak Room." Ryan handed Bill the guitar, and his eyes lit up.

Bill took the guitar lovingly in his hands. "Are you kidding me? I haven't seen a beauty like this in a very long time." Bill laid the guitar on the table and turned on his overhead light. He took in every mark, plane, and angle of the instrument. He checked the strings and noticed the wear and tear on the fingerboard. He removed the capo and turned the guitar over. On the back he saw the years of playing and travel traced across the soundboard. It was a thing of beauty: a well-worn, well-played, and well-loved guitar.

"I'd say it's at least thirty years old. I need to get my dental mirror to check the serial number on the inside, but I can tell you this much: it is a thing of beauty, no longer in production, and worth a lot of money to the right collector. Do you want to sell it?"

Ryan could hardly believe his ears. "No! I most certainly do not want to sell it, and even if I did, it's not mine to sell."

"Got that right," Danny said, even though he knew no one could hear him. Danny didn't like the guitar being anywhere but with Dillon. He felt like it was some sort of sacred link between them and he would be relieved when it was back where it belonged.

Bill shrugged his shoulders and disappeared into the back office. He returned a few minutes later with a small mirror angled at the end of a metal stick. He put the mirror behind the strings and into the belly of the instrument. A moment later he had all the information he needed. He walked over to the computer and put the serial number into the archival database and nodded with satisfaction. This was a pretty special guitar, custom made for one owner. This guitar was a 1967 Fenson Flame VII.

"Did you say this baby was from Memphis?" Bill was practically levitating with excitement.

"No, I didn't. But, yes, it actually is from Memphis, Tennessee."

"Yep. It sure is; in fact I can tell you exactly where in Memphis. Looks like this guitar was delivered to 3600 Highway 51 South, Memphis, Tennessee, in 1967."

"Wow! All that from the serial number?"

"Yep. Do you have any idea who lived at 3600 Highway 51 South?"

Ryan was getting tired of this. It had been a long day, and Bill had to know he was not intimately familiar with the 1967 Memphis yellow pages. In fact, in 1967 the only guy Ryan knew of who lived in Memphis was E. Princely, the World Class Ambassador of the Rock and Roll guitar. Suddenly the penny dropped. Ryan looked at Bill and his mouth opened, but no words came out.

Bill was just about bursting. "This guitar was delivered to none other than Mr. E. Princely's assistant.

Ryan was dumbfounded. Dillon was messing around with a guitar that might have belonged to The Ambassador? How was this even possible?

"Come on, Ryan, please tell me you'll sell it. To a collector this guitar is priceless. I mean put-Dillon-through-school priceless."

Ryan lifted the guitar off the table with a new respect and reverence.

"I'll have to take a rain check on that steak," Ryan called over his shoulder as he headed out the door.

Bill just laughed. "So what else is new?"

Ryan was so excited about this new discovery that he couldn't wait to tell everyone, and on his way home he arranged for a meeting and a pizza at his place.

An hour later Ryan, Maggie, Dillon, Tom, and Thomas were enjoying a soda and a slice, and Ryan could wait no longer. Danny was there too. "Listen up, guys. I have some amazing news to tell you. As you know, I took the guitar to Bill Butler today."

Now he had their attention. Conversation stopped and cheese was left dangling in mid air. "According to Bill, this guitar might have belonged to E. Princely."

"Get outta here!" Thomas' Bronx roots were out in force. "Are you tellin' me *the* E. Princely? As in The Ambassador of the Rock and Roll guitar?"

Thomas was a huge fan and he had a much easier time imagining thought experiments and quantum physics than the fact that the guitar at his feet might have been played by the legendary Ambassador. His son, Tom, burst out laughing.

"Seriously, Dad? Calm down." The twinkle in Tom's eyes gave him away. The way he was smiling let his dad know he knew exactly how cool it would be to have The Ambassador's old guitar.

"I can't believe Danny didn't tell us," Dillon said. Then it occurred to him that maybe Danny didn't even know.

"Look, he said his dad got it for him from Memphis. Maybe he has no idea it might have been played by The Ambassador."

"Actually, he said his dad brought the guitar back from Memphis. He never said that was where his dad got it." Ryan always was such a stickler for details. It's what made him such a good lawyer.

It didn't really matter to Dillon; he was excited to learn more about his guitar. He was getting pretty good at it. When he played, Dillon felt like it spoke for him when he just couldn't find the right words. There was also the undeniable fact that, let's face it, girls notice the guy with the guitar.

"Okay," Maggie made a desperate attempt to bring the guys back to the point of this information. "So now we know a little more about the guitar. We know it was originally delivered to The Ambassador's assistant and that it brought Danny and Dillon together."

Maggie stood up and walked around the couch. Maybe she could hold their attention better if she became a moving target, like a football. One by one she recited a list of what they knew so far.

One, the guitar was sent to The Ambassador's assistant in 1967.

Two, at some point, the guitar found its way to Danny's dad, Clint Charles, and he gave it to Danny in Franklin, Tennessee.

Three, after Danny's death, the guitar went from Franklin to Nashville.

Four, Dillon got the guitar and Danny appeared to him when he began to play.

"Okay. Did I miss anything?" Maggie looked up.

"No, not really." Dillon smiled. "You know, just that I am an awesome guitarist and inter-dimensional time traveler." Everyone laughed, and they finished off the pizza. When he was done, Dillon wiped his hands and took the guitar into his lap like a life preserver.

"You know there is one more thing," Thomas said. "We know that this guitar became important to you. Now we also know that it was created as an important instrument, one likely to be preserved. I wonder if this guitar has more to tell us. Something like this would be a good place to put a message for someone because it is not just some random instrument. It was designed for preservation."

"I guess so." Dillon sighed. "But I have had enough messages from this old thing." Dillon began to strum.

At first no one recognized what he played. Then Maggie's eyes filled with tears.

"My brother, Joe, used to sing that like he was a real outlaw or something. Everyone knew he wanted to play guitar, but he just wasn't very good at it. That's why his friends just gave him a tambourine and told him to sing." Maggie wiped a tear away and Dillon stopped strumming. His mom nudged him to go on. He wished he could have known his Uncle Joe better. They might have had a lot in common, both of them being musicians and all.

It was nice to hear his mom talk about him. Usually, all talk of Uncle Joe was relegated to 9/11 events, and then all they ever said was that he was a firefighter. That he ran in when all others ran out. His uncle died somewhere in Tower Seven that day and the last person to hear from him was his Captain, Fred Dunston. Uncle Joe's last words had been "Play on." No one seemed to get it until Maggie explained it. He had told his band the same thing just before he left for college. The other guys had another year of high school and without Joe they figured the band was over. The night before he left he went down to the garage and painted *PLAY ON* on the bass drum and the black curtain they used behind the band when they were on stage. The guys liked it so much they changed the name of the band to Play On.

"I guess Uncle Joe knew a classic song when he heard it," Dillon said.

"He sounds like he had excellent taste in music," Danny drawled. Then Dillon had an idea.

"Danny! Can you talk to E. Princely?"

"No, fool, I cannot talk to The Ambassador." It came out a bit harsher than Danny meant, but he was in a terrible mood anyway. At least Dillon didn't seem to mind.

It had been a truly poor day for Danny. He might not know much about where he was, or how long he would have to stay here, but today proved one thing to him for sure: he was definitely not in heaven.

Danny tried to relax. He was still unsettled from his visit to check in on his mom and dad. He wasn't ready to tell anyone about it, so instead he just listened to everyone talking about what he already knew about his old six string. While they rambled on, Dillon noticed that Danny could not take his eyes off Maggie. Suddenly, Danny realized that she reminded him of Clint; they both had the same undeniable sadness in their eyes.

Everyone reviewed Maggie's list and Danny filled in that he was twelve when he got the guitar. "My dad brought it back from some business trip and I felt like a real cowboy when I held it for the first time. I played it like a bass at first because it was too big for my lap, but it wasn't too long before it fit, and then I had the greatest love affair of my life. I played my heart and soul into that guitar, and I'm not sure that I could have survived high school without it."

Danny couldn't help wondering about how the heck his dad got a guitar meant for E. Princely. He thought about it until it became like an itch.

Thinking about what he found out in Tennessee only gave him more questions. The most pressing question was *How could this be*? Danny needed some time to think. He just wasn't ready to share what he had found on his parents' farm, not until he had some idea how all these new pieces fit together. Nothing made sense to him. If he hadn't seen it with his own eyes, he would never have believed it. In fact, even now, seeing was still not the same thing as believing.

Dillon knew something was up and he tried to lighten the mood.

"Geez Danny, you look like you've seen a ghost. What's up?"

Danny looked at Dillon. "You have no idea."

A moment later Danny was gone. He had to go back to the farm and think. If he could even just sit under the old copper beech tree, maybe he could figure this out.

It was a moonless night and the stars were infinite in the sky over the Danny's Tennessee home. he lay on his back in the grass. He looked up through the twisted branches of the old beech tree and smelled the air. A sign swinging at the end of the lane proclaimed "The Charles Family Farm." Danny shook his head. What did that even mean? Were they really a family? Danny missed his mom and dad more in that moment than he ever had before. He wished he could walk up to their new house, open the door, and have some of his mom's pecan pie with a ridiculously large glass of milk. Heck, he wished he could just stand on the porch and be seen or heard by his parents.

He didn't like looking over their shoulders and rifling through old papers he didn't understand. He felt dirty going through their secrets and not being able to talk to them. He would give anything to be able to just ask them, just confront them. The whole thing was so hellishly frustrating. All his pent-up emotion gave him a burst of energy and Danny lifted a small rock and tossed it into the pond. The splash was somehow satisfying until he heard his father's voice.

"Who's there? What's going on?" Clint was up like a shot and came around the tree. Danny stood up too and jumped out of the way before he remembered his dad couldn't see him anyway. At the edge of the water he could see his dad's fishing tackle and the line dangling in the water. Danny knew there would be catfish for dinner tomorrow, and he missed it down to his bones; if he still had bones, that is.

Clint walked all around the tree and scratched his head. He knew what he had seen, and he knew that rocks were not usually in the habit of hurling themselves into the pond. Clint also knew there was no wind and no sign of anyone anywhere near him. Still, he relaxed and laughed out loud. Clint didn't know why, but out of nowhere he felt tension drain away. He shrugged his shoulders and went back to fishing. Clint never saw it, but he sure did feel Danny put his hand on his back and lead him back to his lawn chair by the water's edge. Clint felt foolish, but he said it anyway. "Hey Danny, is that you? I miss you, kiddo. I miss you."

OCTOBER 25, 1984

Joe was standing in front of the two-burner stove in his two-room apartment in Brooklyn. He had a new job, a new apartment, and a new girlfriend. No doubt about it, life was good. He had just about everything he wanted; everything, that is, except for one thing. He had no clue how to make a decent pot of chili, and no self-respecting firefighter could take his turn as cook if he couldn't even produce a pot of three-alarm chili.

The buzzing of the door interrupted his thoughts. By the time he washed his hands and put down the towel, he was convinced that the buzzer would be broken by the time he got to the door. Then came the knocking. No doubt about it, Clint was here. He and his wife were in the city to see some kind of special doctor. Everyone knew they were desperate to have a child, but this hotshot in New York was their last chance. It must have been a tough day because Clint had called earlier to say that his wife, Sara, was going to stay at the hotel and try to have an early night.

Clint and Joe had met in college and become fast friends. The cowboy and the city slicker were all but inseparable. Before they knew it, college gave way to new jobs and they each returned to their own hometowns. They tried to keep in touch, but visits like this were a luxury neither one could afford very often.

Maggie stopped by Joe's place on her way home from the hospital where she worked. She opened the door with her key and was surprised to see Clint. "Oh. Hello, Clint. I didn't know you were in town." Maggie gave Clint a big hug.

"You hungry? Chili's almost ready," Joe called from the kitchen. He was equal parts big brother, best friend, and surrogate dad to Maggie ever since their dad passed away.

Maggie joked that she couldn't stay. "I only stopped by to use the bathroom. It's bound to be cleaner than the ones near the subway."

After Maggie left, the guys sat down to enjoy the nastiest chili either one of them had ever tasted.

"Good Lord! What in the heck did you put into this? It's worse than road-kill." Clint pretended he was gagging.

"It may be possible that I put in too much Tabasco." Joe tried to smile. "The good thing is that unlike the Podunk place you come from, here in New York we can order in anything we want."

"No, the sad thing is that you are so pathetic, you have to rely on takeout because you can't make a decent supper."

Joe laughed and called the Mexican restaurant down the street. He ordered chili, nachos, burritos, and deep-fried ice cream for dessert. When Joe came back from the kitchen, they talked about everything from Joe's new job to the bad news from Sara's doctor. It didn't look like Clint and Sara were going to be able to have any kids. Joe didn't know what to say, and they were both a little relieved when the food finally arrived.

After dinner they played Joe's old guitar and sang just about every song they knew until the neighbor knocked on the wall begging them to stop. "She has no respect," Joe laughed. "This old guitar could very well have been played by none other than The Ambassador, Mr. E. Princely! At least that's what the guy who gave it to me said. We pulled him from a burning building and he insisted on rewarding us with his prized possession. I was glad no one else wanted it. I don't think they believed it belonged to The Ambassador of Rock-and-Roll guitar. I don't think I do either, but it's still a really cool guitar." Joe felt like he was back in college, and when his friend was leaving, he made a decision. Joe offered Clint the prized guitar. Joe had no idea that his decision would have cosmic consequences.

OCTOBER 25, 1985

Ryan tried to control the old Ford as it barreled down the street. He was practically standing on the brakes, but it was no use. This thing was out of control. He knew better than to do what he did. He knew better, but that hardly mattered now. He was a freshman at Southern State and it was rush week. He wanted to be a fraternity brother more than anything and now everyone around him would pay for it.

He careened around a corner and tried again to slow down, but the old pick-up truck just picked up speed as it moved down the hill. The traffic light in the distance became his only hope. Just beyond the light was a field that he was sure would stop this wild ride. He would ram it into a barn or a haystack, something that would stop this useless heap of metal.

An hour earlier, Ryan had been in the great room of the fraternity house on bended knee. The president of the chapter was issuing his decree on what kind of hazing Ryan would have to endure to prove he was worthy of becoming a member. After weeks of midnight beer runs and being left naked in a hay field to prove he could find his way back, tonight was the final challenge.

Ryan had to drive the fraternity's old Ford down Main Street at midnight. Everyone knew it had lousy brakes, but when Ryan accepted the keys, he didn't know that it had *no* brakes at all. Now as he held his breath and prayed for a miracle, he felt like a fool. Even if he survived, these fraternity brothers may not be worth all the risk.

The light changed from green to yellow and Ryan

wailed on the horn. In this small town no one would be out this late anyway, but even so, Ryan was praying that he would make it through unscathed. He moved closer and closer to the traffic light and began to look past the intersection to find a spot in the field ahead. It looked like he would make it, and Ryan relaxed his grip on the wheel. But then he looked into the field and saw a woman standing there, watching. At that moment the light turned red.

Ryan once heard someone say that in moments of extreme danger a person's life passes before his or her eyes. That's a little bit like what happened next, only Ryan didn't see his past; when he looked at that woman in the field, he saw his future.

OCTOBER 25, 2011

Danny watched the sunrise and smiled when he smelled his mama's biscuits baking. His dad would be making the coffee by now and bringing it out to the front porch. His parents spent most of their time together, but it had not always been that way. Danny remembered hearing that his parents once spent months apart. It had been during the mid 1980s, when getting the farm to turn a profit was getting harder and harder. There was even the first of a concert series called Farm Aid, to try to help America's farmers. His dad had taken on some extra work as a long-haul truck driver to try and make ends meet. Sara missed him, but he always brought back a magnet for her from every truck stop he ever visited. She developed quite a collection. Then something happened, but Danny had never known what.

Danny remembered hearing about the time that his dad came home just in time for Halloween and a couple of days later his parents had a visitor. A young man arrived on the farm and Sara figured he was looking for work. The young man and Clint went out to the barn to have a chat. When they were finished, Clint and Sara holed up in their room for hours. When Clint came back downstairs, he had his bag in his hand, and he was out the door saying he had to leave again on a very important job. That was the last time she saw him until Christmas Eve.

Sara had said that nobody talked about it, but everyone seemed to know that there was big trouble in the Charles family. Then it was all over as quickly as it began. It still made

Danny smile to hear stories about that Christmas Eve.

Danny didn't realize that even now, Sara could still remember looking out from the upstairs window of the bedroom. The snow was gently falling; it was a picture-perfect Christmas Eve, and then she saw a man in the distance. No car, no truck, not even a sleigh, just one man walking up the driveway with a cowboy hat on his head and a shivering bundle in his arms. Sara nearly fell as she scrambled down the stairs to reach the door. There was only one man she knew who looked like that and it wasn't Santa Claus.

When she opened the door, she got the best Christmas present she could ever remember. Still holding the bundle, Clint's strong hands twirled her around the porch and gave her the biggest and best hug ever. On those rare occasions when she would talk about it, it was as if she could still feel the cold from the snow that was sticking to Clint's beard, and she always smiled just thinking about it.

"Merry Christmas, Sara. I'm hoping this is still a time for miracles." Sara reached out her hand and ushered him inside and out of the cold. Danny never knew that when Clint handed her the little bundle, Sara fell to her knees as tears of joy fell down her face. "I'll tell you all about it later, but I think we'd better warm up some milk first." Sara held the baby bundled in her arms and could barely form the words she needed to ask. "What? How is this possible? Where is his family?" Clint promised to tell her everything, but when the baby let out a howl, they both decided the details could wait; this little one was hungry.

It was years later before Danny knew any part of what had really happened. The young man who came to the barn that night to talk to Clint was not looking for work. In fact, he was in pretty good financial shape. His name was Michael McIntyre and he didn't just have a job at the bank, he owned it.

He had come by the house as a courtesy to let Clint know that the bank was considering foreclosing on the Charles farm. It was a disaster narrowly avoided. Clint went to New York and the "special assignments" he knew his boss could get him. Making deliveries in the New York area meant more money and more runs; the fact that he was delivering cargo with somewhat questionable paperwork was none of his business. Sara had wanted him to stay home and insisted that they go to family and friends to ask for help, but Clint refused. He believed his neighbors were busy trying to save their own farms and he wanted no one's charity. Their fight was epic, but they survived and so did the farm.

OCTOBER 26, 2011

Dillon had the perfect seat in Biology class, just out of the teacher's view and right behind Marie. She was wearing the same pink high-tops she wore at the skate park and everything, from her white leather jacket to her faded blue jeans, was just about perfect. She had smiled at him as she sat down, and now every time she flipped her hair over her shoulder—which seemed to happen a lot—the most wonderful aroma wafted in Dillon's direction.

Dillon's phone pinged. He glanced down. A text from Marie!

"Hello <3"

His teacher may as well have been on the moon and speaking Martian. All Dillon could concentrate on was figuring out what to text back. Something funny, but not stupid, something that meant *please be my girlfriend* but actually gave him a reasonable cover if she said *no*. He was floundering around trying to think of what to text when his phone buzzed again.

"do u want 2 come to the play 2nite? I helped with the set design and the wrap party is right after the show :o) Marie"

Sweet! Dillon had to read it twice before he could calm down enough to answer.

"ok ☺"

When the teacher warned him to sit up straight and focus, he just smiled and slid down in his seat even more. Talk about an out-of-body experience. His body was stuck in class, but the rest of him was home trying to figure out how this miracle happened.

"You are kidding me!" Tom shouted on their way home that afternoon. "Show me the text."

"What? I'm hurt. Don't you trust me? You believe I got a ghost in my guitar, but not that Marie asked me out?" Dillon had a twinkle in his eye as he feigned offense.

"Trust, but verify, my friend. Trust, but verify," Tom said as he scrolled down Dillon's texts.

When they bounded into Dillon's apartment, their first stop was the kitchen. Dillon's mom had left cookies on the counter and twenty bucks for pizza beside the phone. Dillon couldn't see how this day could get any better. Tom placed the order for a large pie with everything, and Dillon went to his room. For the first time in his life, he actually cared about what he wore.

"Put that back!" Tom was behind him. "There is no way you are meeting Marie in that!" Tom shook his head pityingly at Dillon, and then he threw the offending shirt on the bed. "Classic, my man, think classic." Tom pushed Dillon out of the way and rummaged through Dillon's clothes. A minute later he handed Dillon a pair of black pants, a blue oxford shirt, and a black leather jacket. Dillon hated to admit it, but he was impressed—and grateful.

A couple of hours later Dillon was back at school. Kids ran in and out of the auditorium, but there was no sign of Marie. Dillon figured she was probably too busy getting the stage ready so he shrugged and took his seat in the audience. As soon as he sat down he heard Danny from behind.

"I just have to ask, is this your first date?"

"Not that it is any of your business, but no, it is not my first date," Dillon whispered and tried to be serious, but started laughing anyway. "This is my second date. My first date was when I was two and I was the ring bearer at Uncle Joe's wedding. Let me tell you, that flower girl was really nice and an older woman—she was five."

Just when Danny thought he couldn't like Dillon more, he did. In fact, he loved this kid. "Yeah, you just have that look about you."

Dillon was suddenly self-conscious, never a good thing on a first date. "What look? What's wrong? What do you mean?"

"Relax. I can just tell when you're nervous. You run your hands through your hair and you look like a church mouse trying to run the revival."

"What the heck are you talking about?" Dillon whispered.

"It's okay. The truth is, I do the same darn thing." The house lights dimmed and the curtain rose. The opening scene was a mountaintop somewhere in the Alps, and a young girl backed into center stage. She spread her arms wide and turned around singing.

When someone sat down in the empty seat beside him, Dillon wouldn't have even noticed if Danny hadn't gasped. Dillon looked over and then not only did he gasp, he jumped.

"You look like you've seen a ghost." Marie smiled at him and settled in to watch the show.

"Wow, you look beautiful," Dillon stammered.

Marie wore a navy blue dress with a silver shawl that sparkled in the stage lights. Her hair was swept up to one side with a silver clip nestled among the curls. Dillon was really glad he hadn't worn jeans. There was no doubt about it, Marie liked to keep him guessing, and she kept him on his toes for the rest of the evening, but he didn't mind. In fact, he kind of liked it, or her, or whatever.

MARCH 17, 1996

"Guess what?" Maggie was breathless with excitement. "We are going to have the best St. Patrick's Day ever," she gushed. "Come home quick."

Ryan put his key in the lock and thought he heard a cat crying. When he opened the door, he discovered that it was no cat. Maggie held a baby boy in her arms, and she was rocking him and singing him to sleep.

"Look at him; isn't he beautiful?" Ryan took one look and he was hooked. He sat down. "What's going on?"

That was the moment Maggie realized that the whole truth would be too much for Ryan. She had lived it and it was almost too much for her. There was no way she could tell Ryan that an elderly woman she met at the hospital sent her through a time portal to a field in Tennessee where the woman handed her a baby and told her he was to be her son. She couldn't understand how they had gotten there or back, so how could she possibly explain it to Ryan? Even Joe seemed confused when she called him. Joe agreed to help her, but he could hardly believe it himself. In fact, he wouldn't have believed it, but this was Maggie, so he did and together they came up with a cover story.

Ryan was starting to tap his foot; he was losing patience.

"Joe called today and said he needed a favor." Maggie steeled herself. "Joe was headed to Tennessee. He asked me to take care of his buddy's kid for a few days. Apparently the baby's parents were killed in a car wreck and they have no other relatives. Joe went to see if he could locate the grandparents, but no luck." Ryan looked over at his new houseguest and smiled.

"How long is he staying?" Ryan asked. Maggie smiled and rubbed the baby's back. "As long as he likes."

A year later Maggie and Ryan formally adopted Dillon.

OCTOBER 27, 2011

Dillon was completely distracted. In the last couple of months he had gotten used to seeing a ghost and developed a working knowledge of string theory and quantum physics and its relationship to gravity. But right now he couldn't seem to focus for more than a minute on anything that didn't involve Marie. Tom clapped his hands to bring Dillon back from his daydream.

"Man, it's hard to believe you used to spend hours playing the guitar. Lately you seem to have the attention span of a gnat."

Dillon and Marie had spent the last two days stealing glances, sending texts, and even holding hands when Dillon walked her home from school. Compared to this, inter-dimensional time travel was a complete and utter bore.

That night Dillon lay in bed, looking out the window. Even in New York City, the stars were shining bright and seemed so close that he almost felt like he could touch them. It wasn't long before he closed his eyes and began to drift asleep. The last thought he remembered was hoping he would dream about Marie.

Dillon was falling. In his dream, he fell down stairs that were endless and he knew the whole time there was no way he would land on his feet. The stairs were metal and dark, and the railings were covered in spikes. There was a smell of sulfur and rotting garbage, and the more he fell the stronger the smell became. Now instead of wishing for a dream that would include Marie, he was very glad she wasn't there.

Finally he landed with a thud and realized to his horror that he was back on the cold, damp floor of the cave and once again it was covered in broken glass. He was cut and bruised everywhere, and when he tried to stand, he began to wonder if one of his legs was actually broken. He pulled himself to his feet and didn't move for a few minutes. He just stood there panting. The cave was different this time: he couldn't see his hand in front of his face when he was here before, but now there was a dim light glowing all around him.

He realized it was more than just a light; if he listened closely he could hear a distant hum. Dillon looked around and was disgusted when he discovered that what he believed to be broken glass when he landed was actually shards of crushed human bones. That explained the smell of something rotting, but the source of the sulfur smell was still a mystery. Dillon wished he could float. He knew what he had to do, but he wasn't ready to do it. The bones under his feet were smeared with blood and the walls were covered in desperate scratches. He couldn't understand why he kept returning to this place. He didn't understand why any of this was happening to him. Instead of feeling like a fifteen-year-old, he felt very small, and though he hated to admit it, he wished his mom were with him. He should have been more careful what he wished for.

Dillon tried to steady himself. He remembered his Great-Aunt Moya telling him that when your back is against the wall, you have nowhere to go but forward, and so that's what he did. He took the first step forward and heard the sickening sound of the bones crunching under his shoe. He tried to focus on the fact that, at least this time, he could see where he was going, and he headed for what looked like a hallway leading out of the part of the cave that he was in. The last time he followed a breeze, it led him outside. Unfortunately, the outside it led him to was war-torn Afghanistan. There was no breeze this time and Dillon didn't dare to hope that the hallway would lead to a sunny meadow. The truth was that he didn't want to think about where the hallway might lead. All he knew for sure was that, even if he didn't know where he was going, he couldn't stay where he was.

The light grew slightly brighter in the hallway. There were no lanterns or torches and certainly nothing as nice as candlelight either. It was more like green phosphorescence embedded in the walls, like fossilized sea creatures that had died long ago but left a little bit of their light behind. As he continued down the hallway, it became more and more narrow and small, but the distant hum was growing louder all the time.

It wasn't too long before Dillon was faced with an unsettling choice: he would have to crouch down and crawl, maybe even drag himself along on his belly, or else turn around and return to the bone cavern. Even though every fiber of his being recoiled against the idea, he fell to his knees. When he was walking on the floor of the hallway, he hadn't noticed just how soft and wet it really was. Now as he put his hand in front of him to begin to crawl, it felt as though he was crawling on some weird combination of wet sand and jelly. It wasn't glass or shards of bone, but it was nasty and raw. As Dillon thought about it, he realized that *raw* was exactly the right word. As the hallway became more and more of a tunnel and the smell grew stronger, he felt like he was crawling along on some kind of rotting meat or flesh. The tunnel was getting tighter and tighter and he wasn't sure if he could go on much farther. He closed his eyes and listened for the hum. Dillon instinctually knew to follow it. Still, he made no commitment to complete the journey, but in each moment, he made the decision to crawl one step further.

A few minutes later he reached out his hand and was surprised that it didn't land on more of the same, disgusting rot. Instead of feeling slime and decomposing flesh, what he felt was more like dirt. In fact, he realized that the stink was beginning to dissipate.

It was such a relief not to touch the gore that he had been crawling through that Dillon opened his eyes. In his hand he held a fistful of rich, black soil. It was the perfect soil for growing things, his mother would say. Almost as if it was the compost of what he had crawled through. He crawled a little bit faster now, glad to get out of the filth and hoping against hope that the soil he was crawling in would bring him up to the surface on a farm somehow. Who knew? Maybe the worst of this dream was over and now he'd see his grandmother's house in the distance or come up in the middle of Central Park.

On he crawled, and slowly but surely the tunnel grew larger, and it wasn't long before it gave way to something like a hallway again. The light changed from the green glow to more of a cool grey that almost reminded him of moonlight. Even the smell was better, and he realized that most of what he could smell from here was fresh dirt and maybe even grass clippings. Dillon was definitely feeling better as he rose to his feet, dusted off his pants, and began to walk. In fact he was so relieved, he picked up the pace and it wasn't long before he was jogging. He expected an incline, or that at any moment he would turn a corner and see the sky, but every time he turned another corner all he saw was more hallway. Still, the smell was gone and the moonlight was growing brighter, so he went on. Dillon couldn't tell if he had been down in this place for hours or if it had been only a few minutes, but it didn't really matter: he was tired of it and he wanted out. His jog became a run, and he ran on and on with a rising panic. What if he was caught in some sort of inter-dimensional maze? There were no doorways, there was no incline, there was no reason to think that this wouldn't just go on like this forever. Then he rounded the corner and couldn't believe what he saw.

It was a relief not to see more hallway, but only for a moment. Relief turned to frustration when he realized that his path was completely blocked by a large stone wall. The only good thing about this wall was that there was some moss growing on the bottom, and Dillon knew that in order for the moss to grow, the wall must be near the outdoors. This wasn't the kind of stone wall you would see on a farm in Connecticut. These were not big rocks piled on top of each other to keep animals in or intruders out. This was a different kind of wall entirely.

As he ran his fingers over the stones, he discovered more dirt between them. The stones were evenly placed, and it was soon clear that this was more than just a wall: this was the back of a building. Why would a building be blocking this underground tunnel? This made no sense. Why would he be brought here if it were only a dead end? What was he supposed to learn from being more frustrated than ever? Dillon felt trapped and toyed with.

He ran his fingers between the stones and tried to trace the mortar. He was hoping to find the entrance to a doorway or some secret button that would open a passage and let him through. He couldn't imagine that he was supposed to come all this way just to return back through the filth and try and find the merciless stairway that had dropped him into this place.

He felt every inch of the wall from top to bottom and side to side. He traced the mortar with his fingers until they bled. He dug around the sides where the dirt of the hallway met the stones of the wall searching for an opening. Nothing.

He kicked the wall in abject frustration, clenched his fists, and screamed at the top of his lungs. All he heard was the echo of his own voice as he turned around and slid down the wall to just sit there and try to get a hold of himself. He felt cheated that he had come so far and now there was this ridiculous obstacle in his way. He knew life wasn't fair, but why lead him all this way just to leave him here, stuck and alone? Time passed, or at least he thought it did. Didn't Thomas say time is relative? Maybe it existed here and maybe it didn't. Dillon had no idea and he was getting to the point where he didn't even care. He didn't want to go back, but he didn't think he could go forward, so he just sat there and stewed.

Absentmindedly Dillon began pulling at the moss growing at the bottom of the wall. He was exhausted, his body ached, and as much as he tried to stay calm, he couldn't quite quell the rising panic growing inside him. What if he really was trapped? What if this was it? He began to think that the only way out was back the way he had come, when he heard a rumbling and the hum got louder and louder.

He stood up and squinted to look down the hallway from where he had come. He took a few steps and looked around the corner to where the hallway became the narrow tunnel. The thought of crawling back was terrifying. But he needn't have worried about it because in that moment the hum grew into a roar. The walls around him began to shake, and the tunnel collapsed in a pile of dust and rancid smoke.

Dillon turned and ran back toward the stone wall. He

was scared that the hallway would be the next to go. What he saw when he rounded the corner again amazed him. Everything around him was vibrating, and the massive stone wall at the end of the hallway was shuddering. The roar was deafening now, and Dillon ran toward the wall, convinced that his head would explode from the noise before his body was crushed if the wall and hallway collapsed the way the tunnel had. Faster and faster, Dillon barreled down the hallway toward the wall, and as he raced toward it, he knew he should slow down, but he just couldn't. He felt compelled to keep running. In the moments before Dillon hit the wall, he closed his eyes and braced himself for what he was sure would be a stunning impact.

Dillon knew the wall was wet when he leaned against it moments before, but what happened next had him really confused. The cold, hard stones he had leaned against, dissolved into a fine mist. It was like running through a fog in the early morning. Dillon opened his eyes and discovered that his momentum and desperation had moved him through an obstacle that up until a few seconds ago, he believed was impassible. He looked behind him and there stood the stone wall, as impenetrable as ever. He reached for it and was met by the same cold, wet hardness that he felt while he was on the other side. But there was no denying the fact that he had passed through it.

He was just about to congratulate himself. Dillon was already rewriting history to tell himself that he was more smart than desperate. He was so happy that his bravery pushed him through that he was already beginning to convince himself that the fear and desperation he had felt had nothing to do with his flight toward the wall. Then reality returned. The light changed again—not glowing green, not cool moonlight; this was sunlight, and he could see the dust motes floating in the air in front of what looked like a stained glass window. Was he in a church? He walked forward and pressed his face against the glass. No matter how he tried, he couldn't see through it, and there was no recognizable picture depicted in the glass. It was just blue and red glass tiles surrounded in lead. There were two windows on either side of a large iron door. Dillon grasped the handle and was surprised to discover that it was unlocked. He had to pull with all his might because the door was twice his size and just as thick, but slowly, ever so slowly, it opened.

As the sunlight filled the room he was in, Dillon realized for the first time where he was. This was not a church. This was a tomb. It wasn't just any tomb either; this was the place where his grandparents and Uncle Joe were buried. Dillon felt cold all over.

It had been many years since Dillon had been in this place. The last time he was anywhere near it, he was just a kid. Dillon was outside on the grass watching from a distance when his uncle was laid to rest. Now standing in the doorway of his family crypt, he looked around for the first time and realized the remains of his ancestors surrounded him. Some of them he knew through family stories, some of them he knew through the photographs that his mom kept around the house, some of them even visited his dreams, as his grandmother and Uncle Joe did, but he never imagined meeting them in this place. There was room inside the crypt for six bodies. His grandfather had it built years before so that his grandparents, their two kids, and their spouses could all be buried together. Dillon always thought the whole thing was seriously creepy.

Now, looking over at the three vaults that filled half of

the space, Dillon thought they were a lot less creepy than the three empty shelves behind him. He guessed that one was for Uncle Joe's wife, but he had heard that she remarried years ago and moved to Florida. He didn't think she'd have much use for her shelf anymore. Dillon guessed that the other two shelves must have been for his own parents, but it was clear that that wasn't going to work out as his grandfather had planned either.

Dillon stared at the bottom shelf. He didn't want to, but he felt compelled to reach out and run his hand along the side. It was three inches thick and made of white Carrera marble from Italy. Dillon was surprised that there wasn't more dust on the shelves, but then he guessed that tombs were usually sealed so that nothing could get in or get out, not even dust. Nervously, he looked over his shoulder to reassure himself that the door out to the cemetery was still open. Thankfully, it was.

There's something profoundly unnatural about seeing your own mother's resting place from the inside. He wanted to leave, to run outside and never look back, but he couldn't seem to tear himself away. In fact, he had to fight the urge to crawl into his mother's place and wait for her. Dillon knew that was crazy, but there was something about this place that drew him in. He wanted to feel close to his mom, to feel safe, but most of all he wanted to reassure himself that she was still among the living.

Dillon wished he could remember Uncle Joe better. The guy he met in the dream at his grandmother's farmhouse had seemed so nice. He leaned down to get a closer look at the inscription beside Uncle Joe's vault.

Joseph S. Golden
August 15, 1964
September 11, 2001
"The Truth shall set you free."
John 8:32

Dillon knew his family had chosen that Bible verse because they believed that knowing the truth; that we are loved, and forgiven when we screw up, means we can really live the life we dream about. Dillon had never thought about it much before, but he realized now that Uncle Joe had just turned thirty-seven when he died. He had had a lot of dreams he wanted to come true, but they were cut short. Dillon found himself wondering what those dreams might have been.

Dillon looked again at the inscription on the tomb. *The Truth shall set you free.* Dillon wasn't about to take any of it for granted. He was determined to figure out why he was there because he didn't want to have to come back.

Truth. What truth? Maybe it had something to do with the messages he had received. Dillon wracked his brain to remember all the words he had collected so far. *Remember, Death, Honor, Living, Tell,* and now, if he added the inscription to the list, *The Truth shall set you free.* What did it mean? What was so important?

Dillon was lost in his thoughts when he heard music outside. This wasn't the typical funeral music that you might hear at a cemetery. This was no trumpet player playing *Taps.* This was a guitar player strumming an old cowboy song. Dillon turned back toward the open door of the mausoleum.

He stepped outside and was momentarily blinded by the sunlight. As he walked down the two steps and onto the grass, the door behind him slammed shut. Dillon reached for the handle to try and open it again but it was locked. There was no budging it, and there was no doubt he could not return the way he had come.

"I guess even for a time traveler, there is just no going back," Dillon muttered as he walked toward the sound of the music. He knew it was nearby, but he couldn't quite see where the musician was. Still, he walked a little farther and found himself on a path that seemed to lead to the edge of the cemetery. There was a parking lot at the edge of the grass. The parking lot wasn't particularly interesting to Dillon, but what caught his eye was the old Chevy pickup truck parked in front. It was just like the truck his uncle had driven, but that wasn't his uncle behind the wheel. It was a much younger version of his mother, and she was crying.

Dillon wanted to run to her but he didn't even know if she could see him, and even if she could what would he possibly say? He walked closer and he could hear her crying with her head bent over the steering wheel. He could also hear the guitar and someone singing. He would have thought that it was the radio except for the fact that the voice was strangely familiar. Dillon just stood there. He didn't know what to do. His mother raised her head and her tear-filled eyes met his face, but there was no sign of recognition. She just looked through him and off into the horizon.

Dillon was relieved that she couldn't see him, but he still felt like he had eyes watching him. At that moment the music stopped abruptly and the singing turned to laughter.

"Hi, Dillon!" Uncle Joe came into focus on the seat beside his mother.

Dillon was surprised and happy to see him. He had a good feeling just being around his uncle. Dillon came closer to get a better view, and what he saw stopped him in his tracks. Uncle Joe had a guitar in his lap, but not just any guitar: it was the 1967 Fenson that Dillon played at home.

"Uncle Joe, where did you get that guitar?"

"Isn't she a beauty? It was a gift from some guy I barely knew. I don't think it's true, but the guy told me it might have belonged to E. Princely and made me promise never to sell it." Dillon didn't know what to think.

"Uncle Joe," Dillon stammered. "I have that guitar right now in my room, but it wasn't passed down in our family."

"What makes you think it wasn't passed down?" Uncle Joe smiled.

"Gee, I don't know. Maybe because I got it in Nashville while Dad was on a business trip?"

Uncle Joe winked at him. "You know what, Dillon? For a kid raised in New York City, you are pretty gullible. That guitar may not have come to you in the regular way, but it was most definitely meant to be yours. By the way, I get a real kick out of listening to you play."

Dillon was about to say something, to ask more questions, but suddenly they were distracted. His mother's crying had stopped, but not because she was feeling any better.

Uncle Joe explained. "The weeks after 9/11 were a really difficult time. People were taping plastic to their chimneys and windows and stockpiling food because they thought the Taliban was going to fly overhead and drop biohazard over us. People were afraid to ride the subways, and even being in New York City was a scary thing. Your dad wanted to take you far from here, and even though your mom thought it made sense, she just couldn't wrap her mind around living anywhere else."

"Why did you show me this? Did my mom have some kind of break-down or something?" Dillon wanted to know. "I don't understand any of this. Are you the one sending me the notes?"

Uncle Joe reached out and squeezed Dillon's hand and everything began to fade away. Dillon looked around and discovered he was in his own room, and the only thing from the dream that still existed was the guitar leaning against the wall.

OCTOBER 29, 2011

Dillon was in his room again, and he just couldn't bring himself to come out and sit in the kitchen with his mom. He decided he must have been getting better at this inter-dimensional travel because when he woke up yesterday, he was able to come back from his nightmare without a scratch. He left the blood and the bruises behind, but he couldn't leave behind the knowledge of his mother's terrible desperation. He had promised to tell Thomas about every one of his journeys, but to do that now seemed like an unforgivable betrayal of his mother's privacy. Still, if he wasn't straight with Thomas, they could miss some of the most significant clues they had so far.

Dillon had thought about it all day yesterday at the park. He tossed and turned last night and called to Danny, but Danny didn't come. Now here Dillon was, hiding in his room rather than going into the kitchen and talking to his mom about losing Uncle Joe and 9/11. Dillon was disgusted with himself because he knew he'd rather be a coward than have to deal with a discussion he knew he could not avoid forever. He had been avoiding a lot of discussions lately. He couldn't even bring himself to talk to Marie about it. How could he explain this? He didn't want to scare her away, and the truth was, he was a little scared of himself at this point.

This was the first experience he had from this other dimension that didn't involved Danny. The more Dillon thought about it, the more convinced he became that the guitar really was the key to the whole thing. Sometimes he couldn't decide whether he loved it, or hated it. He felt as if his whole world had been turned upside down since the guitar had come into his life. The thing was, even if he wanted to, he couldn't live without it. That guitar was more to him than just a musical instrument; it was a voice. In fact, it was more than just one voice; it was a whole chorus of voices from the past and the present, and maybe even from the future.

These were not voices that could be silenced. Dillon lifted the guitar from the corner, slung it onto his back, and headed out the door. He called good-bye to his mom and told her he was going to his dad's place. Before she could say a word, he closed the front door behind him. He had to talk to someone and he felt like only his dad would understand.

Dillon wasn't the only person avoiding someone. Danny knew full well that Dillon was calling him the night before, but he just didn't know if he was ready to face him yet. Danny was still at his parent's farm because he just couldn't bring himself to leave. It was as though he wanted some kind of confirmation that all of the pain from the past really was over. He watched his mom with a colt she called Rocky and thought about how his mom could train a horse without ever really breaking its spirit. It was as though she had a sixth sense and understood the fine line between defensiveness and defiance. Sara knew how to handle Clint too. Defense and defiance made Danny think about his dad. Danny found himself wandering back into the barn. He went back to the caretaker's apartment. Most of his parents' stuff was cleared out of it now, but there was an old shoebox lying open at the foot of the bed. At the top of the pile of pictures and letters in the shoebox was the picture that changed everything. When Danny saw it, he wanted to scream. Then his dad came into the room. His father noticed the open box, shrugged his shoulders and put the box away again in the back of the tack closet.

After Clint left the room, Danny walked over to the closet, reached inside, and pulled out the box. He put it down on the desk and opened the lid. The box wasn't at all dusty or even old looking. Danny thought it was the kind of thing that looked like it was important to someone—treasured, but very private. Danny removed the envelope and spilled the contents onto the desk. There was the tattered photograph. The picture was out of focus and grainy, but the people were still easy to recognize.

It was Danny's dad, Clint, with another family. They were all lined up outside a decrepit looking truck, and judging from the scared expressions and worn-out clothes, these people had already travelled a long way. Danny didn't recognize most of them, but there was no escaping the fact that the people still seemed eerily familiar. The older lady in the picture held twins. They looked like they were only a few days old. Danny didn't know how he knew, he only knew that he did: that baby looked just like him. Come to think of it, Danny was sure the other baby in the woman's arms looked pretty darn familiar too.

Danny hated it, but he knew what the picture was for. Smugglers in Afghanistan did the same thing. It was an illegal inventory, like a bill of lading for human cargo. His dad must have been driving these people over the border. Searching for a better life, they often sold everything they had just to buy the passage from a *coyote.* Then they were smuggled across the border and treated like cattle. Danny was disgusted. How could this be his dad, and how could Danny be in the picture too? Danny knew the answer, but he still could hardly accept it.

Danny looked at the picture again. He wanted so much to find the truth, but he didn't want to see this truth. He was working to convince himself that all babies look alike and that these twins could be anyone, and then he saw what he knew he could never deny. One of the babies had his foot dangling from the blanket, and there it was, the same damn birthmark that Danny knew so well. He lifted the cuff of his jeans and there it was. All through middle school, he refused to wear shorts because of it—no small feat in Tennessee in July. The same heart-shaped birthmark on the baby's leg was still right above Danny's ankle. So many hours of his childhood were spent trying to turn that thing into anything else. Once he even tried to convince the kids that it was a tattoo, because naturally, lots of ten-year-old boys sported heart shaped tattoos.

That baby in the picture was definitely Danny and there was only one reason he was in that poor woman's arms: he was with her. The twin? Danny just knew it was Dillon. How the hell could this be? There were eleven years between them. How could they be twins? Unless time travel wasn't as new to them as they originally thought. What if someone brought Dillon back eleven years later than Danny? Then they really could be twins who grew up eleven years apart. *Even if it is true, what does it matter now?* Now Danny had a headache, which was weird because up until that moment, there had never been any physical pain where he was.

Danny could not reconcile the daddy he grew up with, with some money-hungry *coyote* smuggling people over the border. He had to find out what was going on. There must be more to this. The problem was how? Was this the reason Dillon was time travelling? Was this what caused the space-time continuum to fold itself? Danny heard his dad's footsteps again and he stood up. He thought about putting the box and its contents away, but he didn't do it.

"Why didn't you tell me?" Danny demanded as Clint lumbered into the room. "I had a right to know. Were you ever going to tell me?" Before he could stop himself, Danny was on a rampage.

"How could you just walk away? What kind of a man are you? You were always preaching at me about doing the right thing and here you are nothing but a hypocrite!"

Danny was so angry that the light in the room began to flicker. Clint checked the switch, shrugged, and walked out again. Danny tried to calm down as he watched his dad walk across the field.

"I guess some things just never change," Danny sighed. "Dead or alive, what I think just doesn't matter much."

Ryan was finishing his fifth mile and his building was finally in sight. He loved to run, but at a moment like this, he loved the fact that he was almost done, even more. All he could think about was the nice hot shower waiting for him at the end of the block. When he got home, he was surprised to find Dillon sitting at his front door.

"Hey buddy, I didn't expect to see you today. How's it going?"

Dillon stood up and looked him in the eye. "I need your help." Ryan nodded, opened the door and they went inside. *So much for a nice, hot shower*, Ryan thought as they went inside.

"Dad, I saw something the other night that I wish I'd never seen. I know I made a deal with everyone to let you know whenever I have a nightmare or time travel or whatever the heck it is that I do, but this time I'm not sure that I can."

Ryan handed his son a bottle of water and they both sat down on the couch.

"The other night it happened again," Dillon continued. "There was a lot to it and I can tell you the details later, but what was most important happened at the end and if it's okay with you, I'd like to start there."

Ryan agreed and Dillon began. It was really hard for Dillon to tell his father what he had seen that night, and it was even harder for his dad to hear it. Ryan closed his eyes and held his head in his hands.

Ryan had long suspected that Maggie couldn't cope when Joe died, but he never imagined that she was completely broken. Now that he knew, things that he never understood began to make sense for the first time. He thought they split because she was tired of him, but now Ryan realized that she didn't grow tired of him; she had grown tired of life.

If he hadn't been so self-absorbed and insecure, maybe he could have helped her, or at the very least, maybe he could have known what was going on, but he was too busy fighting his own demons. He wanted to leave New York and he blamed it on 9/11, but that wasn't the only reason. He wanted to go somewhere where they could be an ordinary family. Somewhere far away, where what Maggie had done couldn't catch up with them.

At first Ryan believed her story about Dillon being the child of Joe's friends, but the lawyer in him compelled him to research. There was no record of an accident, let alone two fatalities. Ryan didn't know how Maggie did it and Joe would never tell, but Ryan was convinced it was way outside of the law. By the time he faced that reality, he had grown too attached to Dillon to care. When 9/11 happened, Ryan took it as a wake-up call. Nothing was protected: not New York and not his family. When Maggie refused to leave, it never occurred to him that she didn't want to leave the city Joe had died trying to protect. Ryan had convinced himself that she just didn't want to leave with him.

OCTOBER 30, 2011

Everyone gathered at Maggie's place. Dillon and his dad had come over earlier that day and told Maggie everything. Ryan was determined that what and how much they shared with the rest of the group had to be Maggie's decision. If she wanted her heartbreak kept out of it, that would be just fine with him. But her response surprised them both. She was not only open to sharing the whole story, she insisted on it.

"It's true, I went through a really bad time after Joe died. It was hard for me, some days it still is hard, but the one thing I've learned for sure is that life is too precious to do anything less than the best we can. We need to tell the whole story if we're going to figure out what's happening to you, Dillon. Your safety is more important to me than my privacy. I'm sorry you had to see that, and I don't understand why you did, but let's keep going."

After Dillon told everyone about his episode in the cemetery, everyone sat around Maggie's living room overwhelmed and a little exhausted. Maggie had gone out of her way to make sure everybody understood that her event was only a part of the story, and now they were all trying to figure out what it could mean. Danny slipped in just in time to hear the worst of it, and he just sat there quietly and listened. Thomas took out a new piece of notepaper and began to put down all the words that had come through so far.

"*Remember, Death, Honor, Living, Tell, the Truth shall set you free.*" Thomas stared at the paper and then a smile began to play around his lips. He looked at Dillon and said, "You know what? I think our little experiment with string theory is finally making some progress. Kind of like that tunnel you were in. You got hurt at first and I know going forward was difficult, but now we may be in a place with some rich soil where things can grow. What I'm saying is, we already have a coherent message: *Remember death and honor the living.* That, right there, is significant. Joe or God or someone is telling us two things. Number one, we should never forget those who went before us, because by remembering the dead we're showing gratitude and understanding that life is precious and finite. Number two, you can also interpret it to mean that we should remember that death, or those who have gone before us, are still here, close to the living." When he said that, Thomas looked directly at Maggie.

"Then take the second part. *Tell and the Truth shall set you free.* Secrets constrict us. There is a lot of energy wasted in keeping a secret, and maybe there is something that is important enough right now in this world that Joe and Danny had to cross dimensions to tell us."

Dillon looked across the room at Danny, but Danny just looked away. Uncle Joe only showed up in dreams so there was no talking to him. As far as Dillon knew, Danny was as confused as he was about why he was there.

Everyone sat quietly mulling over Thomas' words. Ryan could hardly think straight, so he got up to stretch his legs. He picked up the newspaper and let out a wail. "What the hell is this?!"

The headline of the Wall Street World said it all: *Michael McIntyre to Develop Alternative Energy Source.* He was quoted as saying, "Fossil fuels are literally dead and the best way to honor our living world is to tell the whole truth about how fossil fuels are destroying the environment. My company can develop a living energy that will finally set us free." When Ryan finished reading it aloud, he looked more ghostly than Danny.

Dillon could hardly believe his ears. "There is no way that can be a coincidence, but what does dad's client have to do with this?"

Later that night, back in Dillon's room, Danny reappeared. This time it was Danny who picked up the guitar and started to play. Dillon put his head back and closed his eyes and just listened to the music.

"That's really nice," Dillon said. "What is that you're playing?"

Danny smiled and explained it was an old song called "Will the Circle Be Unbroken?" Danny told him it was a song about being together, in this life and in the next.

Dillon smirked. "Sort of a string theory lullaby, I guess." Danny raised his eyebrow but went right on singing:

Will the circle be unbroken? By and by, Lord, by and by.
There's a better home awaitin', in the sky, Lord, in the sky.

OCTOBER 31, 2011

Dillon woke to his phone vibrating across his nightstand. He lifted it and smiled when he saw the text from Marie.

"Happy Halloween ☺"

Dillon texted back; "U 2 ☺"

Dillon couldn't wait to get to school. Even for a Monday, today was starting off just fine. Dillon showered and dressed quickly, but he left the best parts of his costume in his room, and then he headed for the kitchen. His mom was home today, and the smell of pumpkin pancakes filled the house. Maggie seemed more relaxed than Dillon had seen her in a long time.

"Don't put your costume on until after you eat; I don't want you getting syrup on it," Maggie chided Dillon as she placed a plate of pancakes under his nose. The butter melted on top of the stack of pancakes, and Dillon barely waited until he had sat down before he shoved the first forkful into his mouth. No doubt about it, for a Monday this was awesome. Ten minutes later the pancakes were history and so was Dillon as he dashed to his room to finish getting ready for school. In Danny's honor, Dillon was dressing up like a cowboy, and when he came out of his room and Maggie saw him, the dish she was holding went crashing to the floor. "Sorry I startled you, Mom. Don't you like my costume?"

Maggie got on her knees and began cleaning up the shattered dish.

"Yeah, sure, Hon. It's fine. You make a great cowboy," Maggie stuttered, desperately trying to compose herself before

Dillon noticed that she was trembling. "Have fun at school today. Say hi to Tom and Marie for me."

A moment later Dillon slammed the door and Maggie sat back on her knees and wiped off the beads of sweat that spread across her brow. She may have shared one secret, but she had no interest in telling any others. Maggie took a deep breath and made her decision; for the first time in her life, she tried to reach out across the great divide and speak to her brother.

"Joe? What are you up to? A cowboy? Seriously! Stop it! Leave Dillon out of it! Whatever you want, deal with me, not my son!"

It was the first time she said aloud what had been lurking in her heart. Maggie loved Joe with all her heart, and when he died it had all but shattered her. She wanted to believe it was Danny haunting Dillon, but Danny seemed as frustrated and confused as everyone else. How could the brother who made her feel so safe become the brother haunting her son? Why was he revealing her secrets? Why involve Danny, and when would it all stop?

Maggie couldn't see him, but Joe was right beside her, kneeling on the floor. She had no way of knowing it, but he even moved the edge of the broken plate away from her hand when she leaned on the counter to get up. Joe tried to talk to her as he had tried to talk to her at least a thousand times before. This was something too important for her to neglect, but something she seemed determined to ignore. Joe had to find a way to get his sister to talk about it, but he couldn't. He hated to do it this way, but Joe had no choice now but to go on. There was no doubt about it; the stakes were way too high to stop. This wasn't just about Maggie anymore. If she didn't tell Dillon the whole story soon, Dillon and Danny could both be lost.

Halloween in Franklin, Tennessee, was a magical time with a Pumpkin Festival on Main Street and Haunted Hayrides too. This would be the first time in a long time that the Charles Farm would welcome guests for Halloween. Sara was humming as she hung the orange lights around the barn doors and put a fake raven up on the hay hook outside the loft. It would be strange to celebrate without Danny, but Sara needn't have worried. He was right there beside her.

Meanwhile, back in New York, Dillon and Marie walked along West 57th Street after school and stopped at the Mackenzie Brown shop. Marie looked in the window and her eyes lit up.

"This is the coolest store. I want to get a job here after school, but I'm nervous about asking."

Dillon stood beside her and leaned against the glass. He could see her face in the reflection and he was mesmerized. He pretended to study the pottery in the window, just so he could look at her and deal with his own nerves. He spent the last three blocks trying to figure out how to grab her hand in a casual way. It should be no big deal, because it's not as though they had never held hands before, but the longer he waited, the scarier it became.

"Do you *like* me? You know, as in *like* me?" Marie wanted to know.

Without meeting her eyes Dillon mumbled, "You know I do."

Marie smiled and took both of Dillon's hands in her

own. Now he had no choice but to look her in the eye and that was just fine with him. Marie was beautiful. She was dressed as a princess for Halloween, and her tiara sparkled in the window lights. Dillon was lost in her eyes when she reached up and kissed him. It was a warm, wet kiss and he felt it right down to his toes. Before he could speak, she laughed and they were off again on their way home. Of all the Halloween treats Dillon ever got, Marie's kiss was by far the most wonderful.

NOVEMBER 3, 2011

Thomas was in unfamiliar surroundings. In fact, he was ashamed to admit it, but he couldn't remember the last time he had ventured across campus to the English department. He felt more comfortable where everyone had the decency to wear a lab coat and where there was plenty of stainless steel. Here in the English Literature wing of Lewis Hall, Thomas was downright uncomfortable. He felt like he was walking back in time as he passed through the hallowed halls of oak-paneled offices with old-fashioned books everywhere. It was hard to believe the piles of books stacked all over his colleague's office. Had these people totally missed the invention of the e-readers and tablets? Thomas couldn't help but think of the dust mites that had to be all over the place.

Professor Plumston sat on her massive leather chair and reviewed the list of clues Thomas had given her. She looked for quotes, context, or allusion, but found none. "I'm sorry, Thomas. I don't see anything more than you do. It's not an excerpt from anything I know of, and it seems to me like there is no particular code."

"I thought so too, but it's not really my area of expertise. I guess I was hoping I had missed something." Thomas stood up to leave.

Professor Plumston stood as well. "Sorry I can't help you, but good luck."

Remember, death, honor, living, tell, the Truth shall set you free. Thomas mulled it over and over in his mind. Slowly he began to focus on the middle of the message. *Tell the truth.* That had to be significant. Tell what truth? Thomas could hardly imagine that Dillon had a secret so great that he would be thrust into inter-dimensional time travel. Danny might have secrets, but why would Dillon's family be involved? There was the question of Dillon's parentage, but lots of kids were adopted, so Thomas couldn't see how that could be it either. There had to be some reason that the boys had been brought together. The guitar might be the mechanism that joined the boys, but it seemed like it was no longer really necessary to bring the boys into other dimensions.

Still, the guitar figured prominently in many of the experiences. Thomas' brain ached from trying to figure it out, and then it dawned on him. *Dillon doesn't* have *a secret; Dillon* is *a secret. His DNA doesn't match up with his parents'. Maggie seems to know, and she said Ryan knew, but not Dillon? And if he doesn't know, why does it matter now? How does it affect Danny? What makes Dillon's adoption so different, even dangerous? Why should it have cosmic consequences?*

Thomas could feel his brain itch again. There was no doubt about it; he knew he was getting closer to figuring this out. He was definitely on the right track and he was definitely going to be up all night trying to put this puzzle together. The frustrating thing was that he didn't think he had all the pieces.

NOVEMBER 4, 2011

It had been a long night, and when Thomas called Maggie the next morning, he had a list of questions. He didn't want to intrude on her private life, but he needed to know more about Dillon's DNA if they were ever going to figure this out. They agreed to meet an hour later, and Maggie asked Ryan to join them. It was going to be difficult and uncomfortable for sure, but it wasn't just Maggie's story to tell. It was only fair that Ryan should be there when Maggie explained about everything.

Thomas and Ryan arrived at Maggie's place at the same time. Maggie breezed in, and Ryan could tell from her flushed cheeks and bright-red ears that she was nervous. He reached for her hand and gave it a squeeze. "Might as well get started," Maggie said in a voice a little more high-pitched than usual.

Thomas had a list of questions, but Maggie looked like she needed to do this in her own way. Explaining a child's adoption is a delicate thing at best, and Thomas didn't want to make this harder than it had to be. He put away his questions and leaned forward to listen. A moment later Maggie began to speak.

"Wow, this is harder than I thought it would be," Maggie began as she and Ryan sat on the sofa together. "What I'm about to tell you is extremely private and sensitive. Before I begin, I need your word that it will be kept completely confidential." Thomas nodded.

"You are absolutely sure you need this information, right?" Ryan asked.

"I know it's not easy, but yes, it is crucial. You see, I was going over the messages Dillon received and right in the middle it says *Tell the truth.* That got me thinking, *Tell the truth about what*? What secret and who needs to tell it? All along I have wondered what Dillon needs to tell us, and then it finally occurred to me, what if Dillon is not the one with the secret, what if he *is* the secret? That reminded me about the DNA discrepancy and that's why I called you."

"Well, as I guess you already know," Ryan began, "we're not Dillon's biological parents. We are, however, his legal parents and guardians and more importantly, we're the only family he's ever known." Ryan wished he didn't feel as defensive as he sounded. Being Dillon's dad was the most important thing in Ryan's life, but he always felt like he had something to prove. "What if I told you that this is not our first experience with time travel?"

The room fell utterly silent and Thomas tried to get a grip on what Ryan was trying to tell him. At least a million questions flew into his mind, but he said nothing. He just sat back on the couch and retrieved his old notebook. No way he wanted to miss even a word of whatever this was. Maggie looked away and stood up. This was a tough conversation for lots of reasons.

"I'm not sure exactly where to start," Ryan explained, "but I guess 1985 is as good a place as any. I was a freshman in college that October and I was rushing a fraternity. 'Hell Week,' as they liked to call it, was almost over and it had definitely been one hell of a ride. I came through a week of groveling and other miscellaneous embarrassments and there was just one test left to pass. Everyone knew it was crazy, but the last feat I had to endure was driving the old fraternity truck down Main Street at midnight. It should have been a no-brainer, but there was a catch. I guess there is always a catch. The old piece of junk had no brakes."

"Wait a minute. You agreed to drive a vehicle with no brakes?" The question was out of Thomas' mouth before he could stop it.

"I'm afraid so," Ryan sighed. "I didn't realize that 'bad brakes' really meant no brakes at all, but by the time I discovered that, it was too late. Anyway, there I was headed down the street and picking up speed. I pumped the brakes and then pounded them, but it was no use. I saw a field up ahead and a young woman waiting at the edge. I thought that if I could just make it to the field, I could ram that old heap into a haystack, or even the barn, anything at all just to make it stop. I almost made it too. If that light hadn't changed at the last minute, none of this might have happened."

Ryan rubbed his head and sighed. "The light changed, but I couldn't stop. I wailed on the horn, but it was already too late. Another truck came out of nowhere at the last minute. For a moment, I even thought the trailer end would clear the intersection before I got there and it almost happened that way. But at the moment the back of that truck was nearly out of the intersection, I plowed into it. I caught the back of the truck and the force of the impact flipped the whole thing right over. We landed in a pile of twisted metal in the field. It was a disaster."

Thomas was horrified, but he didn't see how this related to Dillon, Danny, or time travel.

"The next thing I knew I was hanging from the steering wheel and I smelled smoke. I must have passed out, and at the time I thought I was hallucinating, but the truth is, I saw the whole thing. Hanging there, peering through the smoke I saw something I would not understand until about fifteen years ago, when Dillon came into our lives.

"I actually saw Maggie walk out through the brush from the field. I watched her go into the back of the mangled truck and an old woman handed her a baby from the wreckage. At first I guessed some Good Samaritan had come to help us. Then I heard sirens in the distance and Maggie began to run. She ran straight into the field and disappeared back the way she came.

"I still don't know exactly how long I was there before I felt these strong arms pull me from the car. There was a cowboy at least six feet tall standing over me muttering and swearing. I'd hit my head pretty hard and I guess I passed out again or something, but when I woke up, I was in the hospital and they told me I had been in a coma for about a month. I tried to tell them what I had seen, but no one believed me. They were convinced it was the head injury talking.

"Later I found out that the truck I hit was full of migrant farm workers from South America. Thank God, everyone got out alive, but they never found the baby or the guy who pulled me out. I guess everyone just ran for the hills. They wanted a description of the other driver, but I couldn't tell them anything more than 'cowboy.' There was no way of knowing who was in the truck because there was no record of those people. It was only the blankets and old clothes left behind that even made the cops suspicious. When they ran the plates, they discovered some kind of illegal trafficking going on.

"They ruled the crash an accident for one reason only: lack of evidence. The wreck was so burned up that there was no way for them to know it had no brakes. They might have suspected it was a stunt, but they couldn't prove it. As for the truck, once again, they knew something wasn't right, but they couldn't prove it. Besides, that cowboy was long gone anyway."

Thomas had stopped taking notes at least twenty minutes before, but he wasn't worried. He would never forget what he just heard. His head was swimming when he muttered, "What happened fifteen years ago that helped you understand all this?"

Maggie smiled and took over. She had a strange look in her eyes. "Fifteen years ago I met an amazing woman. She was at the hospital and we got to talking. She claimed she could time travel, but I didn't believe her, at least not at first." Maggie fiddled with her sweater. "Anyway, she said that she knew how much I wanted to be a mother and that she could help me. She said she could show me where a child would be waiting for me. I didn't understand at first but then she said something that I couldn't ignore."

"You will have a son," the old woman began, "but only if you can claim him. Your child will not come to you by the eagle, not by your kind of medicine or hospital. Your son must come to you by the condor, by the world of spirit and time travel."

"I have to admit I was curious, but still, I thought she was crazy. I thought it was all crazy right up until the moment I discovered it was true."

Ryan shook his head. Maggie continued. "Anyway, the woman said she could show me how to do it, but that there wasn't much time to debate. I went with her to Times Square of all places. I thought I was just imagining things but then even I couldn't deny it. We held hands and then we began to move and I felt like I was falling. The next thing I knew I was standing in the field moments before Ryan's accident." Thomas tried not to look as amazed as he really was.

"The next thing I knew I heard wheels screeching and a crash. It was tragic. There was smoke and fire and then I heard a baby crying. I ran into the burning wreck and saw the old woman pulling Dillon from the back of the truck. I planned to go back into the truck to see if I could help, but there was a cowboy who ran in after me. I brought the baby out of harm's way and that's when I could hear the woman shouting. She yelled at me to run back and to do it quickly before the portal closed. I didn't know what to do. I didn't think. I wanted to go back and help—I'm a nurse for heaven's sake—but I didn't. I ran and ran. I was running so hard that I fell into some kind of a pit. I clutched the baby and together we kept falling and falling."

Ryan continued. "Maggie came back to Times Square with a baby bundled in her arms and she never saw the old woman again. Her first stop was Joe's place where they invented a cover story, but eventually Maggie came clean and told me the truth. The weird thing was that I believed her. It just rang true."

Thomas leaned back and closed his eyes trying to absorb all the implications of this new information. Maggie was a time traveller? Dillon was in the wrong place? Dillon was literally out of time? This had to be the secret, but why was Joe so intent on revealing it? Why did it matter so much now?

"Am I right in assuming that we are the only ones who know about this? What about Dillon's biological family?" Thomas was looking for something, but he didn't know what.

"I'm ashamed to say that there was no one left to look for him after the accident. There was no way to trace an extended family. I don't even know what country they were from. I didn't want anyone to know about how Dillon came to us. Even if we wanted to go public, who would have believed us anyway?" Maggie shrugged.

"As a lawyer," Ryan added, "it was easy enough to get Dillon private adoption papers, so that's what I did."

"Look, Thomas," Maggie added, "I can't pretend I expected to have a child this way, but Dillon is our son. He doesn't even know he was adopted because we would have no agency records for him to see. If I had left him there, he could have died. That's why we didn't tell you all this before. Dillon's sanity was already under pressure; this was just not anything we wanted him to have to deal with now."

"There is just one more thing." Ryan stood up.

"There's more?" Thomas was reeling.

"Michael McIntyre knows everything and never lets us forget it. I don't know how he knew, but he did. He says that's why he keeps me close. I believe he is a time traveler too, but I'm sworn to secrecy. If I tell about his time travel, he'll expose the fact that Dillon isn't ours."

This was definitely a secret worth telling, but to do so now would just hurt and confuse Dillon. Thomas wanted to go home and think.

Danny couldn't stop thinking about that picture in the box at his parents' place. He was going to go there again, but then changed his mind. He didn't need to see it again to remember what it meant, and he knew he couldn't hide away from Dillon forever.

"You ever hear that saying, *You can sleep when you're dead*?" Danny asked Dillon as he appeared in his room. "Well, let me tell you something, it ain't true. There is no sleeping at all."

Dillon was glad to see his friend again. Dillon was trying to change the strings on the guitar, and he was making quite a mess. When Danny saw what he was doing, he thought about letting Dillon struggle along. That was how he learned to do it: trial and error after error after error. The only problem with that plan was that Danny hated to see his favorite guitar suffer through what it looked like could be a long learning curve.

"Stop it. I'm begging you. Please stop strangling our guitar!" Danny took the guitar in his hands and then abruptly dropped it on the bed. "If I can do this! Why can't I make my dad hear me?"

Dillon was confused. "What are you talking about?"

Danny wanted to tell Dillon everything right then and there, but he said, "I've been trying to talk to my dad, to get him a message, and the only thing I can do there is flicker his lights. But there may just be another way."

Dillon asked before he thought it through: "You want me to try and get him a message?"

Danny was tempted, but he knew better. "I'm curious, Dillon. How would something like that go? *Hi, I'm a kid you don't know from New York and I have your dead son's guitar and he has a message for you.* I can tell you right now, he would never believe any of this."

Dillon was relieved because he didn't really want to do it. "Did you ever wonder why you and I can communicate? There must be some reason. We never even met when you were alive. Uncle Joe seems to have a lot to say, but even he can't just talk to me; he has to show me in those awful dreams or whatever they are."

"I may not know what those little adventures are about, but I think we both know that they are not dreams." Danny picked up the guitar again. "Okay, pay attention. I don't ever want you to torture our guitar like this again." He began to untangle the knotted strings. "First off, you never, and I mean never, take off all the strings at once. You might have warped the neck by taking all the tension off it at the same time. From now on, one string at a time. Got it?"

Dillon nodded and watched as Danny put the new strings on the old guitar. When he was finished a few minutes later, he even tuned it. Then he handed the instrument back to Dillon and said, "Play on." When Dillon took the guitar again, Danny disappeared.

A moment later and Danny was back in Tennessee. He used to stay away for years, but now that he knew what was going on, he just had to go there. The box was back in its usual place on the shelf in the closet. Danny tried to relax, to accept the picture as good news, to think of it as a blessing, and not to see it as an indictment of his dad. At first, it didn't work at all. All he felt was angry and then frustrated. Then Danny thought about Dillon playing his guitar up there in New York City. He thought about how nervous Dillon looked waiting for Marie to show up at the theatre, and he smiled. In a way, the snapshot wasn't bad news at all. It explained why Dillon and Danny were in this mess together.

NOVEMBER 8, 2011

Thomas had a headache. It was the same headache he had had yesterday and the day before. He was convinced the pain was caused by the physical stretching his brain must be doing. Dealing with this kind of thing was redefining the term *mind blowing* for him.

He paced in the lab and rubbed his eyes. If someone had told him two months ago that he would be involved in all this, he never would have believed it—time travel, string theory, alternate dimensions? But that wasn't the part that made his head hurt; that was the part that made his heart race with excitement. The part that had him completely upside down was how common these things were.

Thomas prided himself on the fact that he never made assumptions, and yet, in this case, he apparently made them all the time. He assumed that time travel was unusual, but it was happening all around him. Dillon, Maggie, Danny, and, if he took into account the stories from the hospital about people seeing and feeling the presence of loved ones in the moments before death, we are all literally surrounded by string theory in action. People are crossing dimensions all around us, but it is like a conspiracy of silence. We often have dreams about those we've lost, and sometimes the dreams are so vivid that when we wake up, it feels like it was a real visit. What if it was? String theory is believed to be the crossroads between quantum physics and gravity, but what if there were another intersection running right through? What if string theory proved the existence of quantum physics, gravity, and the afterlife?

Good grief! Mediums and psychics, clergy and clerics, and quantum physics and gravity? Is it possible that these are all just variations on the same theme? Vibrations of the same strings? All part of the same whole? Each theory diametrically opposed to the others and yet, all meeting to prove each other true? *In fact, none can be proven without the others,* he thought. Oh boy, now his head was really hurting!

The only thing Thomas was sure of was that this time, he would be sure to make zero assumptions. Before he left them the other day, he made Maggie and Ryan swear that now he had the whole story—no more surprises.

"Yeah, sure. Science is never surprising. Right," Thomas muttered to himself as he sat down at the computer and made another list:

1. Dillon, born 1985 ???
2. Transported as infant to 1995 ?
3. Fifteen years old in 2011
4. Guitar acts as catalyst for initial cross-dimensional travel; Danny to Dillon
5. Danny, born 1985

Coincidence? Thomas didn't believe in coincidence. *So the boys are different ages in 2011 because Danny was born in 1985 and* stayed *in 1985, but Dillon must have made his first leap as an infant*?!?

Thomas rubbed his eyes and sighed.

NOVEMBER 11, 2011

Friday at last! Dillon wished Danny would stop by, but he figured that in a lot of ways, no news was good news. Either way, right now, only one thing mattered and that was his night with sweet Marie. His dad had gotten them tickets to see Jason Austin, and even better, they had backstage passes.

At first, Marie was clueless about Jason Austin, but she was a good sport. Then they turned on GCM, the Great Country Music channel, and there he was, belting out a song and Marie started to smile. Dillon hoped she was smiling because she liked the music, but he had to admit that there was an even more compelling reason for her giggle.

When Dillon had seen Austin on TV, he was so excited that he jumped off the couch and bounced right into the wall.

"Holy Cow! That's Jason Austin? I didn't even know who he was! I heard the song on the radio, but I never put a face with the music before. I know him! Er, well, technically, I met him."

Dillon went on to explain to Marie that this was the guy he had met on his first trip out to Nashville. Dillon told her that it was Jason Austin who had told him that country music was just three chords and the truth, and then Jason had given him the first chord. Dillon had had no idea the guy playing acoustic guitar at the honky tonk for Michael McIntyre was now a superstar. *Cool.*

Now the night was finally here. They were going for burgers and then to the show. Dillon practically danced down the street on his way to pick up Marie. Two hours later she was dancing beside him, his boots were tapping, and their hands were clapping. The show was amazing from the first song to the second encore. Lights, fireworks, and a steel guitar—Dillon was in heaven.

After the show was over, they went backstage. They flashed their passes and were brought into a room full of food and fans. Dillon's ears were ringing, and it took a few seconds for his eyes to adjust to the lights in the room, but he figured that was normal. He was dead wrong.

Dillon rubbed his eyes and then he reached for the wall. He tried to tell Marie that he felt like the room was swaying, but then his eyes rolled into the back of his head and he collapsed. Marie screamed, called 911, and held his hand until the ambulance arrived.

Ryan, Maggie, Thomas, and Tom met them in the ER. Maggie and Ryan disappeared behind the sliding doors. Before Thomas followed, he said, "Wait here and I'll come back and let you know what's happening as soon as I can." Marie and Tom sat down in the waiting room, and Marie wiped away the tears from her eyes.

Danny was still in Tennessee when he felt it. At first he thought it was a headache, but this was different; this was no ache, it was a pain. It was the strangest sensation Danny had ever felt. He felt like his eyes were on fire, but he felt removed from the pain at the same time. He pressed his hands to his eyes and then in an instant, he understood. Dillon's face flashed in front of him and *it* was riddled with pain. Danny could actually feel Dillon's pain.

"Oh God, Dillon! What's wrong?" A moment later he was at Dillon's side in the ER.

"I'm fine. I promise you, I'm okay now. No, I don't

know what happened, but whatever it was, it's over now." Dillon was talking to his parents and getting exasperated and embarrassed. Danny considered both to be good signs. As soon as Dillon saw Danny, he relaxed a little.

"Man. Why can't you just be a normal brother and be seen by everyone?"

Danny's jaw dropped when he heard that, but Ryan and Maggie turned sheet white.

"What did you say?" everyone asked Dillon together.

"For Pete's sake, just look at him!" Dillon was getting tired. He forgot they couldn't see Danny.

"We don't look much alike. Maybe your eyes are more screwed up than you think," Danny stammered.

Dillon was incredulous. "Are you kidding me? When was the last time you looked in a mirror?"

Danny moved over to the mirror, but he wasn't sure what he expected to see. Ghosts don't have reflections. "Dillon, why do you think we're brothers?"

Dillon looked away and heaved a big sigh. It had already been a long night and now, in front of everyone, Dillon had to just say it. Maybe he could salvage his pride by writing this off to the IV drip in his arm.

Probably not.

When Dillon faced them again, he had tears in his eyes.

"I mean that for me, it feels like we are brothers. I don't know, maybe there was a screw-up somewhere, but I just know in my gut that no matter what, we are connected. We have a bond so strong that time and space move out of our way. That can't just be a coincidence. I don't believe in coincidence."

Maggie looked terrified. Did this mean Dillon knew how he came to them? Had Joe shown him more than he was saying? Her mind was a swirl of unanswered questions when Dr. Greene came into the room.

"Well, kiddo, I think you can get ready to go home. You need to see a neurologist on Monday and I would recommend an ophthalmologist too, but for now, everything checks out. My hope is that you passed out from all the excitement. I'm sure that's what the specialists will confirm, but we need to check it out further just to be on the safe side." The doctor then motioned Dillon's parents outside, but it looked like whatever they were discussing was just referrals. Dillon's eyes still burned, but he didn't say a word; he just wanted to go home. Two forms, a discharge order, and ten minutes later they were free. Marie ran up to Dillon and hugged him like she was hanging on for dear life.

"You look better, buddy." Tom smiled as everyone headed outside.

Dillon was so embarrassed about passing out, but all his embarrassment melted into relief when he saw Marie. "Not quite the evening I planned. Sorry."

"Are you kidding? It was great. Really exciting, you know, in a 'permanently scarred' kind of way." Marie smiled and held Dillon's hand.

"What did the doctor say? Are you alright?"

Dillon rubbed his eyes again but he laughed a little when he said, "He said I got too excited. I guess you just have that effect on me."

Now it was Marie's turn to laugh. "Yeah, sure. Guys are always falling all over me."

Dillon looked serious. "*Guys*? What guys?"

NOVEMBER 18, 2011

Dillon was seen by experts in the fields of neurology and ophthalmology and had more tests than a lab rat in the days following the concert. He was exhausted. In the early morning hours he slept. Danny wanted to talk to Dillon about Dillon's suspicions that they were brothers, but Dillon looked so tired, almost smaller somehow. Danny didn't have the heart to wake him. So instead Danny sat nearby, softly strumming the old guitar.

"You play that just as well as your dad. How is that old crow anyway?" Joe startled him.

Danny was shocked. "I can see you."

"Yep. Looks that way."

"Can Dillon?"

"Sometimes, but not like this. Only when he travels. Most of the time, he can't hear me either, but at least you can. I've been here all along, but you guys couldn't see." Uncle Joe smiled and sat down next to Dillon.

"Did you bring us together? Did you want him to know about me?" Danny was so happy to find someone like him. He had to hold himself back from hugging this guy.

"No. I'm not that powerful. I'm just glad for the chance to get a message to both of you. Neither one of you can see what's right in front of you. Open your eyes." Uncle Joe looked frustrated and the more upset he felt, the harder he was to see. Danny reached out, but Uncle Joe was gone. Suddenly Danny's eyes were burning again, but this time it felt different. This time it wasn't a sympathy pain for Dillon; this pain was all his own.

Across town, Thomas was busy working in the lab. He took Dillon's DNA and decided to examine it gene by gene. There was no way he could believe that what happened to Dillon was just excitement. *This kid kept his composure across the space-time continuum; no way he loses it at a concert.*

Isolating each gene took time, but little by little, Thomas extracted each one and breathed a sigh of relief when it was normal. He was beginning to feel like he was wasting his time when he saw it. He didn't know exactly what it meant, but he knew it was anything but normal.

Thomas called Dillon's physician at home. She was an alumnae of Manhattan U. and easy enough to find in the alumnae directory.

"Dr. Serina? This is Dr. Thomas Thurgood over at the University."

"Hospital?" She asked.

"No, not Manhattan Hospital, Manhattan University." From the tone of her voice, the good doctor didn't appreciate being called at home. "Look, I know this is irregular, but I have some information about a patient of yours and I really think you ought to see it." Thomas explained that Dillon was a lab volunteer and that when Thomas typed his genes, he had found a problem.

This time the doctor's tone was different: "I'm on my way."

NOVEMBER 19, 2011

Dr. Antonia Serina was amazed when she saw Thomas' lab, and even a little bit jealous. He had every possible piece of equipment she could imagine and all of it was brand new and in perfect working order. They worked together for two whole days and no matter how they looked at it, Dillon had one heck of a big problem.

Leber's Hereditary Optic Neuropathy is just plain bad news. Leber's Disease, as it is often called, is caused by a change in parts of the genetic code. The disease affects the cells in the optic nerve and destroys the optic nerve's ability to transmit visual information to the brain. If the cells within the optic nerve are irreparably damaged, they die, which results in permanent blindness.

Thomas' phone vibrated and he read a text from his son.

"Hey Dad, mind if I meet Dillon over at Ryan's place? He just got a new video game and --"

"Yeah, sure, fine. Have fun," Thomas texted back before he had even finished reading.

"Thx," Tom replied.

Thomas sat down utterly exhausted and defeated. All this time he thought they were looking for some sort of cosmic secret that would turn the world on its ear, when they had a much bigger problem right in front of them. Thomas couldn't share his questions with Dr. Serina, but he wondered if the change in Dillon's genetic code was a side effect of the inter-dimensional travel. Dillon didn't come back bleeding anymore, but what if damage was still being done? What if the conspiracy of silence around time travel is less about disbelief and more about the simple fact that it is too dangerous? *Maybe that's why it tends to be restricted to the dying and the deceased*, he thought.

"We have to tell his parents. I can't even imagine their devastation. I just wish we had some sort of hope to offer them. These episodes will only become more and more frequent, and then eventually his sight will simply fail to return," Thomas said.

Dr. Serina was trying to be more positive. "There are new medical advances all the time. Maybe he can get into some experimental study. You can't give up hope that easily. That will only make the situation worse, not to mention more frightening. I'll check into any promising studies and set up an appointment with the family for Monday. Can I count on you to let me break this to them?"

Thomas wanted to extend the professional courtesy she wanted. It was appropriate and a required protocol. He really did intend to agree, but he answered with only one word.

"No."

An hour later Thomas was pounding on the door to Ryan's place. When he had called ahead, he asked that Dillon and Tom go out for a while, get a pizza or do some skateboarding. Ryan sent them out with his dry cleaning and a twenty so the boys were set. They didn't even know that Thomas was on his way over. This was an adult discussion, and Thomas wanted Maggie and Ryan to decide how best to tell Dillon that he was going blind.

Maggie opened the door and her eyes were red and swollen.

"It must be bad, right? For you to spend two days with Dr. Serina and now send the boys away for us to talk? I just know this is going to be bad."

Thomas gave her a hug and said nothing until they were seated inside. He had terrible news to deliver, but he had found hope as well.

"First of all, the truth is, yes, the news I have is not good, but we will not let this news become the whole story. I'm going to ask you to hear me out before you respond. I have an idea that might give us a break, but you need all the information first.

"Dillon has suffered a change in the fundamental genetic code of his optic nerve. The result of that mutation is a disease called Leber's Hereditary Optic Neuropathy, or Leber's Disease. It's characterized by progressive episodes of temporary blindness that begin during the teenage years."

"Progressive?" Ryan was sure he knew the answer even before he asked the question.

Thomas nodded and continued. "The blindness becomes permanent fairly quickly and both eyes can be affected in as little as eight weeks. There is another concern. In rare cases, the disease is linked to cardiac arrhythmia. I think that was a major factor in the way Dillon responded to the MRI. Some strains of the disease affect the brain's ability to control muscle movement, muscles like the heart. At this time, there is no cure."

As a nurse, Maggie understood the prognosis all too well. She started to sob, and Ryan could barely move. Thomas didn't want them to get so lost in their grief that they would be unable to keep listening, so he continued. "That is the current reality. Dr. Serina is looking for clinical trials and she will be in touch the moment she has news. She wanted to be the one to tell you this. As Dillon's doctor, it was her right, but I insisted. I need you to just stay with me here for one more minute. I have an idea.

"We all know that Dillon has been able to travel back in time and even forward a few years with Maggie when he was a baby."

"Oh, no. Did I do this to him? Did his genetic code get scrambled from the time travel?" Maggie looked at Thomas with desperation in her eyes.

"No. I'll admit that I worried about that too, at first, but this disease is passed down from the mother's DNA, so I have to believe that he already had it when you brought him forward. Either way, right now, it doesn't really matter how he got it. He has it, and I think I may know how he can get rid of it."

Maggie stopped crying.

"Diseases tend to get cured eventually," Thomas continued. "What if we could figure out when this one will get an effective treatment? What if we could figure out a time and place where Dillon could be treated and *send* him there?" Thomas needed them to believe it was at least possible. They would have to face the hurdle of figuring out *when* and *where* to go later.

Dillon and Tom were digging into their second slice at Lenny's Pizzeria and loving every minute of it. With cheese dripping from his chin and the salt from the pepperoni on his fingers, there was no doubt about it: life was good. As far as the boys knew, there was no real news yet. They knew that Thomas was working with Dr. Serina, but they had no idea how unusual that really was.

"So. Are you gonna ask her or not?" Tom was enjoying making Dillon uncomfortable.

"Yeah, I guess, but I just don't know how exactly." Dillon started to fidget. "You know, it's a big deal. I want to do it right."

The Starlight Ball was a huge deal at Madison Country Day and required a jacket and tie and a heck of a lot of nerve. It was a formal dance with a big band and countless opportunities for embarrassment. The ball was held every year on the winter solstice, to light up the longest night of the year. Tom and Dillon hadn't gone the year before, but now things were looking up. Tom was just finishing up his pizza when he looked up and nearly choked.

Amanda Armstrong walked into the pizzeria and smiled when she saw them.

"You look like you need a napkin," she teased as she put one in Tom's hand. Tom was as red as a tomato, but he cleaned up and offered her his seat.

"You want a slice?" he asked her.

It wasn't long before she helped herself, and Tom's color returned to normal. He gave Dillon the eye, and Dillon took the hint. He excused himself and went to the bathroom. He knew what Tom had in mind and all he could do was hope it turned out all right.

"So, ah Amanda. I was wondering, you know, ah . . . do you have any plans for Starlight this year?" There, he'd said it. Now Tom could breathe.

"Yes. I have plans," Amanda said coyly.

Tom nearly choked again, and he couldn't hide the surprise and disappointment on his face. He didn't know what to say. "Oh."

"I have plans to go with you, idiot," Amanda said, as if Tom should have known.

"Oh, good, that's good." Tom tried to be cool, but he was grinning from ear to ear.

"I'll let you get back to Dillon; thanks for the slice," Amanda said as she stood up. "Listen, Tom, there's just one more thing. Do you think Dillon is going to ask Marie? I told her she should just ask him, but she said no way. She wants him to do the asking." Amanda looked genuinely worried.

"I'm working on it," Tom said, glad for the distraction. "We all know he wants to ask and she wants to go, but, you know, he gets nervous."

Amanda nodded. "Not all cool like you are, huh?"

Tom blushed again, and Amanda gave him a kiss on the cheek and she was gone.

Dillon returned and couldn't resist: "Well? Did you ask her?"

"Let's just say 'mission accomplished.' We are going to Starlight. Now we just need you and Marie to get it figured out." Tom decided the highlights were enough. "Seriously, Dillon, you know Marie will go, so what's the hold-up? Why don't you just ask her?"

Dillon really had thought that he would have asked her by now. He had planned to do it after the concert, but that night certainly didn't go as planned. Now Dillon was trying to find the right opportunity. He wanted it to be special, not just blurted out at school. Still, maybe a well-placed blurt was the best he could hope for.

Back at Ryan's, no one noticed that they weren't alone;

Danny stood in the corner, feeling shell-shocked. He heard most of their conversation and he could barely wrap his head around it. In the last week he had learned that he was adopted, or stolen, or something. That he had a twin. And now his brother was going blind.

He listened to Thomas' plan and he liked it for two reasons. First off, it was a long shot, but not impossible given their recent experiences, and second, it was the only chance they had.

NOVEMBER 21, 2011

Ryan was up before dawn. Everyone agreed not to tell Dillon about his diagnosis until after the weekend. They were desperate to give him the bad news only after they had some good news too—either a trial he could take part in, or some sort of plan to travel into the future to get the cure. It all seemed so reasonable until they realized that they had no way to know when or even if a cure would ever be found. Not to mention the fact that Leber's Disease moved fast. Dillon could have another episode at any time, in either eye. That was bad enough, but there was no way to know when the final episode would come: when would he lose his sight forever?

There was another reason that Ryan couldn't sleep. There had been a lot of talk about sending Dillon forward in time to find the cure, but there was precious little talk about getting him back. What if he was cured, but lost? They didn't talk about it, but Ryan was convinced that a big part of Maggie's tears were about the risk of losing her son in order to save him. They both knew that they were willing to let Dillon go if it meant a cure, but it wouldn't be easy.

They met at Maggie's a couple of hours before the appointment to see Dr. Serina. Thomas let Tom take the day off school to be there for Dillon, and instead of being glad for the chance to play hooky; the boys knew it was a bad sign.

When they were all together, Ryan stood up. No one had any doubt that Danny was there, and he was; standing guard, right behind Dillon. The tension in the room was palpable.

"Dillon, I'm not going to sugarcoat this: we have a big problem," Ryan began. "We also have plans to deal with the problem, so I don't want you to panic. Everything will be okay, I give you my word."

As Dillon heard the details of his condition, and learned that it was almost definitely related to his heart issue, his feelings alternated between fear and anger.

"Why is this happening to me? No one in our family is blind! You said this was hereditary, for Pete's sake."

That was a wrinkle that no one had thought of. The adults in the room knew how Maggie and Ryan got Dillon. Danny knew too, but no one had bothered to tell Dillon yet. Now Dillon would have to hear even more earth-shattering news.

"Dillon, we need to go to see the doctor. Obviously there is a lot more to talk about, but that's enough for now. Let's take this one step at a time," Ryan said.

The doctor's office was across town and located on the fifteenth floor of the hospital. Dillon shuddered when he walked in and smelled the antiseptic. Dr. Serina was waiting for them with a smile on her face.

"I think I may have some good news. I know that by now you must feel frustrated and overwhelmed, Dillon." She spoke as if Dillon was the one in charge and he appreciated it. "I have been in touch with some doctors in England and they are running a clinical trial. They want to see how a drug called Abenone affects Leber's Disease. The initial results are promising and the hope is that this will be a big step toward a cure."

"I have to go to England?" Suddenly all Dillon could

think about was missing the Starlight Ball. The adults were all talking at once after that, and Dillon closed his eyes. This was too much. He just wanted to go home and play the guitar.

NOVEMBER 24, 2011

"Play on, baby, play on," Danny whispered, "and Happy Thanksgiving."

Dillon played the guitar constantly. He didn't know why, but he knew that the old guitar made him feel better—playing guitar and knowing Danny was there. It was good to have someone to talk to when he couldn't fall asleep. Danny hadn't left Dillon's side once all week. There was just too much going on. Danny wanted to go back and confront Clint, he wanted to tell Dillon that they really were brothers, but he didn't want to be the one who pushed Dillon right over the edge.

Marie called, but Dillon didn't know what to say so he just let it go to voicemail. He had to tell her what was happening, but he didn't want to. He just wanted to be normal. Marie knew he was sick, but she had no idea what was really happening.

The trial in England was more complicated than they thought. Dillon would have to be in a city called Newcastle Upon Tyne for at least six months. No school, no dance, no Marie. All of that was bad enough, but there was more. The trial was generally open only to residents of the United Kingdom or Germany. Still, they had a shot at it because Manhattan University had a reciprocal arrangement with the English research facility. They had a shot, but no guarantees. In the meantime, Dillon's vision had blacked out twice in the span of a day and a half. "How ironic: a time traveller, running out of time," Dillon whispered.

Marie was coming over for dessert after having Thanksgiving dinner with her family. Dillon was planning to take her for a walk and ask her to Starlight, but now he didn't know if he could. He felt defective. Why would she want to go with a guy as weird as he was?

"Happy Thanksgiving, Mr. Sunshine," Danny tried again to cheer Dillon up.

"Leave me alone. I don't feel very thankful this year," Dillon sulked.

"Tough. You may not be thankful, but I am. I love this holiday. Great food, great football, and even a chance to laugh at you trying to ask Marie to Starlight."

Dillon glared at Danny and played the guitar louder.

The turkey was just about perfect: golden brown and glistening in the candlelight. Sara had outdone herself. She had even made her special stuffing in the muffin tin. That way, no one had to ask for a corner piece; everyone got their stuffing just the way they liked it.

Clint called their friends to the table, and when everyone was seated, Sara brought in her masterpiece. A cheer went up and the best Thanksgiving they'd had since Danny had died was underway.

Once everyone was settled, Clint proposed a toast. He toasted his son's memory and all the men and women away from their families on Thanksgiving so they could serve their country. Then Clint bowed his head.

"In a world where many feel alone, we are thankful to be together. In a time when many don't have enough to eat, we are thankful for this beautiful meal. Most of all, we are thankful for every day we had with Danny. God bless him. Happy Thanksgiving and let's eat."

Danny slipped in during his dad's prayer.

Sara was smiling because she felt warm and happy inside. Danny's place at the table was empty, but she could swear she felt him nearby. Danny wanted to get back to Dillon in New York, but it was Thanksgiving and he felt he had to see his mom and dad too. He tried not to think about it, but he couldn't help but wonder whether these people who had raised him were his real family. Danny remembered asking his mom when he was a kid about why he didn't look much like them, but she had brushed it off, saying that he looked a lot like her grandpa. Come to think of it, he never did see a picture of that man.

Back in New York, they were just sitting down to dinner. Danny winked at Dillon and said he would wait for him in his room. It was time to talk about what couldn't wait any longer.

Dillon came in after dinner and found Danny strumming the guitar. *There has to be something special about that guitar*, Dillon thought. *Some reason it delivers messages...*

"Mailbox! Why didn't I think of this before?" Dillon was getting excited. "That guitar is more than a musical instrument, it's a freakin' mailbox. What if the answers we need will still come out of it, like the words we found before?"

"I don't know, Dillon, maybe, but I don't think we have time to just sit around and wait for the guitar or Uncle Joe to tell us what to do next."

They spent the next hour talking about Thomas' plan to figure out how and then where and when to send Dillon into the future to find the cure for Leber's Disease. Danny nodded and then fidgeted.

"Look, I don't really know how to figure that out, but I think I have some information that we need to discuss."

NOVEMBER 25, 2011

A lot of people get up early on the day after Thanksgiving. There are great deals at the malls and Black Friday means a place like New York is even busier than usual. Ryan was busy too, but he wasn't going shopping; he was going to see his client, Michael McIntyre, the most powerful man he knew.

Rockefeller Center was impressive any time of year, but when it was dressed for Christmas, it literally sparkled. Trumpeting angels led the way to the biggest Christmas tree in New York City, and the ice skating rink below the tree was always a sea of happy people. Crews were lifting the mammoth evergreen into place, and excitement was in the air.

Ryan knew exactly where he was going, but he was still trying to figure out exactly what he was going to say when he got there. Michael McIntyre Industries spanned the entire fiftieth floor of One Rockefeller Plaza, and it was at twice as impressive as the tree going up outside. Every time he walked in, Ryan marveled at the fine art, the antiques, and, most of all, the fact that he got to be Michael's personal attorney, the keeper of his secrets.

Jeanine, Michael's personal assistant, was a wonderful older lady with a no-nonsense style. She handled the press, the pressure, and her position with indefatigable grace and wit. Ryan smiled when he saw her and put out his hand.

"Hello, Jeanine, I know I don't have an appointment, but I really do need a few minutes of Michael's time. Is he in?"

"No, you don't have an appointment and yes, he is in.

Let me tell him you are here," Jeanine chided Ryan as she lifted her phone to call her boss.

A moment later Ryan was seated on a kidd leather club chair with a silk and wool rug under his old leather loafers. The light glowed softly around them, and Ryan picked up a small crystal on the table beside him. He was waiting for Michael to turn to face him, and he was nervous. How the heck could he ever hope to convince Michael to help? He nearly backed out of the office while Michael's back was still turned, but the little crystal from the end table distracted him.

"Funny place for a paperweight," Ryan mused as he turned it over in his hand. The lights in the room flickered and Michael whirled around. Michael was on the phone with his representative in Asia and he was not pleased.

"What do you mean the earthquake continues to affect production? Get it done, or your career is done. Clear?" He hung up and unclenched his gnarled fist.

Ryan put down the crystal and sat up to face Michael. There was no turning back now. Michael looked tired and ticked off, but there wasn't much Ryan could do about that. Ryan used to wonder if all the pressures of success made him age faster, but it was more likely to be the pressures of his three ex-wives and his current young wife or nurse or whatever. Dillon had been a good sport the day Ryan took him to the McIntyre's place for a Fourth of July party. Michael's son was just a little guy, but Ryan knew that little boy was still talking about his friend Dillon. Ryan could only hope that Michael remembered.

"Michael, I came to see you today on a personal matter. I need your help and I hope that as a father you will understand just how important this is to me." Ryan knew how long

Michael had waited to become a dad and how much it meant him. He was known for rescheduling meetings to see his son play soccer, and it was a totally different side to the otherwise fierce man.

Michael sat up and listened. Ryan explained that Dillon had been recently diagnosed with Leber's Disease and what that diagnosis meant. That was the easy part. Then he had to confirm Michael's suspicions that Dillon had a unique ability that could put the cure within his reach. "If you can help us find out about a future cure for Leber's Disease, I believe that Dillon can go and get it."

At first, Ryan was hoping that Michael would see an opportunity to make millions by helping them bring back a cure from the future. On the way over, it seemed like a good idea in Ryan's head. A man like Michael McIntyre could access the latest research and pay for experts in any field. Ryan knew that McIntyre Industries had vast holdings in technology and bioengineering. If any group was even close to knowing how to time travel to a specific time and place, to knowing about future cures, or even if any group was close to a breakthrough, medical or otherwise, Ryan was sure Michael McIntyre could find out. Now though, as he spilled it all out in this mogul's office, Ryan felt ridiculous. Maybe the best thing to do was to forget it and try to get out of the office before he was thrown out, but Michael didn't let him get that far.

"Are you saying Dillon can cross dimensions and time travel?" Michael's eyes widened.

"Yes."

Michael was quiet for a few minutes as he tried to figure out the best way to play this new development. There was no doubt he could help Ryan; the question was whether it was in his best interest to do so. As a father, he felt sorry for Ryan. Still, he was about to wash his hands of the whole mess when he had a thought. Unbidden, it flashed before his eyes like it always did when he least expected it: a church not far from where they stood now, and a young man desperate to make his troubles go away. Michael wasn't proud of what he had done and he wished he could forget about it, but it haunted him and weakened his resolve not to get involved. For a moment, all he could think of was the basket and the bundles he had left behind him at the church that day so long ago. Michael sighed and asked only one more question. "Have you told anyone else?"

"No, I came to you first because . . ."

Ryan expected to have to try to prove his claim or explain it. The lights flickered again and Michael looked almost nervously at the crystals on his desk. There were a few small crystals glowing on the corner of Michael's desk, and Ryan realized something he hadn't noticed before: the crystals glowed, but had no power source—no battery and no plug. For that matter, there was nothing plugged in anywhere, as if there was no electricity in the room; but everything around them was switched on and working. The lights, the computers, the fan—everything was wireless, but it was more than that. The soft glow in the room wasn't like regular lighting. It was more of a glow than a glare. Ryan wondered why he had never noticed this before. Absentmindedly, he touched the crystal paperweight beside him. Ryan guessed it must be some new kind of bulb or something when the lights flickered again.

"Would you please stop touching that." Michael looked annoyed. Ryan quickly put the crystal paperweight down again. He hadn't even realized he was holding it again.

The lights returned to normal.

Ryan suddenly realized that the computer in his own briefcase was vibrating. He stopped talking and opened his briefcase. The computer was on and it was transferring files from his computer to Michael's. The crystals around them were practically humming now.

"Wait a minute. What the hell is going on here? It's like your office is some kind of machine vacuuming all kinds of private information from all of us."

When Ryan looked at Michael's monitor, he saw Jeanine's shopping list beside his own letters to Dillon's doctors. Ryan stood and was about to throw the monitor and the glowing crystals right off Michael's desk.

"Wait! Wait! I can explain." Michael held up his hands.

Suddenly Ryan understood why he didn't have to prove Dillon's time travel was possible. Could it be that Michael was already an expert? "That's how you do it," Ryan gasped as his long held suspicions were finally confirmed. "It's easy for you to always stay ahead of the curve: you're peeking. You make money by bringing the ideas from the future back to us and you are using these crystals to power the trips and collect the information. How? How do you know when and where to go?"

Michael had expected to answer questions about the crystals, not about his other secrets. "These crystals are the future of alternative energy. They not only replace electricity and fossil fuel, they provide security through transparency. Everyone behaves when they know that anyone can see what they are up to. It is the key to peace in our time. No fuel wars and no secrets!"

"We are definitely going to talk about this; the implications are magnificent and utterly terrifying, but right now, I just want to figure out how to help my boy," Ryan hissed.

Michael did not want to share the secret of his success. "It's complicated and I really wouldn't know the first thing about teaching someone else how to do it, and besides, it's almost impossible to know when and even if Leber's gets a cure."

Ryan was through being impressed. "I will give this crystal to every media outlet in the world and tell the Pentagon all about what you are doing if you don't help me. I mean it, Michael; you won't just be collecting other people's secrets anymore. I'll tell the world yours! I'll make sure you can't siphon off other people's research, because once they know what you're doing in the future, they will have plenty of time to block you from here, in the present. When you visit the future, they will have already had years to freeze you out."

"I suggest you reconsider and remember just who you are trying to threaten." Michael's low growl was more terrifying than a lion's roar. "I can access the future and if you don't watch your step, I'll destroy yours! Word gets out that you believe any of this and I'll make sure you get committed and permanently medicated."

Ryan's mind was racing. How could he make Michael help him? Then it came to him, an old trick he learned in law school: find your opponent's weakness. Michael's weakness was easy to find, and Ryan began to feel less and less afraid.

"Tell you what, Michael," Ryan began. "You help my son and I won't tell your son who you really are. I won't tell him that you had him practically engineered from a donor and a surrogate, a donor and a surrogate who are no longer alive. I won't tell him that you keep his mother on a payroll to take care of him, that that woman he calls mommy is paid to play a role so that people won't find out what kind of monster you really are. Most of all I won't tell him that you keep his genetic material on file in your compound while your company tries to perfect the human clone. You shouldn't forget that as your lawyer I have access to all of your information."

The blood drained from Michael's face, and he looked as pale as one of his crystals. "You can't do that. You can't prove any of it," Michael breathed.

"I don't have to, Michael. Like you said, security through transparency. I would lose my license happily to spill your secrets. Perception is reality. You might win in a courtroom, but you will have lost your son's love and respect, and we both know you can't handle that."

Michael's eyes shone with rage. "You will never threaten me or my son again."

Ryan was almost starting to enjoy this. He winked at Michael as he put the crystal paperweight and the glowing crystals in his briefcase. "I'll just keep these with me. It would be a real shame for the Securities Exchange Commission to find out that you have been insider-trading and siphoning confidential information off everyone else's computers." Ryan leaned in and was inches from Michael's face. "I will ruin you, personally, professionally and financially. You will help me, or you will lose your own future."

Michael pretended to laugh. "I guess that's what makes you such a good lawyer. You are willing to do whatever it takes to win. I'll help you, but first give me back my crystals."

Ryan dropped the last crystal into his briefcase and

locked it. "No chance. Now we are both willing to do whatever it takes to find the cure."

Danny took a deep breath. "Dillon, I need to tell you something."

Dillon didn't know what Danny was going to say, but he could tell from the look on Danny's face that it was going to be big.

"What is it, Danny? More bad news?"

Danny smiled and tried to lighten the mood. "Well, I guess you could see it that way, but I'm hoping you won't. Remember when you were at the emergency room and you made that crack about us being like brothers?"

Dillon nodded and felt his heart beat a little faster. "What are you getting at, Danny?"

Danny took another deep breath and blurted, "I think we are brothers. More than that, I think we are twins and I can prove it." Danny told Dillon about the old picture from the box on his father's farm.

At first it was hard to believe, but when Dillon heard the whole thing,,he gasped. Danny said it was a picture of a huddled group of people who looked scared and tired, but right in the center there was a proud old woman. In her arms she carried two babies. There was a heart-shaped birthmark on one of the baby's legs.

"No way! No damn way!" Dillon shouted.

Danny wasn't quite sure what to say. Danny knew how he figured out who the babies were; he had suffered with having that lousy birthmark all his life. But how could Dillon put it together so fast? Danny straightened up and tried to show Dillon his birthmark.

Dillon pushed back from the desk like it had a bad smell. When he looked at Danny, Dillon was the one who was as white as a ghost. Danny pulled up his pant leg and hoped Dillon could see the birthmark but there was no need. Without saying a word, Dillon did the same thing. There on Dillon's leg was the identical mark. As Dillon and Danny exchanged stunned glances, they said in unison, "Twins."

NOVEMBER 26, 2011

The farm was a busy place as Sara and Clint got ready for another Christmas. The decorations were coming right along, and the carriage looked almost ready to ride, but something kept nagging at Danny's dad.

Clint walked out to the barn and it wasn't long before he drifted upstairs to look at the picture again. It had been an awful accident, but it was also the beginning of their life as a family. Sometimes Clint wished he could go back. He would handle things differently this time, starting with telling Danny the truth. Clint had no regrets about having brought Danny home, but he could not forgive himself for keeping the truth hidden. They always had planned to tell Danny, but it never seemed to be the right time. At first, they thought he was too young to understand, and then they thought it would upset him to find out just before he deployed. The night he left, Sara and Clint made a pact to tell him when he came home; they just never imagined that by then it would be too late.

This unfinished business made Clint more and more uncomfortable. Danny had had a right to know where he came from, but Clint didn't know what to do about it. He fingered the photograph again and kissed the picture. He remembered what the grief counselor told him when Danny died; that anytime he needed to say something to Danny, he could still write a letter. "Aw Danny, I wish we could just go fishing and have a good, long talk," he said to the air. Danny watched as his dad paced.

"Come on, Dad, we still can talk about it. Tell me

now!" Danny screamed in frustration. Clint sat down at the desk and took out a pen and some paper.

"I sure enough feel stupid having to do it this way, but I guess better late than never," Clint continued to mutter. "Damn grief counselor. Sure, just write him a letter and say whatever you need to say. Put it on his grave and let it go. Blah, blah, blah. Whatever." He made fun of the advice, but he still took it. Clint wrote for over an hour and cried at one point when he was near the end. Danny tried to read it, but whenever he got too close, Clint stopped writing.

Finally, Clint took the letter and went outside. He walked for two miles over to the Franklin Cross Cemetery and kneeled down at Danny's grave. It was the first time Danny read his own epitaph:

Daniel Charles
Beloved son and patriot
An unexpected gift and an intolerable absence
"And the truth shall set you free."
John 8:32

Clint touched the headstone lovingly and wiped away the tear in his eye. Danny watched him put the letter next to the stone and leave. Now that he had it within his reach, Danny could hardly move. The answer was written down for him to see, but he could barely bring himself to read it. All the anticipation and excitement drained out of him, and Danny felt as tired as he had on the floor of that awful warehouse where he died half a world away.

There is something unnatural and uncomfortable about being at your own grave. Danny preferred to avoid it because he didn't feel dead and he hated to be reminded. Now, reading his epitaph, Danny wondered if his dad knew he couldn't move on without knowing the truth about how he came to be Clint's son. Maybe the truth really could set Danny free. When he finally did open the letter, he had to sit down, right there, next to his own grave.

Dearest Danny,

I feel like a fool writing to you like this and I don't want to bother you up in heaven, but I need to get this off my chest and I guess there just isn't any other way at this point. I want to let you know that your mom and I always wanted to tell you, but it's complicated. By the time we felt like you were old enough to understand, it seemed like it was just too crazy for you to believe. To tell you the truth, if I were you, I wouldn't believe it either. Before I go on, I just want to say one more thing: your mom and I love you. I hope you can forgive us for not telling you this before.

I did a terrible thing and then I got rewarded for it. You see, back in '85 we were a hair's breadth from losing this farm. I just couldn't let that happen, but there was no work to be found around here. I knew a guy in New York who was always looking for drivers, so I went up there to see him. He gave me a truck and an address and told me to pick up the cargo at night. I guess I knew it was not a good situation, but I was desperate and I agreed.

I took the truck and I went to the address, someplace just outside of San Antonio in Texas. I waited 'til dark and I rang the bell. I thought I was picking up cheap TVs or something, but what I discovered was much worse. The man who opened the door was missing a tooth and reeked of alcohol. He said something in Spanish and at least ten people scurried out of the house and into the back of my truck. I was shocked. I was stupid and I just stood there trying to figure out what to do. I tried to talk to the man, but it was no use. At one point, I tried to force the people out of the back of the truck, but they were afraid to go. When I turned around again, the man was gone and the house was locked up. I didn't know what to do, so I drove.

The next morning, I got twenty bacon, egg and cheese sandwiches and had my first Spanish lesson. We were all starving, so I handed out the food and then I saw the old lady with the babies. She smiled and I couldn't resist. That was the first time I held you, Danny. I never dreamed you would be mine, but I loved you and your brother.

We took the picture and became friends in spite of ourselves. It was a long drive from Texas to New York and I'll never forget it. We almost made it too. We traveled at night to avoid suspicion. During the day, we tried to lay low and parked behind barns or in mall parking lots. Then one night our luck just ran out.

We were outside Southern University, a kid in a beat up wreck came out of nowhere and plowed into the back of the truck. I tried to control the impact, but it was no use. We flipped over into a field and the vehicle that hit us got impaled on the back. I ran around to check on everyone and it was bedlam. Everyone ran away because they were afraid of what would happen if the police discovered them. Only the old lady and the babies were there. At least I thought they were both there.

I was so relieved to hear the crying that I guess I got confused.

The lady smiled and handed you to me and I took you in my arms. When I looked back again, she was gone. I didn't look for her for very long. I knew I had to get out of there. Once I checked on the kid driving the other car, I left. I searched for your family for a couple of months, but it was no use. Eventually, I left the whole mess behind us and took you home. My friend down at town hall helped with the paperwork and it was official. You were ours to foster and we adopted you a year later. I never knew what happened to your brother or the lady, but I never stopped thanking her for giving you to me.

I may not have been your father, but it was the best part of my life to be your daddy. I hope you can forgive me for not telling you sooner.

Love,
Dad

Danny had already put together most of the story, but seeing it written out in his dad's handwriting somehow made it all the more real. In his dad's shoes, he didn't know what he would have done. Danny wondered how the other baby got away, and where the woman had gone. It seemed like the answers only led to more questions. He looked again at his epitaph. The truth did set him free of one thing: he wasn't angry anymore. And now that he understood his own journey, he wondered even more about Dillon's.

He wished he could talk to his dad, give him a hug, and let him know he was okay. Danny didn't understand a lot of what he was learning, but he knew he was still a part of the Charles family, and he always would be. He may have had another family somewhere, but he saw them as a bonus not a replacement. He just wished there was some way to let his dad know.

NOVEMBER 28, 2011

When Dillon woke up, he just knew it was going to be one of those days. He had already chickened out twice over Thanksgiving and he knew if he didn't ask Marie to Starlight today, it would be too late. He probably should have been thinking about a million other things, but really, what was the point? Dillon felt like he knew a fair amount about life and death, and the one thing he knew for sure was that life is short, really short. No way he was going to waste his because he was too gutless to ask his girlfriend to the dance.

"Good Lord! Are you wearing that? I knew you had trouble with your eyes, but I didn't know it was this bad." Danny was back, and Dillon was glad.

"Shut up. There's more to life than jeans and boots." Dillon adjusted his blazer and slipped on his loafers.

"Well, in that case, you look mighty purdy," Danny joked.

"What part of *shut up* do you not understand?" Dillon smiled as he headed out the door. "I'll see you later. I got an important job to do and I don't need any help from the peanut gallery. I'll meet you here after school."

"Well, then I guess I'm dismissed," Danny teased as he picked up the guitar. What was it about that guitar that drew him in so irresistibly? Danny played and played, and the more he did, the more he lost himself in his own memories. He knew no one else could hear him, but still, that guitar was his connection to life—past, present, and maybe even future. Danny couldn't wait until Dillon got home. As far as he was concerned, he and his brother had a lot of time to make up for.

Marie greeted Dillon with a big hug and slipped her hand into his. What was his problem? It should be so easy to ask her; he knew she wanted to go with him, but he still felt a little nauseated.

"I've got to do this, and it has to be now," Dillon muttered to himself. Marie looked confused, but she let him lead her through the doors of the school lobby. He pulled her around a quiet corner and all his plans of romance and charm melted in his sweaty palms. "I would really love to take you to the Starlight Ball. Will you go with me?"

Marie smiled up at him, but she didn't answer. She gave him another hug and whispered in his ear, "I'll think about it." With that she was gone, and she disappeared down the hall at the sound of the first bell. After keeping her waiting so long, Marie was enjoying making Dillon wait for her answer, even though they both knew she would say yes.

"Did she just say she'd *think* about it?" he muttered to himself as he got swept down the hall in the throng of hustling students.

Maggie, Thomas, and Ryan were hurrying downtown. When they finally made their way through the tourists, they were at least fifteen minutes later than they wanted to be. They didn't have an appointment exactly—they had an emergency. There was no doubt the sooner they got to Michael, the better. There was no telling when he might change his mind. The elevator seemed to take forever, and then they arrived. Michael's office was deserted as they stepped inside, but there was the sound of a commotion coming from behind the back wall. They heard loud voices and unfamiliar words.

"Ay, Dios mío. No," an old woman's voice said.

"Tienes que ayudarme. Absolutamente." Michael's voice was trembling.

In all the years that Ryan had been Michael's lawyer, he had not known this room behind Michael's office even existed.

If the office was impressive, the back room was opulent. Gold was everywhere, from the desktop to the frames along the walls and the ceiling lights. The sparkle from the gold danced along the edges of the space to bathe the whole room in a warm glow. The person behind the gold desk was small, but fierce. She wore a lace shawl around her linen dress and her skin was the color of a warm sunset. Ryan guessed who she was in an instant, but he could not imagine why she was there.

He wished he had paid better attention in his high school Spanish class. Michael stood and waved them in. It was the first time Ryan ever saw Michael look uncomfortable. "Let me introduce Señora Rosa De La Joya."

Ryan nearly fell over. This was not the meeting he had expected to attend.

Maggie reached her hand across the desk and smiled. "Yo soy Maggie; me recuerda?"

The old woman smiled and nodded. "I know who you are. I know all of you and I know why you have come. I guess I always knew you would."

Thomas started. "You speak English?"

"I speak many languages. I am from many places."

Maggie stepped forward again. "If you know why we have come, please tell us you can help us."

"Do you know the legend of the condor and the eagle?" Rosa looked Maggie in the eye, seemingly willing her to think about the last time they met. "The condor soars for the spirit world and the eagle flies for strength in this one. One without the other is unbalanced." Rosa's voice took on a pitch higher with excitement. "We believe that the Americas are a blessed land because it is the only place where the people of the condor and the people of the eagle can unite to bring balance to this world. Humanity needs both, but few can hold the mighty power of the condor and the eagle in one person. Still, some children are born to unite these worlds, and they must live their destinies without interference. Dillon is such a child, and so was Danny."

"You are the one who brought him into our lives, who separated him from his brother. Please, he needs your help again. He can't meet his destiny like this!" Maggie was on her feet begging this woman for help even she couldn't fully understand. "That night, in the back of the truck, you were the one who gave me this boy. You protected him and told me to raise him to be kind and strong. He is . . . he is gentle with the spirit of a fighter, but this fight is too much for one kid. You are the one who made these boys time travelers. Why bring them back together now if you won't help them travel to a place where Dillon can be healed?" Her eyes were tired and tearing up. "Dillon can't fulfill a destiny to bring balance to the world if we lose him. With or without you we will find a way to save his sight and his life."

Maggie made one last plea. "Dillon, and Danny too, need you now like they did the night of the accident. You were there for them once; don't let them down now."

Rosa turned to Michael and looked right through him. "I will show them what I can and you will help them. You have used my gift for profit. Now you will use it to restore balance to what you once destroyed." Michael only nodded. Ryan marveled at the way this old woman reduced Michael, the most powerful man in the world, to an afterthought. When she spoke again, her voice was like rolling thunder.

"Let the condor and the eagle fly together."

Señora De La Joya stood and held out her hands. Everyone joined hands and the room began to spin. The golden swirls grew warmer and warmer, and soon it felt as though they were hurtling toward the sun. Maggie shut her eyes, and when she opened them again a moment later, they were all standing in a field at the mouth of a dark cave. Ryan recognized the place in an instant. Any business traveller would. Newark Airport rose in the distance. "We're in New Jersey???"

"This is a crossroads of time. Enter here and travel between the dimensions, but you must know where and when to go. I have shown you all I can. There will be a cure, but it is for Michael to show you." Rosa spoke as they stood outside the cave. "I can show you only where to begin. Michael must be the one to take you to the time you need to access. Only then can the balance Michael altered be restored."

Back at his mom's place Danny and Dillon were up talking all night. They had a lot to say. At about five in the morning, they realized they needed to know more; there just had to be more information. How did Danny and Dillon get split up? Dillon was waiting at Ryan's place when Ryan got back from his run an hour later.

NOVEMBER 29, 2011

Ryan told them everything, and for the first time since the whole mess had started, things were beginning to make sense to Dillon.

"Your mom brought you to us across time. I think Danny stayed in 1985 and grew up from there. Now, even though you are twins, Danny is still eleven years older than you today. Get it?"

Danny and Dillon nodded, but of course Ryan could only see Dillon. Ryan continued.

"Now that everyone's time travel is out in the open, we just need to figure out how to use it to find the cure."

Dillon was thinking out loud again. "Danny and I are brothers and we were born to bring together the spirit and the physical? That lady, Rosa, she said that, right? Condor and eagle, spirit and physical, balance. . . . Okay, so let's get it done."

Ryan admired his son's enthusiasm, but couldn't help but think he was being naïve. "I don't think it's that easy."

"Yeah, it is exactly that easy. We've been doing it for months now. The only difference is that from now on, we go on purpose, not just by accident," Dillon said.

Danny rubbed his eyes.

"Danny, what is it? Are you okay?" Dillon looked worried, and Ryan wished he could see what was going on.

"That Leber's thing, it's hereditary, right? Oh man, I've been blind all along. Not literally, but I just couldn't see the forest for the trees. I can't believe it's been in front of me this whole time." The moment he said this, a light came on all around Danny. Dillon could see the glow, but everything else was too bright to decipher. Danny looked around at a new world. He could still see Dillon and Ryan, but now he was surrounded. Joe was there, and Rosa too. Had they been there all along? Who were all these others? Danny looked around him and saw where he was for the first time.

It was as though knowing about his brother and seeing the community of support around them really helped Danny open up to the possibility of help from both dimensions. Now, looking into the light, Danny realized he had never been alone.

DECEMBER 1, 2011

Clint and Sara were just about as busy as they had ever been.

"Looks like a white Christmas may not be completely out of the question if this week is anything to go by," Sara said, laughing.

The barn was undergoing a complete transformation from working stable to party central, and Clint had to admit that he loved it. Maybe that counselor had been right after all. He really did feel better after writing to Danny. He might even agree to play Santa this year. Sara and Clint worked into the night, but that was fine; it was exciting to be a part of all the fun.

Things in New York were decidedly less festive.

Dillon's head hurt again. This time both eyes were burning and he wished he could just sleep. He wished he could take a break from his own life. Dillon didn't for a minute think that wish was a side effect of time travel; he figured it was more likely a side effect of being a teenager. When his cell phone started vibrating, he opened one eye to check it out. It was a text from Marie and it made Dillon feel much better.

"YES. I'll go to Starlight w/U! ☺"

Dillon flew off the bed and cheered. "Yes!" Things were looking up again.

DECEMBER 2, 2011

Dillon was playing the guitar again. An old love song filled the air. In the other room Ryan and Maggie stopped what they were doing and just listened. He had no way of knowing that they had sung the same song years ago. It was its own kind of time travel to hear it now. Maggie wondered if Dillon had any idea how his music affected people. Maybe that was the destiny Rosa De La Joya was talking about.

Dillon played a while, and then just as he was reaching for the high note at the end, he screamed. Maggie and Ryan flew into his room to find him on the floor in agony. He clutched his eyes and rolled on his side. The guitar lay beside him and the soundboard was split down the middle from the fall. Dillon peeled a hand away from his eyes and felt the break in the guitar. It was a fast trip from agony to panic.

"My guitar! NO!" Dillon shrieked and his parents tried to calm him down. "Oh God! I can't see! Where is it? I can't see!" The doctors had warned them that this insidious disease moved fast, but they had honestly believed they would have more time.

Maggie held him and Ryan reached for the guitar. He would never be able to say why he did it: in that moment he acted on sheer instinct.

The soundboard was held together by one slim piece of wood. Looking at it from the inside out, Ryan could hardly believe his own eyes. There was a brass plaque mounted inside the soundboard. On it was the most beautiful thing Ryan had ever seen:

September 13, 2046

"I got it! Get him up. I know where we have to go! I'll get the car." Maggie didn't know what he was talking about until she saw the plaque.

"Dillon, you need to listen to me. Everything is going to be all right now. Just trust us. You will be fine."

DECEMBER 3, 2011

They drove through the night with only two stops: one to pick up Thomas and one to get Michael. By the time they got to the field, Dillon was pale and covered in a cold sweat. His mother worried about him making the trip, but she worried more about what might happen if he didn't. It was rare that Leber's Disease affected the heart, but when it did, it affected it severely. She knew her son was starting to have trouble breathing and that all she could do was pray they would make it in time. It was the first time she appreciated the speed of Ryan's car.

They carried Dillon into the cave and looked expectantly at Michael. He nodded and said that only one of them could follow. Maggie wanted to go because she was a nurse, but Ryan couldn't risk losing both of them.

"There will be help where we are going. I swear to you, I'll bring him home," Ryan tried to smile. With that he, Michael, and Dillon disappeared into the cave. They had only gone a few yards when Dillon heard Danny.

"Hey," Dillon panted, "where you been?" Michael thought Dillon was delirious, but Ryan knew better.

"Danny, tell me we got this right," Ryan's voice trembled.

Danny ran beside Ryan and helped to carry his brother through. Before long, they reached a tunnel and Dillon worried that if this tunnel was anything like the others, they would never make it through in time. It was getting harder and harder to breathe, and his lips and fingers were already tingling from the lack of oxygen. They ran forward, and the ground slipped out from under them.

Here we go, thought Dillon as they fell into the abyss.

Danny knew they would get there quickly because they were surrounded: Uncle Joe, Dillon's grandparents, Danny's relatives, and crowds of others were all there and surrounding them in a circle of light. This was nothing like the trips Danny and Dillon had taken alone.

SEPTEMBER 13, 2046

When they landed, it wasn't onto a pile of bones or broken glass like before: they landed on a plush Aubusson rug. Ryan stood up, sure they must be in some sort of parallel universe. Michael was so comfortable, it was almost as if he had been there before.

"Dillon! Where are you?" Michael bellowed. Dillon was confused. *Were Michael's eyes affected?* Dillon was still on the floor right beside him, gasping for breath.

A man burst into the room. He had a commanding presence and a confident air as well as gray hair and a muscular build. He lifted a now-unconscious Dillon from the floor to a bed in the center of the room. Ryan followed, unable to take his eyes off his son.

"Can you help us? Do you know what to do?" Ryan was fighting a rising panic as Dillon's body began to seize.

The voice that answered him was vaguely familiar but Ryan didn't have time to place it. "I know exactly what to do. What took you so long? I thought you would get here much sooner. His muscles are seizing up and our window of opportunity is closing."

Michael stepped back and watched in fascination as the doctor placed oxygen over Dillon's face and an IV into his arm. A moment later the seizing stopped, and Dillon became deathly still.

Now it was Danny's turn to panic. "Oh no. *No*, sir. I did not go through all this to drop-kick you into my world. Damn it, you need to live for both of us you selfish little . . ."

Danny was shocked when the doctor told him to knock it off.

"You can hear me?"

"Yeah, and so can Dillon. He's going to be fine, and he doesn't need flack from his brother right now. He just needs to breathe."

Ryan noticed that the doctor seemed a little winded and guessed it was just from all the excitement. Still, the doctor's hand shook when he applied a second syringe to the IV. A few minutes later Dillon stirred. He mumbled something that only Danny understood. He was calling for Marie. Yeah, he would be just fine.

"You'll have to stay here for the night. I don't think he can travel for the time being. It will be a few hours, but he'll be okay. His sight may take a little longer, but he's already on his way." With that the doctor sat down at a desk, looking exhausted.

"I don't know what to say. *Thank you* doesn't seem like nearly enough. Can I ask? How did you know we would be here? Who are you?"

The doctor looked Ryan in the eye and smiled. He didn't have to say a word. Now it was Ryan who had to catch his breath. He was looking into the eyes of his own son, only now, they were just about the same age. The older Dillon had gray hair and the same green eyes. A moment later he stood to embrace his father. The way Dillon hugged him was so tender that Ryan couldn't help the tears in his eyes.

"Dad, it's so good to see you."

Ryan had to sit down. This was so far beyond weird: his own son looking as old as Ryan was. "Dillon, are you doing all right? Is this your home?"

"Yeah, Dad. I'm doing great, especially now that I know that I'll eventually make it here." Dillon gestured over to his teenage self, asleep across the room. "I'm a doctor now."

Dillon felt like he was cheating. It wasn't fair that he could see his family like this. Millions of people wished for this, but only a few could do it. He wanted to tell his dad that he had travelled all over South America and merged North American technology and research with South American alternative and herbal practices. He wanted to tell him that they had cures to all kinds of diseases now and that breakthroughs were happening all the time. He wanted to tell his dad that the answers had always been right there in front of them, but it had taken years to see them.

He wanted to tell his dad to stay home on the twenty-fifth of June, 2020, but he said none of these things. Instead, he showed him an old family picture. Ryan saw himself and Dillon along with a beaming Maggie with two grandchildren on her lap. The young woman in the picture bore a striking resemblance to Marie.

SEPTEMBER 14, 2046

There was no doubt about it. It was the longest night of Dillon's life, at any age. It wasn't a good idea for Dillon to be out of his own time any longer than he had to, but he was just starting to come around. This was the tricky part. Dillon was awake, but he still couldn't see.

"Danny? Dad? Is anyone here?"

They were at his side in an instant.

"We're right here and you're going to be just fine. How do you feel?" Ryan asked.

"Okay, I guess, you know, apart from being BLIND!"

"Dillon." The doctor's voice was calm and commanding. "Your sight will return very soon. Just try to relax. Maybe this will help." With that the doctor put the guitar into Dillon's hands.

"How can this be? I broke it. But I know this is my guitar." Dillon was confused and distracted, and that was fine.

"Actually, I broke it. I had the soundboard opened and I installed the plaque you found inside with the date on it. It was the one place I could be sure you would find it. I just wish you had found it sooner."

"Yeah," Dillon said. "Me too." His sight was starting to return and he could make out some shadows. "I think I see something, shapes, or shadows or something.

"You know what they say, right? Never fear the shadows because it just means that a light must be shining nearby." Doctor Dillon was smiling at his own comment. Ryan was admiring his son's awards and wishing he could ask him how everything would turn out. He ventured to the window and gasped at what he saw. It was New York City as he had never seen it before: no power lines, no exhaust, and a warm glow from every light.

"Crystals. That's how I know they are going to work." Michael was looking out too, and he was practically levitating with excitement. "These babies will revolutionize the world. We don't need oil any more; we have our own self-sustaining power supply that actually protects the environment instead of threatening it. I feel like Ben Franklin and Thomas Edison all rolled into one."

Ryan couldn't resist. "I'm just curious. How will you get around the massive security glitch? You know, when it just sucks up everyone's information for public use?"

Michael looked annoyed. "I'm working on it. I still don't think it's such a big deal. Privacy is so pre 9/11 anyway. I'm sure it's completely out of fashion by now."

Dillon was grinning from ear to ear. He looked right into his own green eyes. "I can see! I can see. Holy smokes! Are you me?" Doctor Dillon smiled and nodded.

"If I wasn't you, I would never have known to send you the message in the guitar or work so hard to find the cure to our little problem."

Dillon only wanted to know one thing. "Did Marie and I have fun at Starlight?"

Everyone laughed and even Dillon realized it was a stupid question. Of course they had had fun. Duh.

The rest of the day was spent in a weird kind of family reunion. They learned that string theory was a well-accepted concept in this time and that some people, like Dillon, had a natural aptitude for hearing and even traveling between dimensions. In fact, there was a movement afoot to try to use string theory to visit heaven, under the hypothesis that heaven was just another dimension. So far, not so much progress. Danny could have told them that.

Soon it was just about time to head back. They got ready to go back to the field and Doctor Dillon called for a car to be brought around. It was hard to say good-bye even though they knew they would meet again. Dillon sat for a moment behind the desk that would one day be his and saw his future family picture on the shelf. Yeah, they definitely had fun at Starlight.

Finally it was time for the two Dillons to say good-bye. "Guess I'll see you in the mirror. Do me a favor, will you? Try to find a cure for going prematurely gray," teenage Dillon joked.

"Play on, kid. I promise, it matters." It was surreal for Ryan to watch them hug each other. He turned away with a tear in his eye, and that was the moment Ryan saw the piece of paper that would change the rest of his life: his own obituary was in a frame behind the door.

Doctor Dillon knew it was a lousy thing to do, and he knew he couldn't tell his dad that he would never live to see the world he had just visited. Still, he didn't want him to keep wasting time. Everyone knew he and Maggie belonged together, and Doctor Dillon hoped this was the nudge his dad needed to make the next years really count.

DECEMBER 3, 2011

This time they ran through the tunnel trying to keep up with Dillon, and it was Ryan and Michael who were panting. Feeling like an expert when the ground beneath them began to shift, Dillon dived in and felt like a cliff diver instead of a lead balloon. When they landed, they expected to find Maggie and Thomas waiting for them. Instead, they found Rosa.

"Each of you has received the gift of time that was not yours and knowledge that you didn't earn. That is a privilege not to be wasted." She looked right at Ryan, and he nodded. "I have a message for all of you. You are loved beyond anything you can imagine, and now you must share the gift you have received. It is your destiny to bring this light to others."

In an instant she was gone, and Maggie ran to them. She held Dillon and Ryan, and even Michael. "I'm so glad you are back. Dillon, are you alright? You really had me worried."

"Mom, I am fantastic and improving. Marie and I are getting married!"

Maggie looked at Ryan. "Did he hit his head?" Everyone laughed because they knew the car ride back to the city would be full of the best conversation they had ever had.

Dillon filled them in, and Thomas asked so many questions that they were more than halfway home when Maggie realized that Ryan had barely said a word. He looked fine, but something was different. She didn't know what it was, but she knew she would make it her business to find out.

Danny was very happy for Dillon. He'd made it, he'd

survived. He knew some of his dreams were sure to come true. Danny knew the score. For Pete's sake, he knew he didn't make it; he was dead. His mom and dad were moving on and that was a good thing. Wasn't it? Danny was disgusted with himself. He knew how he was supposed to feel, but he just didn't feel it. He didn't want anyone else to be miserable, he just wished he could move on too.

Danny was pretty sure that Dillon didn't need him much in that fancy future he was headed for. For that matter, maybe Dillon didn't need him much now, either. Danny figured it was time to say good-bye.

DECEMBER 5, 2011

Sara was excited about the trip to New York and she was ready to get organized. She checked her list again: tickets to the city, tickets to see two Broadway shows, and reservations at the Plaza. They would be paying for this trip for months, but so what? It was time.

Uncle Joe just did not get it. Where the heck was that kid? He thought this whole thing was settled. The rescue was accomplished. Dillon was saved and Danny knew they were brothers. That should have been it. In a way, it was like the boys were both going blind. Dillon literally, and Danny was blind to all the souls around him trying to help him find his way home. Danny had to learn where he came from in order to get where he was going, right? So, where was he? He saw them all there surrounding him in the cave. How had Danny missed the point? Could he really think they were there for just one twin? No way.

There was no chance he was going to leave Danny behind. Wandering around in the space-time continuum was fine for a little while, but it was no way to spend eternity. Uncle Joe had been given a job and he wasn't going to leave a man behind. Not now, not ever.

Dillon and Marie were having a great day. Finals were next week, and then the Starlight Ball was on the following Saturday night. It was supposed to light the longest night of the year, but it happened a full twelve days before the winter solstice. That seemed just about normal in the world of high school.

Marie noticed a big change in Dillon. It was hard to believe this was the same guy who took two weeks to ask her to Starlight. He had a whole new, relaxed confidence. She liked him a lot before, but now he was just about irresistible.

"Hey Sweets, let's grab Tom and Amanda for a movie later." Dillon didn't want to be overconfident, but there was no getting around the fact that now he knew this was a sure thing.

"You do realize finals are next week?" Marie feigned a scandalized expression. "Still, if you want to see *Vampires in Love,* I'm in.

Well, that had certainly backfired. "*Vampires in Love*? Really? I was thinking we could catch that new remake of *A Christmas Crisis.* You know, the one with the zombie as the ghost of Christmas?"

"Zombies, vampires, how romantic." Marie laughed. "Maybe we should grab a pizza and meet at my house to study bio."

Dillon smiled. "Yeah, that sounds about right." It didn't much matter to him anyway. He just wanted to be near her, and he really didn't care where they went. Dillon wished Danny would come around, but he hadn't seen him.

Maggie had a double shift that night so she was glad Dillon had plans for dinner. It used to bother her that Dillon was alone so often, but it didn't seem as though that would be a problem anymore. Ryan offered to pick him up around nine, and Maggie was surprised to find herself hoping Ryan would still be there when she got home.

The hospital was quiet when she got there, and as her

shift wore on, Maggie found herself daydreaming about the future Ryan described. Looking into the ER waiting room, she couldn't wait until there was a cure available to help ease some of the suffering all around her. In the meantime, they had to do the best they could.

When Ryan went to Marie's house to pick up Dillon, he stayed a few minutes to have coffee with her dad. Given what he now knew, he wanted to get to know Marie and her family a little bit better. Ryan was different too. That trip to the future rocked his world. Ryan wished his obituary had said how he was going to die. Maybe it didn't list the cause of death to keep time travellers, like him, from becoming neurotic.

Dillon was practically floating as they drove home. There was nothing like falling in love, especially for the first time. It was glorious. Then there was the added confidence boost that comes from seeing that you actually get to keep the girl.

What Ryan wouldn't do to have a piece of news like that in his back pocket. He hadn't really planned to stay when they got to Maggie's, but Dillon wanted to see the Country Music Institute awards and his enthusiasm was contagious.

DECEMBER 6, 2011

Danny walked past a bakery at about four in the morning and it smelled ridiculously good. Fresh-baked bread and brewing coffee made him wish he could just walk right in and order breakfast. He wasn't hungry, he was just human, or used to be. It was weird to be stuck as he was. He had no physical needs, but he still had wants. He wanted the bread and coffee, and maybe a doughnut. Why not? It wasn't like he needed to watch his diet. Danny stayed there another minute or so and then moved on.

He liked this part of New York. If things had worked out differently, he could imagine moving to a place like this after MIT, maybe a small apartment in a five-story walk-up and falling in love with the girl next door. Danny laughed at the thought of it. Here he was daydreaming about being single in the most dynamic city in the world and all he could think about was falling in love with the girl next door.

"I guess what they say is true: you can take the boy out of the country, but there ain't no taking the country out of the boy," Danny muttered to himself.

He figured he would stop by Dillon's later on, but he knew he couldn't keep it up much longer. From the looks of things, Dillon had a pretty nice life ahead of him and he wouldn't need Danny much anymore. Danny figured he was in Dillon's life to help him find the cure Dillon needed. Now that his part was done, Danny felt more like a third wheel than a big brother. As for Clint and Sara, they looked like they were getting on with their lives too. These were good things, things any good brother and son would want. So why did Danny feel like the loneliest guy in the world?

He decided to spend the day the way he figured lots of New Yorkers do. He had no laptop and he couldn't drink the coffee, but he joined all the other laptop hobos in a coffeehouse and watched the tourists walk up and down Fifth Avenue.

That night he went to visit Dillon. Dillon was hunched over his desk, crunching numbers. Danny thought he could actually see the smoke coming from Dillon's ears.

"You gonna be okay there?" Danny teased. "You look like you might burn your brain."

"Oh, be quiet. MIT isn't exactly beating down my door, so I got enough math to make up to last until I go to college. Apparently, what I understood as necessary absences, my teachers understood as unexcused. Now I have a pile of make-up work that's bigger than me."

"Five point three seven two nine," said Danny.

"Excuse me?" Dillon looked up, confused.

"The answer is five point three seven two nine, or do you want me to carry out the decimals further?"

"Seriously? You make me sick. I've been trying to figure this out for at least fifteen minutes and you just look over my shoulder and announce the answer?"

"Yep." Danny would really miss these moments torturing his brother.

"Feel free to shut up."

"Are you sure that's really what you want? I can go, no problem, but your pitiful math skills suggest you might want to reconsider your order, Captain."

Dillon clenched his frustrated fist. "I'm sorry. Will you help me?"

"Yep. Three point seven nine eight two."

"Look, I appreciate the answers and all, but it's possible that I'll need to know *how* to do this." Dillon was erasing his latest mistake. Danny sat down and explained the finer points of the problem. Once he understood the concepts, Dillon caught on quickly, and it wasn't long before they were racing each other to the answers. Danny won most of the time, but Dillon was definitely getting faster.

"You know, it might have been like this," Danny said. Dillon looked confused, so Danny continued. "If things were different, if we were just regular brothers. I bet we would have had some fun."

"In no possible scenario could we be *regular* anything. We are clearly irregular to say the least. But I know what you mean. It would have been cool and annoying."

"Annoying?" Danny asked.

"Yeah, I'm used to being the smart one."

It was a late night for Ryan too. He wanted his Maggie back home, but he knew she wouldn't make it easy. The way he figured it, he had about eight and a half years left. Eight Christmases, eight birthdays, eight more summers. Ryan felt a kind of liberating pressure to make them count. He wanted to do something important with the time he had left.

He was sure that he had more time than a lot of people, but now that he knew when he would die, each day seemed more precious. He had the same number of days he always had, they just seemed more fragile somehow. Ryan sat down and looked over the bucket list he was creating:

1. Spend time with Dillon
2. Win Maggie back

3. Help Michael develop the crystal
4. Go to Hawaii . . . *every year!*

Ryan was pleased with his new agenda. If he could move through this list, then his life would have meaning. The only question left was how? It was overwhelming until he realized he was already well on his way. He and Dillon were becoming allies instead of adversaries, and they were even talking about spending Christmas together. That was progress; now for momentum.

Michael sat in his Chesterfield leather chair and put his feet on the golden desk. Ryan knew about the crystal, but that couldn't be helped, and besides, it could be handled. It wouldn't be the first time Michael had to take out a little garbage. It was nothing he couldn't take care of. It was a shame though, as Michael actually liked Ryan, but he could hardly count on attorney–client privilege now. A do-gooder like Ryan would be a real pain in the neck when Michael began to sell shares in the crystal. Ryan would have to be neutralized. It simply could not be avoided.

DECEMBER 8, 2011

Clint walked up and down Main Street, looking for the perfect gift for Sara. He needed something that would travel well, for her to open on Christmas Day in New York. He knew he could get a fancy present in the city, but he wanted to give her something from home. Besides, he didn't want to have to worry about sneaking away to shop once they were there.

He considered a gift card, but shook his head. Yeah, that was real romantic. Nothing says I'm thinking of you better than, "Here, go get yourself something."

Clint wanted something easy to carry that would last *and* remind Sara that he loved her. Why was this so hard?

"Oh, hell. Maybe I should just get the gift card," Clint muttered as he crossed the road. A car full of kids flew by with the windows open and the ground vibrating beneath them from the music they played. Seeing the teenagers singing along gave him an idea. He tipped his hat as they drove out of sight and whispered, "Thank you."

Sitting in a study room at the library with his friends, Dillon was practically pulling out his hair. He was far behind and finals were less than a week away.

"At least try to pull out the gray ones," Marie joked.

"What do you mean, gray *ones*? I am not going gray. I had one gray hair and it's gone."

Tom laughed. "Sensitive, aren't we?

Dillon was in no mood to be teased. He had to cover a semester's worth of work in a week and there were huge holes in his notes. At least math was under control. Bio was fine too, but how could he read *Pride and Prejudice* in three days? He did not understand why Marie liked it so much. She was even quoting it when she teased him.

"'My good opinion, once lost, is lost forever.' Darcy, Chapter 11. You really should give it a chance, Dillon. It's a beautiful love story about things not being as they seem."

"I think it's sadistic. I can't believe the teacher based her whole exam on the parts of the book that aren't even in the movie. What is she trying to do?"

"I think she wants you to read the book." Marie shook her head.

"Really? I had no idea." Dillon was smiling now.

Danny needed to talk to Dillon but he knew that now was not the time. Finals required all Dillon's attention and that was all right. Danny wasn't in a hurry to have this conversation anyway. Another few days either way wouldn't matter. Maybe he would even stay 'til Christmas. Then that was it. Danny didn't know where he was going, but he knew it was time to go.

DECEMBER 12, 2011

"Ladies and gentlemen, pencils down."

It was a relief and a worry at the same time. One exam done and four more to go. Dillon never knew how well he scored at the end of an exam. He was usually so fried, all he knew for sure was it was over.

When he stepped out into the afternoon sun, he was surprised to see his dad waiting for him.

"I thought you could use this." Ryan handed him a paper cup. Dillon put it to his lips expecting whipped cream and hot chocolate; what he got was hot, black coffee.

"How did you know?"

"I noticed you drinking black coffee when you thought no one was looking at Thomas' lab, or at home. I know you're not a kid anymore. Besides, you're gonna need a lot of coffee if you are going to survive exams."

They walked toward Ryan's place and stopped outside the florist. They had a row of truly pathetic Christmas trees leaning against the window.

"Only in New York can you have a tree so amazing that people come from all over the world to see it and apartment trees that would put Charlie Brown's to shame." Ryan chuckled as he bought the worst one.

"Why that one? Pity? A mercy killing? That has to be the worst Christmas tree in the whole city." Dillon was convinced he would never understand his dad.

Ryan explained that he kind of liked it and it wouldn't take long to decorate. Dillon carried it, and an hour later they stood back and admired their handiwork. The spindly little tree took one strand of lights and bent under the weight of Ryan's five ornaments.

"I like it," Ryan declared. Dillon wasn't sure if Ryan meant it, or if he was just trying to convince himself. It was weird to see his dad in any kind of Christmas spirit. Usually he was the king of Bah Humbug. Dillon had to hit the books again, but as he headed out the door, he reminded his dad that he would get out tomorrow at the same time.

"Coffee?"

"How about a mocha? You know, a little of both?" Dillon figured he'd throw his dad a bone and not grow up too fast.

DECEMBER 17, 2011

The rest of exam week was a blur, but it ended. Now it was time to celebrate. Dillon had his first tux hanging behind the door and even a rose for Marie to wear in her auburn curls. In about an hour he would pick her up and take her to the dance. He could hardly wait. They were going with Tom and Amanda, and everyone was ready to blow off some steam. Dillon was really looking forward to a night of fun.

When he came out of his room ready to go, he felt equal parts excited and ridiculous. His tie was almost as annoying as his cummerbund, but he comforted himself with the fact that at least he didn't have to wear heels. Ryan and Maggie took pictures, and he was out the door. Walking down the street in his tux, he had a rose in one hand and his phone in the other.

"I'm on my way. Are you ready?" Dillon had promised Marie he would give her fair warning. He wasn't too surprised when Danny fell into step beside him.

"You remind me of an old ad for cologne."

"Thanks, that's the look I was going for. Old cologne ad." Danny laughed and was gone. Dillon arrived at Marie's place and knocked on the door.

"Hi, Mrs. Watson, is Marie ready?"

"Almost, Dillon. Why don't you wait in the living room with my husband and I'll go and get her." Marie's parents were nice people, but Dillon hadn't rented this suit to hang out with them. They had a glass of water and then another, and Dillon thought there was a distinct possibility that he would float away if Marie wasn't ready soon. That's when he saw her.

Marie wore a silk gown of royal blue that matched her eyes. Her hair was a mass of curls swept up and off to one side. A couple of loose curls danced around her face and played peek-a-boo with the pearl earrings that dangled from her ears. Dillon stood up when she crossed the room, and she gave him a hug. She smelled like roses, and Dillon held onto her hand when she pulled back. He could hardly believe she was going with him. He could hardly believe she was real.

Dillon gave her the rose and she smiled and put it up in her hair. He knew he would never forget the way she looked at that moment.

The Plaza Hotel was a sight to behold. The lobby was awash in holly, stargazer lilies, and boxwood. It was a long trip from Tennessee, but now that they were finally here, Sara wondered why they had waited so long. She squeezed Clint's hand and they followed the bellhop to the elevators. There was a lot of noise coming from one of the ballrooms, but that was okay. After all, Sara had heard that New York was the city that never sleeps.

When they arrived at the Starlight Ball, they could hear the music thumping from the moment they walked inside. Dillon knew the Plaza Hotel well. His parents used to take him there for Afternoon Tea and he enjoyed it just about as much as getting a root canal. Still, there was no denying that it was cool. You never knew whom you might see in the lobby. Celebrities and politicians were a common sight in New York, but at the Plaza, they were an expected part of the scenery.

The DJ welcomed the crowd and played a favorite high school dance anthem that had everyone on the floor.

On the other side of Central Park, Michael paced around his Park Avenue apartment. Something was wrong; he could just feel it. He had already put into place most of what he needed to bring the crystal to the highest bidder. He almost felt bad about what he had done when he saw Ryan and Dillon together. The father and son bond was a sacred one, but that's why he just couldn't back down. This technology would mean that James was set for life. He already had plenty of money, but handled in just the right way, the crystal meant power. Michael had been travelling around time for while, looking for an opportunity like this. Technology brought back from the future was easy money, but power was elusive and power was the only currency Michael needed. With the crystals, it was clear that he could have more personal power than any one family had ever had. Michael didn't want to make a score: he wanted to start a dynasty.

Three hours later Dillon led Marie back out onto the dance floor for the last dance. When they dimmed the lights and the last song began to play, Dillon knew that song would be his favorite for the rest of his life. It almost didn't matter what the music was. Holding Marie in his arms was the closest thing to heaven Dillon had ever known. Dillon could never forget the night they fell irrevocably and utterly in love.

DECEMBER 18, 2011

Ryan and Thomas decided to get together for coffee near the lab. In the last few months they had become good friends, and Ryan knew that if anyone could understand the crystal, it was Thomas. It was another strange conversation in what seemed like a never-ending dialogue that always started the same way: "I know this sounds crazy, but . . ."

Ryan told Thomas about most of what happened in Michael's office and in the future, how this little rock could create enough energy to power a whole city, but with a big drawback. It seemed to run on information, so it sucked up whatever data it could access from the computers around it. Michael seemed to consider that a bonus, but Ryan was not so sure having private information in the public domain was such a good idea.

"If you're right, then what we really need is some kind of shield around it. That way we could *feed* it a loop of recycled information to keep it busy, but safeguard current secure information," Thomas said. He was excited about this whole idea. "This kind of thing really could change the world."

Ryan laughed. "Yeah, that whole interdimensional travel thing is so dated."

Michael was in the office and he was furious. Sunday was his day with his current wife and their young son. He was beginning to get a little tired of the mother, but the boy was his dynasty, his legacy, and his future. Michael knew he had to deal with Ryan if he was going to provide for James. The fact that he was already a billionaire didn't matter.

He had to figure out a way to get the crystals back from Ryan and then for Ryan to just disappear. The last thing he needed was Ryan talking to anyone. Michael smiled when the solution danced across his twisted mind. He was so preoccupied with his own plans, he didn't notice that Rosa was standing in the shadows and making some plans of her own.

Rosa De La Joya loved Michael. She had helped him move from the streets of Jackson Heights to Park Avenue and she was proud of his progress. She knew he was willful when he was young and she had liked that. She needed someone with guts to help her realize her dream.

Rosa had grown up in the Amazon jungle. Her father was the village shaman and her mother was a healer. She was well versed in herbal medicine and also in spiritual healing. That was the reason that traveling between dimensions of time and space came so easily to her. One day, her father took her away from the village and up a steep incline to a cave. When they reached the top, he took her inside and she took the first step on the path she followed even today.

It was her father who explained to her about the eagle and the condor. Her mother explained that she could bring much healing to the world if she found a way to bring these two great spirits together. Then her father brought her further into the cave and she discovered the tunnel that led to the abyss. Her father grabbed her hand and they flew down and through the opening. They landed in a future unlike anything Rosa had ever imagined.

There were cars whizzing by and the streets were full of people. Rosa had never seen anything like it and she squeezed her father's hand a little bit tighter. Up ahead, she saw crowds of excited people all moving toward a big plaza where bright lights flashed everywhere. The people were bundled up against the cold but they were laughing and dancing. Her father smiled when he saw her bewildered expression.

"This is why I chose this time and this place. It is very different from our jungle, isn't it, little one?" Rosa's dad grinned.

It was dark and the stars should have been blazing, but only the twinkling lights could be seen, and then the moment everyone seemed to be waiting for finally arrived. The people began to count down: "Ten, nine, eight…" Rosa wondered what was happening. "Seven, six, five, four . . ." The excitement and anticipation were at a fever pitch. "Three, two, one, Happy New Year!"

People began to cheer and a marvelous crystal ball descended over the crowd. At that moment, the ball opened and released a bald eagle and a condor that flew off at break-neck speed over the crowd. Rosa could not believe her eyes. The sign above her read "Welcome, 2050!"

She looked at her father with confusion on her face. Why was he showing this to her? Her father took her hand. A moment later they were in a church that was quiet and empty. The only light came from the candles around the altar. Rosa took a few steps forward to get a better look, and there it was: a basket behind the candles with two little babies sleeping inside.

"These boys are your destiny," her father whispered.

Now Rosa was completely confused. She was just about to ask her father what he meant when a noise startled her. She turned and saw an old woman who looked remarkably like herself. She was dressed in the traditional clothes of Rosa's village and she seemed to know exactly where to find the basket. She smiled as she passed them and winked at Rosa. A moment later she was gone.

"There will come a time when you will bring these boys to the time and place they belong. With your help, they will be great teachers and healers. Keep them safe and give each one to the right person."

Rosa had a million questions, but she didn't get a chance to ask even one. In the next second, her father was gone, and she felt herself falling and falling as if the ground just swallowed her whole. When she finally stopped falling, she discovered that she was back in her bed in the hut she shared with her family. She could hear the cicadas and the wind blowing through the moonlit jungle. Across the room, she saw her father. He sat up and smiled at her and then he put his fingers across his lips and winked. Rosa knew it was not a dream and she knew what she had to do. She even knew *when* and *where* to go, but what she did not know was that they had not been alone in the church. In the back pew sat Michael McIntyre and he had seen the whole thing.

It wasn't long before Rosa heard a thud outside. Her parents were snoring as she tiptoed out of her home. There he was in a suit and tie, looking completely baffled and delighted all at once. Michael McIntyre followed her back in time. She was naïve enough to believe he did it for love, that he had somehow seen her and his passion had driven him back through time. In a way, she was right. His passion did drive him. Michael McIntyre had travelled back in time for the love of money, power, and adventure, but Rosa didn't know that yet.

She hid him and taught him about the special places in the world where the space-time continuum could fold. For a long time, she thought they would work together to fulfill her destiny to help bring healing to the world, but Rosa soon learned that Michael was more interested in bringing profit to his pocket.

Rosa held out hope for many years that he would change, but now, watching him plan Ryan's demise Rosa knew it could never be. Michael had to be stopped, even if it broke her heart to stop him.

DECEMBER 21, 2011

Dillon and Marie finished their Christmas shopping, and Dillon could not wait to get outside. He held Marie's hand tightly as they made their way through the crowds. Dillon was dragging her along 34th Street when she stopped abruptly.

"Hey! What gives? Why are we in such a hurry?"

Dillon shrugged his shoulders. "I guess I just don't like crowds much."

As they trudged through Times Square twenty minutes later, Dillon realized it was only four days 'til Christmas and no matter what he did, he could not contact Danny. He didn't know where Danny was or how he was doing, and it didn't feel anything like a holiday without him.

Worse than that, Dillon felt like a hypocrite. Dillon loved Marie, but he was hiding the biggest part of his life from her. He just didn't know how to tell her. *Guess what? I'm a time traveler and I also discovered that I have a brother. He happens to be dead, but we don't like to let that get in the way of a good jam session.*

He needed to talk to Danny. Danny was the only one who could help him figure everything out. That's when Dillon stopped short. Dillon spent all his time thinking about how this whole situation affected him, but he wasn't the only one affected. In fact, Danny seemed to be lost between dimensions and yet he had never even asked for help. For the second time, Marie looked at Dillon like he was nuts.

"I'm such a loser."

Marie would have answered him, but he didn't seem to

be talking to her.

"What a freakin' narcissist. Not everything was about me. Danny needs me and I didn't even notice." Finally Dillon looked at Marie.

"Who is Danny?" Marie wanted to know.

"I'm sorry. I have to get you a cab. My brother needs me."

Dillon burst through the door of his home and ran up the stairs. He almost made it, too, but then he stopped short. What was that in the living room? Dillon turned and went back down the stairs. He sat down on the bottom step and looked again. Maggie *and* Ryan were decorating the biggest tree ever. It was no secret that Maggie loved Christmas, but even she never chose a tree like this. They were playing Christmas carols and laughing and actually working together. Weird.

Dillon stared for another minute, just to make sure he wasn't hallucinating or something, and then he shook his head. This was too much. He had to talk to Danny. Seeing the future, talking to the dead? No problem. Seeing his parents look happy *together?* No way.

Dillon went up to his room and closed the door. His newly repaired Fenson guitar was lying on his bed. Dillon picked it up and began to play and sing softly.

"Will the circle be unbroken? By and by, Lord, by and by. There's a better home awaiting, in the sky, Lord, in the sky."

Dillon knew it was one of Danny's favorites, and he was sure that if any song could coax Danny back, it was that one. Dillon was just getting into the second verse when he heard that old familiar harmony and he knew Danny was near. Dillon couldn't see Danny yet, but he sure could hear him.

"Man, you sound so lonesome when you sing that. Don't you know it's Christmas?" Danny said as he floated into view. "Even so, I do love that old song. Makes me think of home."

Dillon looked at his brother and for the first time wished he could just give him a hug or something. For someone who really ought to be in heaven, he looked seriously miserable.

"Where are you, Danny?"

"What are you talkin' about? I'm right here in front of you. For Pete's sake, you're looking right at me."

"No, I don't mean right now. I mean when we are not together. Where do you go? What's it like?" Dillon was about to ask Danny if he was happy, but he stopped before he did. He knew Danny was proud and that he would never tell Dillon anything that might worry him. Dillon knew this had to be handled very carefully.

"When I'm not with you, I go back to Tennessee. I see my mom and dad, and sometimes I just walk around the places I used to like to go. Once I even went to see an old girlfriend, but that was a huge mistake. I don't know what I expected. I guess a part of me hoped she'd still be pining away over a fallen hero, but she wasn't. She was knee deep in dirty laundry with a baby on her hip and a *husband* mowing the lawn. I did not expect that. I'm happy for her though, sort of."

Dillon knew that this was his opening. "Why do you think you're stuck, Danny? Why don't you just let go and go to heaven?"

"Just let go and go to heaven? That's it. You are not allowed to watch any more daytime talk shows!" Danny chuckled. "Don't you think if I could get to heaven, I would be there by now? I thought there would be a guide or an angel or something to whisk me off into the clouds, but I can't see anyone over here. I saw your Uncle Joe one time and there were people all around us that night we were in the cave headed for your future, but otherwise, the only time I'm not alone is when I make my visits here."

The moment Danny said this, he regretted it. "That's not to say I'm unhappy or anything. Not at all. I can go anywhere I want, see anything I want, and know that the people I care about are okay, so don't worry about me. I'm in my own kind of heaven. It's just not exactly like I thought it would be.

"Danny? What would you say if I told you that you don't have to be alone?"

Before he could say another word, Danny interrupted him. "Forget it. I'm not alone; I can visit any time I want to. And besides, you still get to be a kid at Christmas, so no worrying about stuff neither one of us understands."

"You helped me. Neither one of us understood what was happening to me, but you stuck it out with me. You went with me to places neither of us wanted to go, saw stuff neither of us wanted to see, and discovered that there was a really good reason for it. We needed to learn about those things. *We,* not just *me.* I don't think we're done. I think there is more."

Danny looked Dillon in the eye. Up until that moment, Danny figured he was there to help Dillon; it never occurred to him that there might be help for him too. "Maybe those talk shows are on to something after all. Maybe I do need a little help."

There was a huge crash downstairs and then silence. Dillon ran down the stairs two at a time and stopped cold at the bottom. Ryan was frozen. He just stared at the shattered tea set on the floor at his feet. The tea set belonged to Maggie's grandmother. They rarely used it, and brought it out only at Christmas. It was great for holding the flowers Maggie loved to have around the house. For years, Dillon had walked gingerly around the table with the tiny cups and saucers and just plain avoided the mammoth teapot overflowing with blooms. No one wanted to imagine what would happen if they broke; now imagination would not be necessary. They were all about to find out.

Maggie looked at the shattered pieces and up to Ryan's ashen face. Dillon braced himself for what was bound to be a tirade. Everyone knew Maggie's grandmother had carried the set with her from Ireland at least a hundred years ago.

"What a relief!" Maggie definitely took Ryan by surprise. "It's okay, really. I always felt like it was my job to keep them safe, for the next generation. Like it was the only link to the past. Like somehow it made my family history more real. The truth is, I never really liked that set. That's why I only used it at Christmas. Let's face it, I don't even like tea."

Ryan was convinced Maggie had popped a blood vessel somewhere in her brain. "I'm so sorry. The box just slipped out of my hands. I know you loved that set. I'm so very sorry—"

Maggie cut him off. "I love my grandmother and I still do, but that tea set was just a reminder. I still have her picture and I think this is really okay. I need to start to let go of the past." Maggie looked around at all the old pictures and antiques that surrounded them, and she took the broken porcelain out of Ryan's hand. "Maybe my best times aren't all behind me."

Okay, thought Dillon, this was weird, but kind of wonderful all at the same time.

DECEMBER 22, 2011

It was just like old times. Everyone was gathered together for a new meeting on an old topic. After the *Tea Set Incident*, Dillon told his parents about wanting to help Danny move on in much of the same way that they were starting to move on. Ryan called Thomas, and he and Tom agreed to meet at Maggie's place right away.

"Looks like we're getting the band back together," Thomas joked as they took their seats. No one could see him, but everyone knew Danny was in the room with them. It took a minute, but it wasn't too long before they knew that Uncle Joe was there as well. It was like a breeze or familiar scent: they couldn't see him, but they could sense his presence.

After a quick check of their lists and notes from earlier sessions, they began to realize the one thing all of their time travel had taught them was time was too precious to waste. Everyone assumed that only Dillon was in jeopardy. After all, Danny was already dead. Now they began to consider a much more disturbing thought: Danny may have a limited time to move on.

"Dillon, I want to talk to Uncle Joe, can you tell me what he says? I really feel like he is listening," Maggie reasoned. Dillon nodded and Maggie looked uncomfortable, but she carried on. "Joe? Listen to me. You have always been there for me and for Dillon as well. Dillon knows where he is from now and how he came to us. We told him the whole story. I understand that you were trying to tell us that Dillon was at risk and I understand that you took him to the places you did because it was the only way he would learn about where he is from. I also understand that you could have done it at anytime, but you waited until Danny came into Dillon's life. I guess I thought Danny was there to support Dillon. Now I realize that they are brothers who must support each other. That means that we are going to need your help again and this time I want it to be out in the open. No more scare tactics. What do you say?"

Dillon listened for a response, but when he heard it, he was a little afraid to repeat it to his mother. It was still hard for him to hear Uncle Joe. The connection was never as strong as it was with Danny, but he heard this response loud and clear.

"He says, 'The twins may have been going blind, but you are deaf'." Dillon's face turned bright red. He'd never heard anyone speak that way to his mom.

Uncle Joe went on to say that he had been waiting all along for the chance to talk to her but she was never ready. She couldn't hear him now because she was too preoccupied with his memory. He also said that he was worried about Danny.

"Dillon, your eyes are fine now, but Danny still can't see much of what is around him," Uncle Joe continued.

Danny didn't have a clue what Uncle Joe was talking about. *I can see just fine*, he thought.

Dillon continued to repeat Uncle Joe word for word. "Danny, I know you have always felt a little alone in this world. I think there is some part of you that knew you were out of step with this time. Whatever the reason, you need to believe that you are not alone. You never have been. Even in Afghanistan, you were not alone. Your buddies risked their lives to bring you out, even though they knew it was too late to save you. Your family has surrounded you, and not just in Tennessee.

Right now, you have family all around you waiting to welcome you home to them, but you can't see them. It's like a kind of emotional blindness."

Danny looked supremely uncomfortable and Dillon was afraid he might bolt. "Look, it ain't that I don't appreciate the intervention and all, but if I am blind, it ain't by choice and it ain't like there is some twelve-step program I can follow to learn to see."

Thomas was writing again furiously. He was making calculations and shaking his head. It was almost as though he wasn't even interested in what was going on around him. "We need to find her," he mumbled.

"Who?" Tom asked his dad.

"The old woman who gave the twins away. She is the only link to their real past, their real identity. Damn, I hate it when I make assumptions. I assumed that the boys belonged to her, or to the people in the back of the truck that night in 1985. Now I don't think they did. Dillon and Ryan can do it. Michael McIntyre can do it. Why not the old woman? What if Danny can't see where he is going because he needs to know more about where he is from. What if there is one more piece to this puzzle? Something they left behind them in the place they were born. Something they are incomplete without. What if Danny can't move on until he finds it?"

Ryan was impressed. Everyone was overwhelmed. But Thomas was busy developing a hypothesis, and a good one to boot. If Thomas was right, then they had to return to the time before the boys were in the back of the truck. They needed to know how they got to Rosa De La Joya. Only if the boys discovered their whole story could Danny, and someday Dillon, discover eternity. *You have to know where you've been in order to get where you're going.* That made a lot of sense to Ryan, and he knew just where to start.

DECEMBER 23, 2011

Ryan, Dillon, and Danny went back to Michael's office and were surprised at the warm welcome they received. Michael handed them each a cup of eggnog and turned down the carols on the radio. Michael wasn't just full of Christmas spirit, he was practically possessed by it. It was creepy.

"Hi, guys! I'm so happy to see you. Listen, I've been thinking about everything and I hope we can figure out a way to work together." Michael took one look at Dillon and it was clear Dillon knew about the crystal.

"Where is she? Is the old woman here all the time, or do you have to call her?" Ryan was in no mood to play games.

"Her name is Rosa De La Joya, and yes, I can call her whenever I like." Michael didn't bother to mention the fact that she was never very far away.

"Call her here right now," Dillon demanded.

Michael feigned offense. "Gentlemen, haven't I always helped you in any way I could? Tell me what's going on."

"What's going on is that you have been stealing ideas and technology from the future with no hesitation whatsoever, but you were still reluctant to help my son. We are not friends. I will personally give the crystal to the government and then we both know you will never make a dime from it, unless you call Rosa, right now," Ryan snarled.

Rosa stormed into the room and took everyone by surprise. She didn't know what she might find, but she knew Ryan and Michael in the same room was dangerous enough to have cosmic consequences.

"What is the meaning of this? What is going on?" Rosa demanded.

Ryan's whole attitude changed once he saw her. "Please, Rosa, we need your help again. We need to know where you found Dillon and Danny. We have to piece together their story from the beginning so that Danny can move on."

Rosa looked at Michael. She made her decision.

"We will all go. Give me a day to make the preparations and we will go tomorrow. I will meet you in Times Square at dawn." With that, she rushed out of the room.

Dillon and Ryan looked at each other in surprise. "Times Square?"

DECEMBER 24, 2011

Marie woke up earlier than usual. This time of the year, the mornings were so dark that she relished the idea of sleeping late, but today was different. It was Christmas Eve. Her family would have a full house tonight, and it wouldn't be long before her mom was up and peeling shrimp in the kitchen. Her mom was from a long line of Italian moms who prided themselves on the special dinner of seven fishes for Christmas Eve. Marie liked the shrimp, but she could do without the eel. Still, her mom insisted on serving it all. Shrimp, baccalà (a dried cod fish that took her mom days to make), mussels, calamari, crab, whitefish, and the dreaded eel for Uncle Bob.

Marie got dressed quickly and went downstairs to leave a note. She wanted to surprise Dillon with breakfast and then spend the day looking at the windows at Saks Fifth Avenue. She knew it would be a day they would never forget.

As she headed out the door, the wind whipped around her face. By the time she reached the end of the block, she was already rethinking spending the day outside looking at the decorations on Fifth Avenue. Maybe a little quality time at the Plaza Food Hall was in order. The more she thought about it, the more she liked that idea.

Marie was glad to get to the coffee shop, and even happier when they handed her a peppermint mocha and hot chocolate to go. She got a bag of Christmas cookies and was on her way. The street lights turned off as the sun broke over the horizon. It was 7:30. When she rounded the corner of Dillon's block, she got a surprise. Dillon and his dad were already up and headed down the front steps.

Marie wished she had thought to bring more hot chocolate. She planned to text Dillon and meet him on the street, but she never counted on Ryan being over there so early. Still, she was up, dressed, and standing twenty feet away with breakfast. She had come too far not to at least say hello. She could always beg off if it looked like they had other plans.

Marie picked up her pace and called out to Dillon. Naturally, that was the moment the garbage truck groaned in down the street. She tried to catch up, but by the time the truck moved out of her way, Dillon and his dad had already turned the corner and were headed downtown. Marie called again, but it was no use. If they couldn't hear her before, there was no chance that they would hear her calling after them on Fifth Avenue.

"Okay," she grumbled. "This is getting stupid. If they get in a cab I will just turn around and go home." This was not turning into the Christmas Eve morning that Marie planned. Even peeling shrimp would be better than this.

They didn't get into a cab, but they took off at a run. Marie ran after them. The dawn was breaking and Dillon and his dad knew they had no time to lose.

"Maybe there is some use for all that cross-country practice," Dillon joked as he struggled to keep up with his dad. They rounded the corner and there it was, Times Square twinkling in all its early morning glory. Dillon wondered where to meet Rosa, but he needn't have worried. She was easy to find. Rosa and Michael were waiting for them between the TKTS booth and the iconic statue of George M. Cohan in Father Duffy Square, right in the middle of everything. It was too early for the usual line of tourists hoping for bargain seats at Broadway shows, so there was no one blocking Dillon's view. Rosa and Michael were on the top step of the pavilion.

The sun was rising higher and higher, and when Dillon reached them, he found Danny already there. Before he realized what he was doing, Dillon blurted out, "Why here? The cave I understand, but right here in the middle of Times Square? I don't get it."

"There are many things you don't get, but you will learn," Rosa said. "Time travel can occur anywhere there is a great energy source and someone prepared to use it. The cave works because of what is underneath. Hundreds of miles below the surface of that cave is a massive deposit of plutonium. That untapped energy provides the power needed to travel to another dimension."

"Don't tell me there is a plutonium mine waiting to be discovered under Times Square," Ryan said.

"Of course not. What surrounds us here is much more powerful. It is the most powerful, renewable energy in the world," Michael said, practically salivating.

Danny and Dillon looked at each other and shrugged. As a budding scientist, Danny was desperately hunting through his memory for what might be more powerful than plutonium. "It can't be solar. Even at the equator, it couldn't be solar, right?"

Rosa looked right at him and it was clear she could easily see Danny. "You are right. It is not solar. Let me tell you a story. We believe at the dawn of time, the Great Creator made human beings and he wanted them always to be able to find him again. There was a special key that would always bring them back into his presence. His servant asked him where he would put the key so that humanity would not lose it. The Great Creator smiled and told his servant that he would put it in a place where they could never lose it, but that sadly, because it was so safely tucked away, only a few would ever find it. Then he put this key, this greatest source of energy inside us: the power of thought, faith, and love. Times Square is the crossroads of the world. People come from all over and add their gifts to this place. The gifts of thought, faith, and love are the only gifts that grow greater the more they are shared, and so this is the place of the most powerful energy in the universe. It remains unharnessed because so few of us discover its power. That is why time travel eludes most; they are overwhelmed in one dimension and cannot access the key that would allow them to expand into others." Then Rosa looked squarely at Michael. "Even some who are given the key can never fully use it. Some never move beyond their thoughts and so they need to borrow faith and even love in order to access the power of the key. Thought alone is only a beginning."

Dillon and Danny didn't know what to make of that. It sounded good in theory, but surely it was just some indigenous legend describing the energy of certain places all over the world, energy patterns that Rosa must have recognized in Times Square.

"Wait a minute," Dillon gasped. "Is that why they named it *Times* Square?"

It would have been much easier to dismiss if they hadn't seen what happened next. Rosa raised her hands and the wind around them began to blow. It lifted dust and papers, and soon it was so fierce that even some of the neon signs began to swing. Marie was only a few yards away now, watching the whirlwind take shape.

The wind continued to move all around them, and

Dillon and Danny began to feel like they were in the eye of a storm. Soon the winds began to spark as they moved, and the energy discharged with loud cracks. Ryan reached for Dillon, but Ryan was blown back. Dillon didn't know what to expect as the cyclone around them grew tighter and tighter. It looked like a freak storm to the other people in Times Square and most of them ran inside, but Marie moved closer, utterly entranced. Another second and Rosa began to shout prayers or incantations or something else that Dillon and Danny could not understand. She opened her arms wide and blasted Michael and Ryan out of the circle as Marie was swept in. Suddenly, the ground shifted beneath them and Dillon could see it open up as if to swallow them whole. Dillon squeezed his eyes shut and reached out for something to hold on to, and he caught hold of a hand. He was sure it must be Rosa's. Then he opened his eyes. Shock replaced relief when he realized that Marie was falling with him through a great abyss.

As they fell, Dillon cried out for Danny. He couldn't see him but he knew for sure that Danny was right beside them. Marie's eyes were wide with terror and she gripped Dillon's hand for dear life. Dillon tried to close his eyes and relax. He knew from experience that this kind of travel always went better with a relaxed mind, but it was almost impossible. He worried about telling Marie about this and now she was right here in the middle of it all. The wind whistled in their ears and it was a bumpy ride as they fell through the icy air.

Soon the ground was rushing up at them and Dillon knew it wouldn't be long before impact. Rosa landed gracefully on her feet, but the others didn't do quite as well. Danny tumbled down and rolled to a stop on his side at Rosa's feet. Dillon tried to pull Marie closer to him so he could catch her and maybe even break her fall, but no such luck. Dillon came down with a thud, and Marie finally released her grip on his hand. When he rolled over, he understood why. Marie was lying on the ground a few feet away and she wasn't moving.

NEW YEAR'S EVE 2049

"Marie!" Dillon yelled as he raced over to her motionless form. Danny was already at her side and the look in his eyes told Dillon all he didn't want to know. Carefully Dillon rolled her over and wiped the blood from her forehead. She was never intended to make this trip with them and now she might never make it back. Dillon knew they had a future together, but now that she was here in this place, it seemed like she was literally out of time and that everything could change.

Rosa knelt beside her and took Marie's wrist in her hand. Marie's pulse was weak and her lips were starting to turn blue. Danny knew from basic training that if they didn't do something soon, Marie would not wake up. Rosa removed her shawl and wrapped it around Marie. Without saying a word, she lifted Marie's feet a little higher than her head and put her bag underneath them. Then she stood.

"Dillon, you must bring me a very special herb. *Cleome monophylla*. It's about a foot high and it grows in places just like this." That was the first moment Dillon took his eyes off Marie and looked around. They had landed in a wasteland of dry brush and dirt.

"Nothing could grow here but weeds," Dillon said with a rising panic.

"It is a weed. Now go and hurry."

Dillon bolted and Rosa leaned over to listen to Marie's heart. To Danny, Rosa gave another instruction. "You go and find me two rocks. When he finds the weed, we will need to pound the roots to make a fine powder."

Danny was on his feet in an instant, but he worried that it might be a waste of time. "What makes you so sure he will find the root she needs anyway?"

Rosa looked at him with a serene expression. "This is why we have come. This is the reason that you must bring balance between the physical and spiritual, the eagle and the condor. People need this healing. Now it is Marie, but the whole world needs the balance you will bring. This is part of your journey. The weed will be here because Dillon needs to find it, and you will find the means to crush it because you must. That is your journey. That is my faith."

Danny found Dillon on his hands and knees in the underbrush. Dawn had broken and they could clearly see Marie and Rosa a few yards away. "I don't even know what the heck I'm looking for. Danny, what am I gonna do?"

"I'll tell you what we are not gonna do. We are not giving up." Danny sounded a lot more confident than he actually felt. He looked around for a big flat rock, but found nothing. He tried to find a rock he could use as a hammer, but there wasn't anything the right size or shape. In the distance, Marie began to moan.

Then Danny did something he hadn't done since he was a small boy. Even in his own last moments, he thought about it, but he was gone before he could begin. "Oh dear God, please help us help her. She loves Dillon and he's gonna need her. Please show me how to grind the root and show Dillon where to find it."

The place around them darkened and then was bright, as though a lightning bolt had flashed across the sky. Danny looked over at Dillon, but he didn't seem to see it. When the sky cleared Danny saw a mortar and pestle and shouted to

Dillon that the plant they needed was right under their feet. Danny didn't know how he knew, but he was sure that the plant they needed was right beside them.

When they returned to Rosa's side, there were tiny beads of sweat forming across Marie's face. She was pale and her breathing was shallow. Dillon had seen his future and knew he would become a doctor. He figured he must have made that choice so he would be able to cure himself of Leber's Disease when the time came. But now, looking down at Marie, unconscious and struggling to breathe, he knew that wasn't true. He would become a doctor so that he would never feel this helpless again.

Rosa was surprised to see the mortar and pestle, but she took it gratefully. She ground the roots until they were reduced to a fine, brown powder. Very carefully, Rosa put the powder on Marie's lips. Dillon and Danny didn't know quite what to expect. They hoped she would sputter back to life, cough, or even moan, but there was nothing. Rosa put a little more on her lips, then reached for Marie's small hands. She put one in Danny's hand and one in Dillon's. Dillon trembled when he held it and thought of the first time he held her hand, skateboarding in the park—he had been trembling then too.

Rosa began her incantations and brought to bear all of her training as a healer and a shaman. She chanted and shook the flowers of the plant over Marie. Dillon thought she looked like sleeping beauty with the tiny white flowers in her hair. The wind began to rise again, but this time it didn't whip itself into a froth as it had in Times Square. This time it blew in only one direction. It blew over them and soon all the flowers and powder were at Marie's feet. Whether it was wishful thinking or the result of the wind Dillon didn't know, but Marie's cheeks began to pink up and even her lips were starting to look red.

Dillon felt it before he saw it. Hardly at all, at first, but then stronger and stronger, he felt Marie squeezing his hand. The wind kept blowing and Marie began to stir. At the precise moment that she opened her eyes, the wind ceased and everything became very still and quiet.

"What happened?" Marie asked as she tried to sit up. Dillon and Danny's hands both held her still.

"What happened is that you scared us nearly to death," Dillon said as he brushed the hair from around her eyes. "Try to take it easy for a minute before you sit up. You've been out for a while."

Marie was about to tell Dillon about the strangest dream she just had when she looked around and realized that it wasn't a dream, and it wasn't over.

"How do you feel?" Rosa wanted to know. "I think you will be okay, but go slowly for now." With that, she held out her hand and Marie took it.

"Thank you . . . I, I feel okay now," Marie stammered. Rosa helped her up and steadied Marie on her feet. Dillon and Danny flanked her on either side when Rosa stood back. "We must go," Rosa declared. "We have much to do here and time is running out."

Dillon and Danny looked at each other, and then Marie did the strangest thing. She looked right at Danny and said, "Thank you."

Dillon just had to know: "Can you see him?"

Marie nodded. "Yeah, but I'm sure it's just the head injury talking. I see a guy a little older than us, but I don't know who he is. Is he a relative of yours? You guys look a little alike, but he seems kind of pale."

CHRISTMAS EVE 2011

Back in Times Square, Michael and Ryan glared at each other with shocked expressions on their faces. At first neither of them understood what just happened. The cyclone was whizzing around them and sparks were flying. Then the loud cracks in the air made it clear that something big was about to take place, and then it was over. A single *pop* and that was it. Dillon, Danny, Rosa, and someone else just disappeared. Ryan couldn't see who brushed past him in the last seconds before the pop. All that was left now was the hot chocolate spilling down the steps.

Ryan looked accusingly at Michael. "What have you done?"

"Me? What have you done? Who was that girl who went with them? Don't you realize that the more people involved in this, the worse it is for everyone? If they change the wrong thing, our whole existence could be threatened." Michael looked a little sick.

All around them, the city was springing to life. Cabbies honked their horns and store owners lifted the metal gates that protected their stores through the night. It was Christmas Eve and every shopping second mattered. People were moving in and out of the area, and no one even noticed the two men near the TKTS booth who looked like they might very well kill each other.

"Take us to them. I know you know how. Bring me to my son." Ryan clenched his fist. He didn't know what awaited the boys when they got wherever Rosa took them; he only knew he didn't want them facing it alone.

"Give me back my crystal and I'll take you," Michael said with a quiet stillness that made Ryan shiver. All at once Ryan was out of words. The man who made his living drafting documents and making compelling arguments had absolutely nothing left to say, so he used body language instead.

Ryan hurled himself at Michael and together they tumbled down the stairs in front of the TKTS booth. When they landed at the bottom, Ryan tore into Michael and pounded all his fear and frustration into Michael's chest. The weird thing was Michael didn't hit back. In fact, he smiled, almost as though he was enjoying seeing just how unglued Ryan had become.

Michael had been looking for an opportunity like this. He needed Ryan out of the way and this forced Ryan to play right into his hands. Michael let Ryan hit him for a few more minutes, just to make sure the security cameras all over Times Square caught the whole thing, and then he made his move when he saw the cops running toward them.

Michael reached up and grabbed Ryan by the collar. He threw Ryan off and used momentum and sheer brute strength to fire Ryan right into the oncoming traffic. Ryan looked up in time to confirm that the cab coming at him would never have enough time to stop.

NEW YEARS EVE 2049

Rosa led the group through what looked like miles of bramble, and as the sun set, Danny began to wonder if they were in the right place. Until this trip, when he and Dillon crossed into another dimension, they were always right where they needed to be. Danny was trying to figure out a polite way to ask if maybe she was lost when Rosa turned around. She whispered for them to be very quiet.

"Be quiet and stay out of sight; we don't want to frighten her," Rosa warned. "This is a time in the future, but it is also a time in your past." They took a few more steps and saw a young girl writhing on the ground under a big tree. She was bright red and sweating, and her hands were bunched into fists. She sat up and groaned and then there was a gush of blood underneath her. That's when Danny understood. He wanted to rush over to try to help, but Rosa held up her hand.

"That poor girl is giving birth!" Danny hissed. Dillon wasn't so sure until they heard the sounds of the first baby's cries. They expected her to be relieved, but the baby's cries were met with screams from the mother instead, and soon it was obvious that she was still in agony. A couple of minutes later two babies were crying and the mother was silent. She had lost a lot of blood, and when they saw her face, it looked almost peaceful. This time it was Dillon who started over to her but again Rosa held them back.

"You must stay here. You may witness, *not* interfere," Rosa warned. Dillon and Danny looked at each other and knew in an instant where they were. This was the place they were born, in a field on the outskirts of some future skyline of a big city.

Dillon looked again. "Oh my gosh, is that New York?"

Rosa crouched down again and beckoned them beside her. A moment later they saw what they would never believe: a much younger looking Michael McIntyre arriving in a space-age car. He stepped over the mother's body and put the two babies in the large basket he carried. He got back into the car and took off. Rosa held out her hands and they all linked up. More incantations, and soon they found themselves in the futuristic city. It looked a little different to be sure, but Dillon recognized it in an instant.

"This is New York," he stammered as they came down behind a small church around the corner from Times Square. Times Square was crowded with people and the lights were so bright it was hard to believe it was nighttime. They went inside the church and waited.

Soon the younger-looking Michael hurried inside with the basket in his arms. He placed the babies up near the altar and disappeared into the shadows. You had to know exactly where to look, to see him take a seat in the last pew. Outside, the crowd was cheering as a new year was welcomed in Times Square. Danny was stunned when he heard the announcer wish everyone "Happy 2050!"

A moment later they watched a young Rosa and her father enter the church. They only stayed a moment and then they left. When they were gone, another Rosa, as she looked now, hurried up the aisle. She knew exactly where to look and she was so focused on her task that she didn't even see Michael following her. Within ten minutes they were all gone. It was bizarre to hide with Rosa as she watched herself play her part.

"I believe you know the story from there. I took you to the families you would need in order to fulfill your destiny."

Danny and Dillon and Marie just looked at each other. Dillon stammered "Is Michael McIntyre our father? He just left our mother to die in some field? How did he know where she would be? Who is she?" Dillon was still trying to understand, but Danny had already made his decision: Michael McIntyre would pay for this with his life.

CHRISTMAS EVE 2011

The Plaza Hotel was bustling with activity. Flowers were being delivered and the lobby was festooned with holiday decorations of every kind. This would be a whole new kind of Christmas Eve for Sara. Instead of baking pies, she was going to the spa. She had a facial appointment, a hot stone massage and then a manicure and pedicure to round out the day. That would give her and Clint enough time for a great dinner before they headed to St. Patrick's Cathedral for Midnight Mass.

Clint left early and promised to be back soon. He said something about wanting to see if the lights went off in Times Square at dawn. Sara doubted that they ever went off, but she also doubted that was the only reason Clint went out. If she knew him, he would be up to some last-minute Christmas shopping.

On that account Sara was right. Clint was almost done with his shopping and proud of his gifts. He had bought Sara some new running shoes and a jacket with reflectors on the back, but he was most proud of the little white box. Inside was a new smart phone that contained the gift he knew she would love the most. When they were dating, he used to make her mix tapes where he recorded all their favorite songs. She especially liked the love songs.

The way Clint saw it, a guy could still get the old "mix tape mojo" with a little technology update. So he spent at least five hours last week putting together a playlist. Clint was convinced he was a real techie now except for one thing: when he wrapped the gizmo, he realized that Sara would need better earphones if she was ever going to hear it.

That was the real reason he went to Times Square. He wanted to try to beat the crowds and be back at the hotel in time to watch the Jacksonville Jaguars get trounced, by the Tennessee Titans. Football on Christmas Eve was Clint's gift to himself.

Now, riding along in the cab through Times Square, Clint thought about what an amazing, fun, and alive place this was. No wonder Danny had always wanted to go. It was exactly the right place for someone who was young, strong, and full of life.

He was jolted from his happy reflections when the cabby swore loudly and slammed on the brakes. The cab began to skid on an oil slick and Clint lurched forward in his seat. He could barely tell what was happening until they screeched to a halt inches in front of a man lying on the street. Clint leapt from the back of the cab and rounded the hood of the car a moment later. What he saw changed his life forever.

JANUARY 1, 2050

Rosa looked directly at Danny. It was almost as though she knew what he planned to do to get justice for his mother. "You will not stain your soul with murder. There is always another way."

Dillon looked at Danny and nodded. There really was a special connection between twins, and Dillon understood what Danny must have been thinking about. "I'd like to make him pay too, Danny, but right now we have a bigger problem. We left my dad alone with Michael back in Times Square."

"Wait a minute. Can somebody help me understand what the heck is going on? I know I hit my head, but it seems like I am still missing huge pieces of this puzzle." Marie's gaze settled on Dillon.

"Marie, what I'm about to tell you is quite simply unbelievable, but I need you to believe it anyway," Dillon began. "The short version is that I have a twin brother named Danny. We were separated at birth and didn't even know about each other 'til this past summer."

Marie looked amazed. "That's incredible! How did you find out . . ."

Dillon raised his hands. "Hold on, that's not even the crazy part." He took a deep breath and plunged in. "Danny and I were born in that field we just came from. Apparently we were born on New Year's Eve in 2049, but we didn't stay there for very long. This part is a little sketchy, but I'm guessing Michael McIntyre was or will be or whatever way you say it, Michael McIntyre is our father. After that poor woman, our mother, died giving birth to us, he took us to the church. I guess he didn't feel like having to take care of twins." The gravity of what Dillon had just learned hit him as he spoke.

"I guess he abandoned us at that church on New Year's Eve and Rosa came to get us. Rosa?" Dillon asked. "You knew where to come because that man brought you when you were younger? Is that right?"

Rosa nodded. "My people have been healers and time travelers for generations. That was my father who brought me to the church. He said it was my job to bring you to the families and times that would fulfill your destinies." Rosa looked sad. "I brought Danny back to 1985 and there we met the family that would raise him." Danny's hand covered his mouth and he shook his head trying to take it all in.

"Dillon, you had a more complicated journey. That night in 1985, there was another young woman who learned to time travel. I met her in 1996 and I knew she was for you. I sent her back to the field in 1985 to collect you. That woman became your mother, Maggie. Your father, Ryan, was also there, but he was too young to help you."

Marie was overwhelmed. "So you are twins who are eleven years apart?"

Dillon smiled and nodded. "Now for the hard part."

Marie felt behind her for a church pew and sat down on the first one she found. "The hard part?"

"OK, here goes." Dillon looked nervous. "My brother is technically eleven years older, but there's more. He died in 2004. When I met him, he was technically a ghost. Turns out he owned my guitar before I did and when I started to play it, we were able to communicate," Dillon blurted out in a rush.

Rosa took over from this point so Dillon could catch

his breath. "The boys have time traveled to the past and the future. Coming together was necessary for them because they are learning to bridge the gap between the spiritual and physical worlds. My people are more spiritual, like the condor. You, from the north are more physical, like the eagle. The world needs both to find cures and discover lasting peace. That is the destiny of my sons."

Dillon and Danny looked at each other stunned. "*Your* sons? What?" Danny looked like he might faint.

"You are mine. I have lived to become an old woman only because I am literally living on borrowed time. I was in love with Michael but he betrayed me. I have waited a long time to give him what he deserves."

Dillon and Danny were on overload and Marie was still figuring out what she had just heard, but the thought of giving Michael what he deserved snapped them all back into focus. Michael was a dangerous and cruel man, and Ryan was back in 2011 with him right now. There would be time for long discussions later. Right now Dillon just needed to get back to his dad.

Dillon looked at Rosa pleadingly and she nodded at him. "We must return at once. Danny? Do I have your word? Michael is mine and mine alone to handle."

Danny nodded but said nothing. In that moment he was all about plausible deniability.

It wasn't long before they were out of the church and back at the site of the future New Year's Eve celebration around the corner in Times Square. 2050 looked like it would get quite a welcome, but they weren't there to celebrate. The crowds of people were singing and lining the streets. People wore funny glasses that said "2050" around the eyeholes, and balloons and confetti were everywhere. Dillon, Danny, Rosa, and Marie struggled to the top of the TKTS booth steps and made their way to the same spot where they had stood back in 2011. This time, Danny and Dillon surround Marie and told her to try to relax her mind during the fall. Experience had taught them that it was the only way to arrive unscathed.

Once more Rosa lifted her arms and began to chant. Danny, Dillon, and Marie held onto Rosa and each other. Soon the gentle breeze around them became a fierce wind that created a vertical tunnel around them. Revelers nearby barely even noticed the flashes and loud cracks as the light encircled them. Those nearby seemed to think it was all a part of the celebration. The air grew colder and then they were on their way. Again the ground opened to swallow them, but this time they were ready. They fell and fell, and then they could see the lights of New York City shining below them. On they went and soon they were able to make out a commotion on the street. A cab was twisting itself up and onto the curb and it looked like there was a man on the street right in the line of the cab's front tire.

CHRISTMAS EVE 2011

When they landed back on the steps, no one even noticed because everyone was staring at the accident unfolding before their eyes. Dillon raced down the steps, pushing past a laughing Michael. He got to the bottom just in time to see his dad close his eyes as the cab lurched forward.

Ryan knew they were back. He would never be able to say just how he knew, but he did. He also knew there was no way the cab driver could stop in time. Ryan felt the grit and salt hit his face as the tires skidded toward him. He smelled the oil and asphalt and heard the cab's gears grinding in a last-ditch effort to stop. Ryan felt sorry for the driver.

The sun set early in New York at this time of year, but it still felt like the longest day of Dillon's life. It was about 5:30 in the afternoon when they finally let Dillon, Marie, Maggie, and (even though they didn't know it) Danny in to see Ryan. He was sitting up on a stretcher in the ER looking equal parts embarrassed and relieved. St. Vincent's Hospital was a busy place any time of the year, but it was especially nuts today. Not only was it Christmas Eve, it was a Saturday, so there were people everywhere.

Ryan looked tired and sore, but apart from the cuts and bruises on his face and hands, the only sign of the impact was the yards of bandage around his chest. Maggie spoke to the doctor and Dillon overheard something about "broken ribs" and "very lucky."

The moment the doctor left the room Ryan whispered

to Dillon, "Where is he?"

"Who, Dad? Danny is right here. Are you okay?"

"Michael! Stay away from him. That man is dangerous."

Dillon agreed and told his dad about their adventures with Rosa. Ryan wanted Marie to call her parents and get checked out by a doctor, but he backed off when he heard the rest of the story and learned she was okay.

"So you weren't born in 1985, it had to be the last hours of 2049?" Ryan tried to clear his head. "Man, if that doctor hears me talking like this, he'll think I have a head injury for sure. I'm sorry for all you guys have been through. I wanted to be there with you, but I got a little sidetracked." Ryan touched the goose egg that was forming on his head.

Danny was glad Ryan was going to be okay, but he had another pressing matter to attend to. He had to find Michael. Even if it meant looking for him in hell, Danny was determined to deal with the man who put this whole chain of events in motion, and he had to do it fast. When Michael had followed the young Rosa and her father back in time, he'd started a race with destiny that they were all still trying to win. Michael had already proved he was willing to kill, and now he was under an intolerable threat. If his time travel was exposed, it could mean the end of everything for him. Danny knew a madman like Michael would not go gently.

Before he could deal with that though, Danny had to do something else. Clint was in that cab and right now he and Sara were sitting in a waiting room down the hall hoping they might be able to find out if Ryan was all right. The police had reviewed the security tapes and declared the whole mess nothing more than an accident. In fact, it was Clint who pulled Ryan away from the wreckage, but Danny knew they would want to be sure Ryan was going to be all right. Rosa and Michael had disappeared into the crowd, but Clint stayed with Ryan through the whole ordeal.

"I'll be back in a little while," Danny said to Dillon as he turned to go. He was stunned when Dillon reached out and caught his arm and even more surprised that he felt it.

"From now on, we stick together. Wherever you need to go, I'll go with you."

Danny didn't know exactly what to say. He was touched, but he just couldn't imagine telling Dillon that the guy in the cab was his dad, Clint. But while Danny couldn't imagine it, he didn't have to worry. Maggie came back into the room and took Ryan by the hand. "I don't know how to tell you all this, so I'm just gonna say it. Danny's parents are downstairs. His father was in the cab that hit you and they haven't left the hospital yet, hoping for news of your condition. By the way, you have been upgraded to good condition now and we might even get you home in time for Christmas." Maggie winked at Ryan. "I went down to thank the man who pulled you free of the wreck and realized it was an old friend of Joe's, Clint Charles. I don't know why I didn't recognize Danny's last name before. He told me about his son, and when his wife showed me the boy's picture, it looked too much like Dillon not to be Danny."

Danny looked at his shoes, and then he got another surprise. Dillon hugged him, and he not only felt it, he could feel his brother's energy coursing through him.

"Please, Maggie, ask them to come up," Ryan said. "We can't lose the opportunity to talk with these people. I don't believe in coincidence. There is some reason that our paths literally crossed today. We need to meet."

Ryan tried to ease himself off the bed and winced a little when his feet hit the floor. This was too important to him to greet Danny's parents lying down. He reached for the bag with his shirt in it and winced again. The paramedics must have cut it off him because it was shredded.

"Maggie? Can we just go home?" Ryan sounded exhausted. Maggie didn't quite know what to say. She could probably convince the doctor to release him into her care, since she was a nurse and it was Christmas Eve, but did Ryan realize what he was asking? Did he know he couldn't go home to his place alone?

"I thought you wanted to see Danny's family," Maggie began.

"I do, I really do, but not like this. I feel pathetic." Ryan felt frustrated and dizzy too, so he backed onto the bed and sat down again. Maggie took charge. She disappeared for about fifteen minutes and came back with a triumphant smile on her face.

"Okay, here it is. You can come back with Dillon and me tonight; there is just no way you can be alone. It's not the Ritz, but it's not the hospital either. Mr. and Mrs. Charles have agreed to come by tomorrow to visit. And Dillon? I believe you and Marie can still make it to her house for Christmas Eve. Now, if that is settled, Ryan, I got you a lovely sweatshirt from the gift shop. Put it on and let's get out of here."

Ryan had never loved her more.

CHRISTMAS DAY

Dillon woke up to sights and sounds he hadn't been a part of for years. His mom and dad were in the kitchen together and they were laughing. Bacon and eggs were on the stove and Bing Crosby's "White Christmas" echoed throughout the house. Dillon would have thought he was dreaming, but Dillon didn't usually have dreams like this.

When Dillon walked into the room, he saw a huge pile of presents under the tree. It was going to be quite a Christmas.

"Man, Santa sure does like you," Danny joked as Dillon sat down. Ryan and Maggie joined them and for a little while, they got to be a nearly normal family; no time travel, no cosmic catastrophes, just almost normal. Dillon was wiping the bacon grease from his chin when the doorbell rang. It was still too early for it to be the Clint and Sara Charles so Dillon hurried into his room to get dressed. He didn't want to start the day feeling embarrassed to be in PJs in front of company.

Twenty minutes later he appeared, showered and dressed, and he really thought he was ready for anything. He was wrong. When he came into the living room, Rosa was there, and Ryan was on the phone with Thomas. Danny began to pace around the room and Dillon wished someone would just tell him what was going on.

Maggie explained to him that for the first time in about seventy-five years, Rosa couldn't find Michael. He always spent Christmas on Long Island with his little boy, but he wasn't there. Before he disappeared, he told Rosa that he wished he had left the twins to die when they were born. Rosa was worried that he might travel through time and make good on his threat. He had tried to kill Ryan yesterday; would he try to kill the boys today?

An hour later they were all together again in Maggie's living room. Thomas and Tom were there with Marie and Clint and Sara. Rosa went into another room to pray and prepare.

Ryan smiled. "Clint, I think we owe you an explanation. Danny stood behind his parents and was surprised to find his mother's hand unconsciously reaching for his own.

"Our sons both came to us in unusual ways. There were unusual circumstances to say the least." Ryan began.

Clint started to look uncomfortable and then his eyes grew as wide as saucers. Rosa came in from the other room and sat down. She told Clint the whole story of Danny's birth and abandonment. She told them about her own history, and then she told them the news that shook them to the core.

"Your son, Danny, is here with us now and he has a brother." Rosa smiled and pointed to Dillon. Maggie could see Clint and Sara struggling to understand, and she wanted to help them. Her first thought was to make another of her famous lists with all the information they had now. It could read:

1. 2049: twins born, abandoned by Michael and collected bt Rosa.
2. 1985: twins brought to their families after the truck accident. Danny adopted by Clint. Dillon brought to 1996.
3. 1996: Maggie brings Dillon to their family after the accident.

Then, in the midst of her imagined list-making, Maggie realized there was a much better way. "Dillon, go get the guitar."

Dillon returned and the look on Clint and Sara's faces made it clear they believed.

"I think you know this guitar."

Dillon was hoping they wouldn't ask for it back. Clint reached out his hands and held it in his arms. He plucked the strings and Danny was mortified to discover that he had tears in his eyes. The tender way that Clint played the guitar made Danny cry. It was like he was sending Danny a message only meant for him, and Danny felt a huge piece of his broken heart heal.

"Will the circle be unbroken . . ." Dillon smiled as he heard Clint's rich baritone fill the room. When Clint was finished, he handed the guitar back to Dillon. "I expect this is meant to belong to you now. Especially if it keeps you in contact with Danny."

"Dillon?" Danny needed his help. "Dillon? I need you to tell them something for me." Dillon nodded and listened.

"Danny wants me to tell you two things. First, Sara, he really misses your pie, especially something called Fruits of the Forest?" Dillon got distracted and turned to Danny. "What is that?" Danny told him he would have to wait and see. Then Dillon got back to relaying.

"Second, he wants you to know that he is so grateful and glad that you took him in as your son. He says no kid ever had better parents or more chances to be happy. He didn't always see that then, but he knows it now." Now it was Sara's turn to cry. "Oh and one more thing," Dillon continued repeating every word Danny said. "Now I want you to go ahead and adopt Dillon and his parents too."

Dillon said the words before he realized their meaning. Danny thought the look on their faces was hysterical. Ryan was the only one who seemed to get it.

"I agree with Danny. We should stick together. Our boys deserve to have all of us and not just to avert disaster, but to share whatever time we can."

Maggie walked across the room to her photographs. She picked one up and laughed out loud. "Clint, you have been before my eyes for years and I never saw it. I knew that name sounded familiar, but I couldn't place it. You were a friend of my brother, Joe." She was still laughing as she passed around the old picture.

Rosa stood up. "Please, I'm sorry to do this, but really we must go. Michael McIntyre is on the loose and it will take all of us to stop him."

It didn't take long to figure out *when* and *where* to start looking. They knew they needed to make sure that Michael didn't make good on his threat to kill the twins. The sun was high in the sky by the time they returned to the TKTS booth in Times Square.

"TKTS?" wondered Maggie when she realized where they were headed. Rosa nodded and lifted her arms in the air. Clint, Sara, Thomas, Tom, Ryan, Maggie, Marie, Dillon, and Danny linked arms and prepared to ride. Times Square was all but deserted and no one either noticed or cared when the breeze around them began to stir. It wasn't long before the wind whirled around them and tightened their circle. Around and around it whipped until sparks ignited. Dillon closed his eyes and waited for the inevitable crack. In the last moments before the fall he opened his eyes again and looked for Danny.

Dillon had the terrible feeling that only one of them would be coming back.

The next thing they knew, the ground opened up and Maggie began to scream. Dillon wished he had thought to warn her about having a relaxed mind, but it was too late now. Down and down they fell as the edges of the great abyss rose around them on all sides. Dillon expected that any minute they would land with a thud on the parched ground they found on their first visit. As they fell, he realized they were falling into a mist and that lush vegetation was everywhere. He looked down and saw the canopy of a rain forest rushing up at them. Dillon was confused, but he knew he would have some answers soon.

TIMELESS

When they finally landed, there was a small hill to break their fall. They rolled down a few feet and came to a stop in front of an ancient temple. Dillon looked at Rosa for explanation, but she looked as confused as he felt. More than confused, in fact: Rosa looked afraid.

Everyone scrambled to their feet and Marie grasped Dillon's hand.

"You sure know how to impress a girl," she whispered, and then she asked the question on everyone's mind: "Where are we?"

"I said the right incantations," Rosa said. "I did everything just the way I always do, but I have never been here before. Not even in my dreams."

Danny was busy looking over Thomas' shoulder. As usual, Thomas had his notebook out and was writing furiously. "Dillon ask her what the incantations mean," Danny said.

Dillon didn't need to translate because Rosa heard every word. They all did. And then Sara screamed.

"I can see you! Oh Danny! You are alive!"

Now it was Thomas' turn. "Okay, that tells us something very important. Since we can all see and hear Danny in this place, then it stands to reason that this place is not just a different time; this must be another dimension. It also stands to reason that we can't really drive this thing. We can only put in a request. Rosa, tell me again about the most powerful kinds of energy?"

"Thought, faith, and love," Rosa answered.

"Okay, so maybe we are exactly where we should be. I wasn't thinking about a date. Were any of you?" Thomas asked. Everyone shook their heads. But a big smile spread across Danny's face.

"Wait a minute, I think I get it," Danny said. "We were all thinking about stopping Michael. That's why we are here. This must be the best place to do it."

Michael was hurrying through the jungle. The whole situation didn't seem real to him. How the hell did he let this go so far? Michael cursed himself for not being more careful, more careful with his story and more careful with the crystals. He knew where he was going and he knew he had to get there fast. Once the others discovered the crystal mines it would be over. The world would have the energy source and Michael would have nothing for his trouble.

When he had discovered, by traveling into the future, that digital downloads would revolutionize the music industry, he thought that would be enough. For a little while he convinced himself that he could leave the rest alone. But as the war in the Middle East kept going, Michael realized that finding an alternative energy source was just too big a pie for him to miss getting a slice. Then he discovered that the crystal was going to power whole cities in the future, and he realized that a piece of the pie would never be enough: Michael planned to own the whole bakery.

On and on he climbed through the steep hills of the jungle. When he slid down through the mud, he just dug in deeper and pulled himself along on the vines.

"Not much farther," he muttered to himself, and then he saw them. Over the crest of the next hill he saw Danny and Dillon and everyone with them. They looked like they had just landed there and were still getting their bearings. Michael looked again and things went from bad to worse as far as he was concerned: they were standing around the temple entrance to the mine.

Ryan didn't know anything about where they were, but he trusted that they were there for a reason. It didn't make sense to him to land in front of the temple and not start there, so he walked over to it to get a better look. It wasn't long before the others joined him, and together they entered the ruin. Clint took Sara's hand and Danny smiled at them.

The temple was like a big gateway to a smaller cave. The altar sparkled in the sunlight, and there was a large stone table beneath an opening in the wall on the far side. Behind the table they saw more sparkling light and realized that this must be some kind of entrance to another room. When they got closer, they saw thousands of tiny crystals lighting a small cave within. The inside of the cave was a lot like what Danny and Dillon had grown to expect: a cave that was damp and dark with some kind of slime on the walls. No one really wanted to, but they pressed on. Bad got worse, and they realized that the large anteroom gave way to a narrow tunnel. Dillon looked at Danny. He knew only too well what this meant: a long walk through tight, dark spaces.

As the tunnel got narrower, they walked hand in hand and single file. It was so dark that Ryan had to put his hand out ahead of him to feel his way. Dillon wished he could tell his dad what to look for and when to move and when to wait, but he could offer him nothing. There was no rhyme or reason to this kind of place. There was only darkness and instinct until you reached the light.

On they went, and soon the entrance behind them was completely out of sight. Ryan slowed down the pace because he thought he felt a breeze up ahead. Surely that was a good sign. It must mean that soon they would emerge into a light-filled cavern, somewhere big enough for air to move around. Ryan took another step and reached out to touch the wall and steady himself. When he put out his hand, he expected the damp, moss-covered stones he had come to know. He did not expect what he got. Another hand grabbed his, and before he realized what was happening, Ryan and everyone else fell down into a deep crevasse.

It took every ounce of self-control he had, but Dillon let go at the last moment and now found himself alone with Danny up in the tunnel. He could see nothing, but he knew that whoever pulled everyone else into the ditch was nearby. They also knew that it had to be Michael. Logic dictated that Dillon and Danny should turn back and try to find something to help, a vine or a light that they could use to help get the others out. But this wasn't about logic, and retreat was not on their minds. Danny took the lead and together they ran around the opening in front of them.

"We'll be back. I swear to you. We'll be back," Dillon called down to the others and he and Danny moved on into the darkness. Running faster now, they covered the length of the tunnel in no time. They were sure that Michael was there and had pulled the others over the edge. They were on his turf. He knew the pitfalls, but Dillon and Danny didn't care; they knew what had to be done.

Danny felt like he was back in Afghanistan as they got

down and crawled forward on their bellies. Danny knew the only way out was through and nothing could stop them now. This wasn't about alternative energy or curing a disease; this was about family, and their family would not be destroyed by Michael ever again. On they crawled and Dillon felt sick as they reached across the ground through the old familiar filth. The cave was like Michael, sparkling on the outside and rotten at its core. The smell nearly overcame him, but Danny kept making jokes that somehow made it easier to bear.

"Good Lord! We must be in the belly of the beast. Some big, fat, disgusting, burrito-eating, bean-belching, seething pot of shut-the-heck up. This place stinks worse than an outhouse in August."

"Really? We are going to do that whole Southern humor thing now? Did you forget we were born on the outskirts of New York?" Dillon teased.

"The only reason I was born north of the Mason-Dixon line is because that's where our poor mother was and I felt it was important to be with her on that day. I tell you what, I just wish we were big enough to fix that rat who left her. I'm going to enjoy this. I trained for a long time. I'm looking forward to putting some of that training to work."

"Knock it off. You are freaking me out," Dillon said as the tunnel began to open up again. Soon they were on their feet and there it was, right ahead of them: the stone wall. This time Dillon knew exactly what to do. He grabbed Danny and together they raced toward it shouting a battle cry into the air. In the last moments, they jumped up and pushed their feet through the wall. Stone and glass and mortar shattered all around them.

Dillon expected to be in the back end of a tomb.

Danny expected to be in Michael's lair. Both of them were wrong. Instead they discovered that they were in a beautiful garden.

The Garden

"Wow, it's not even a cemetery this time," Dillon stammered. There were birds singing, bees buzzing, and the sun was shining. Danny tried to step forward, but he discovered he couldn't. It was too perfect, too beautiful to be real and Danny smelled a trap. Dillon didn't know what to think. Dillon looked around and saw a small brook babbling in the distance. He thought about following it, but he didn't. He was distracted by the man in white heading toward them. The man was tall and slim, and he reminded Dillon of a sticky, stretched marshmallow oozing toward them with a sickly sweetness.

"Gentlemen, so good of you to come." The man smiled a syrupy grin and held out his arms. "I believe you are looking for someone. Please, allow me to be of service. This place belongs to me, I can help."

"Dillon, it's a trap." Every hair on the back on Danny's neck stood up and that was never a good sign. Danny struggled to move, but he couldn't break free. He could go back, but not forward. "Dillon, don't trust him."

Dillon heard every word, but he smiled a big, happy teenager smile that smacked of "Golly gee, Mister, would you really?" Dillon walked toward the man and joined him at a table laid out in a gazebo.

The man poured tea and Dillon took the cup in his hands. He had no intention of drinking it, but this nut didn't need to know that.

"My brother and I, we'd be real grateful if you could tell

Michael we came to see him. He took something that belongs to us and we came to get it back."

"Took something? I can't imagine what you could possibly have that would interest Michael." The man in white looked intrigued.

"He took our past, our future, and he even tried to take our family." Dillon's voice sounded stronger than he actually felt. The man in white burst out laughing and when he did, Dillon could see a sickening filth on his yellow teeth.

Danny was frantically trying to break free. What was it that was holding him back? Any second now Dillon might need him and he would be useless. Danny raged against his trap.

Dillon stood and moved closer to the man. "Bring Michael to me!"

The man rose and towered over Dillon. He said nothing; he merely looked into Dillon's eyes, which sent a shock right through him. Dillon was thrown about twenty feet and landed next to Danny.

"Get up! Get up!" Danny yelled. The man in white walked slowly to where Dillon lay trying to clear his head.

"Let us remember our manners, shall we?"

Dillon's hands were shaking and Danny was frantic. They expected to deal with Michael, but this guy was a whole different matter. Danny never took his eyes off the man. He learned about turning his back on the enemy in Afghanistan and he did not intend to make that mistake again.

Dillon summoned all his courage and looked him in the eyes again. "So you can push me around. So what? Everyone can push me around. It seems to me like Michael must be worried to send a guy like you to keep us busy."

Danny wondered if taunting this guy was really the best

way to go, but he couldn't do much about it now.

The man raised one arm and Dillon crashed into the remains of the stone wall in ruins behind him. That was it for Danny. He was not going to just stand there and watch his brother get pulverized.

When Dillon stood he had a wildness in his eyes. That's when Danny saw it: the man in white was flickering.

"Fear!" Danny yelled. "That thing is powered by fear!" The moment he said it, Danny could move. Dillon let his rage overcome his fear, and together he and Danny pounced. The man in white laughed as they ripped into him. Danny landed a punch and it was clear that he was seen and felt in this place. It was also clear that Danny's military training was excellent.

Dillon grabbed the man by the collar and demanded, "Michael! Where is that evil snake?" The man in white cackled again and then, in a flash he was gone and Michael stood above them.

"Well, you can thank me later, but it seems to me that my actions have turned you two into quite a tough team. It's not just anyone who can overcome the latest in the next century's personal security."

Danny was on his feet in an instant. Every soldier instinct was firing and searching Michael for the most efficient vulnerability. Michael, on the other hand, was in the mood for a chat.

"Come now, boys, vengeance isn't your style. I'll share with you. Together we could accomplish three times as much. The crystals are only the beginning unless you let your misguided loyalties obscure your real destiny."

Dillon and Danny moved together as one finely tuned machine. They dragged Michael to the ground and knew they had to end this. To let him go would be to condemn them all to a life of looking over their shoulders. There was no doubt that Michael would keep coming until he killed everyone who knew about the crystals and inter-dimensional travel. Danny considered drowning Michael in the brook. He had to be stopped, they knew that, but not like this. Still, Dillon and Danny dragged Michael over to the brook. It gurgled and flowed along over the stones beneath the water. When Dillon looked again, he realized those weren't just ordinary stones: they were crystals and they were glowing as the ground began to shake. Danny thought there was something familiar about them, like a certain grenade he had seen in Afghanistan, but right now, he didn't have time to think about it.

Michael noticed it too and he looked worried. He knew what the glowing meant because he had seen it once before, just before he threw it in Afghanistan. Michael was a time traveler. He had already lived this moment once before and he never expected to face it again. He thought he had handled this when he abandoned the twins in the first place. Michael had never guessed that Rosa's blood in their veins made Dillon and Danny natural time travelers and spirit walkers.

When Danny died, Michael was sure he was in the clear. The insurgents loved his crystals and thought they were some kind of concentrated grenade. When he threw it in the warehouse that day in 2004, Michael was sure he would never have to worry about facing Danny again. As for Dillon, Michael never expected Dillon to survive the Leber's once it attacked his heart. He never expected their trip to the future to actually cure Dillon. Now, here he was, fighting his own sons to survive.

They were surrounded by these unstable crystals

and Michael knew there wasn't much time. If that day in Afghanistan was anything to go by, the glowing would lead to explosion in about thirty seconds. Danny looked at them in the water and realized exactly where he had seen them before.

"My own father?" Danny finally understood what happened on the day he died. He let go of Michael, grabbed Dillon and ran for what was left of the stone wall. Dillon didn't understand until the crystals began exploding behind him. One crystal set off another until the ground shook with the release of the massive force of energy. A tidal wave of light and heat crashed over them, but Danny and Dillon ran on. The tunnel was collapsing in on itself from the force of the first blast and still they ran.

"We have to get to the crevasse! We have to get them out!" Danny yelled as they rounded the corner just ahead of Michael. The tunnel was lit with the crystals they could now see all around them. The crystals were glowing and the heat that was coming from them was overpowering. A second blast went off behind them and threw them onto the side of the crevasse. Michael ran past them and Dillon and Danny dropped down into the hole to free the others. At that moment, there was an explosion bigger and hotter than all the rest. The whole cave shuddered and began to fold in on itself.

Dillon and Danny found Rosa and the others on their way up through the debris. As the cave collapsed, the ditch rose up from below and Rosa began to chant. Not sure what else to do, they clasped hands and waited for the fall. This time though, it was different. The wind that surrounded them lifted them up, and as the last parts of the cave fell around them, they began to move. Higher and higher they flew until they could see only the stars. Everything was strangely peaceful. Danny was mesmerized. He saw a magnificent light that sparkled and had even more colors than a rainbow.

"Do you see it? That light, is it the sun?" Danny asked Dillon.

Dillon wondered if the explosions had hurt Danny's eyes. The only light he saw was from the Empire State Building that was coming into view as they returned to their own time. When they touched down a few minutes later, Dillon couldn't believe it was over. He was sure that Michael was somewhere far away buried under the rubble of the crystals he loved so much. Marie held him and Dillon breathed in her perfume. They made it. Michael was gone, and they were safe Everyone was talking and checking on each other to make sure no one was hurt. Ryan held a crystal in each hand and then tossed one to Thomas. "Here's a little something for your research." Ryan smiled. Dillon couldn't take his eyes off his sweet Marie, even as he spoke.

"Danny, I can't believe it. We made it!" Dillon cheered. "Danny?" Dillon looked around and saw that his brother was nowhere to be found. Maggie and Ryan looked confused, Clint and Sara looked concerned. Rosa smiled and pointed to the stars. She knew Danny was finally where he needed to be.

That night in his room, Dillon pulled out the old guitar. He played for a while, but he knew Danny was long gone. Still he played on.

"Will the circle be unbroken? By and by, Lord, by and by . . ." and in the distance Dillon always swore he heard Danny answer.

"There's a better home awaiting, in the sky, Lord, in the sky."

TODAY

Dillon never saw Danny again, but he had no doubt that Danny was alive and well and that they would one day be reunited. Years later Dillon would see his brother's grin on his own son's face, and Marie liked to say that it was just proof of what they already knew. When it comes to family, love will always play on.

ACKNOWLEDGEMENTS

Writing is all about relationship. I have been blessed by a beautiful constellation of talented people willing to help light my path, and now it is my pleasure to offer my thanks.

To David Rust who believed in this project from the first word to the final edit. Your faith, humor, and skill helped to make the dream of this book come true. To Carla Jablonski, editor, mentor, and teacher: working with you has been both an education and adventure requiring the courage to grow as a writer and storyteller. To Renata M. Brunner Jass, copyeditor extraordinaire whose attention to detail is unparalleled. To Virginia Anagnos, gifted in public relations and generous in friendship. To Jennifer Marcus for welcoming me to the world of social media. To Jennifer Brod for energy and enthusiasm, and to Caroline Capute for time and talent. To Goodman Media for rooting for the underdog. To Vic Lau for skill as a web master and vision as an artist. To Elizabeth Lezama for being the world's best intern and a treasured friend. To Mike Dominguez for making video my friend. To Stephen Bosak and Elena Bosak for lending a hand and reading an early draft. To Stephanie Weller for willingness to enjoy the sport of extreme proofreading.

To my children, Katherine, Elizabeth, Alexandra, and George, you are my inspiration, my motivation, my favorite readers and my living proof that dreams come true. To my dear husband, Stephen, the brightest star in my darkest night, your faith in me fuels every word. There would be no me without us. I love you. Lastly, to my mom and dad, Kay and Pat Melville, who taught me that the love of my family will always play on.

ABOUT THE AUTHOR

Marilynn Halas lives in rural Connecticut with her four children, two dogs, and one husband. As founder and creative director of 4 Sunflowers Media, LLC, Marilynn believes wholeheartedly in celebrating and supporting families and empowering the next generation.

Visit her on the web at www.4sunflowersmedia.com/teen.